D1029018

The
Black Tolts

Center Point
Large Print

Also by William MacLeod Raine
and available from Center Point Large Print:

Desert Feud
Border Breed
Courage Stout
Clattering Hoofs

**This Large Print Book carries the
Seal of Approval of N.A.V.H.**

The Black Tolts

William MacLeod Raine

CENTER POINT LARGE PRINT
THORNDIKE, MAINE

This Center Point Large Print edition
is published in the year 2015 by arrangement with
Golden West Literary Agency.

First US Edition: Houghton Mifflin
First UK Edition: Hodder & Stoughton

The text of this Large Print edition is unabridged.
In other aspects, this book may vary
from the original edition.
Printed in the United States of America
on permanent paper.
Set in 16-point Times New Roman type.

ISBN: 978-1-62899-667-8 (hardcover)
ISBN: 978-1-62899-672-2 (paperback)

Library of Congress Cataloging-in-Publication Data

Raine, William MacLeod, 1871–1954.
 The black tolts / William MacLeod Raine. — Center Point Large Print
edition.
 pages cm
 Summary: "The Tolt Brothers made history when they robbed two
trains at the same time. Now they will became a legend when they rob
two banks at once"—Provided by publisher.
 ISBN 978-1-62899-667-8 (hardcover : alk. paper)
 ISBN 978-1-62899-672-2 (pbk. : alk. paper)
 1. Large type books. I. Title.
 PS3535.A385B57 2015
 813′.52—dc23

2015022006

I

Eavesdropping

As Dave Tolt drove his string up to the stable, he could see that his brothers were discussing some matter both secret and important. Their black heads were close, their voices low. Even before he had swung from the saddle, he realized his presence was an embarrassment, and with the sensitive bitterness of youth he resented his exclusion.

They watched him unsaddle, conversation suspended.

"Well, I got back," he said. "They're rounding up the Bald Knob country. I didn't figure many of our strays had got that far south, so I left Buck as our rep."

"Pick up many of our slick ears?" Caldwell asked, with an interest only perfunctory.

He was the oldest of Dave's full brothers, a big broad-shouldered man of about thirty with a long reach of well-muscled limb. The bony contour of his brown face was marked, an inheritance from the small percentage of Indian blood in him. Hair, eyebrows, and mustache were black. Except when he talked his lips were close-shut. He looked a man both forceful and reckless.

"We branded seventeen J. T. calves."

"Good. Better run up to the house and have Mother fix you up some breakfast."

"I found that pieded bull, the one with the twisted horn, bogged down in the quicksand below the ford, so I stopped to yank him out."

"Fine. Run along, kid." This was Cole's contribution. He looked very much like Caldwell, though he wore an imperial beard. The black Tolts all had a strong family resemblance. They were big rangy men, strongly individual and yet clannish, known to be daring and turbulent, suspected of lawlessness.

David carried the saddle to the stable and hung it to a peg driven into the wall. He wondered jealously what was in the air. There was a conspiracy among his brothers, so he felt, to keep him out of things. The reason was clear enough to him. He was not yet nineteen, his mother's youngest, and they did not want to encourage him to follow in their footsteps. Between him and Steve there was a gap of four years. They thought of him as a kid.

This he considered an affront. On the frontier men and women matured early. Going-on-nineteen, Dave felt, meant manhood. He had given his proofs. Already he had ridden out blizzards, been up the trail, stood on his own among the rufflers at Dodge and Ellsworth. He had even known that electric moment when time stood still while a bully whose bluff he had called made up his mind whether to back down or carry through.

"When you've had breakfast, better hook up and drive to town, kid," Luke suggested. "We're needing supplies. There's a list at the house. Don't forget the cartridges."

"Here's your hat. Do you have to hurry?" Dave drawled ironically.

"Someone has to go," Steve said.

"Sure, and you've all broke your legs, I reckon," Dave flung out in dudgeon. "Send the kid! He ain't been working but eighteen hours a day for the last week."

"Scoot along to the house and get some grub under your belt, boy," Caldwell told him with easy good-nature. "You'll feel better after you're fed."

Over his shoulder Dave left with them an irritated protest. "Looks like I'm welcome as the smallpox."

A murmur of indulgent laughter reached him, and it stung as a spur does a spirited horse. Possibly it deflected the whole current of his life, though that may be an overstress. It may have been written in his horoscope that because he was what he was he had to do what he did.

Dave walked toward the house. . . . All right. Let them laugh. He would find out what all that huddle of heads meant. . . . As soon as he passed the willow thicket and was out of sight, he dodged in among the young trees and plunged through them to the creek. For a hundred yards he followed the devious stream, then cut across the meadow to the back of the barn. Noiselessly he shinned up the adobe wall, as he had done several times before, using a window-ledge, a projecting brick, and the floor of the loft as foot and hand holds.

Creeping forward over the hay, he could hear a drone of voices which became less faint as he approached. He wriggled close to the edge of the floor and listened. Even from here he caught only occasional snatches of sentences.

". . . if there's no slip-up."

That was Steve's voice. Dave did not catch the answer, but presently the name Jack Bray came to him. After that there were more unintelligible murmurs, followed by a question from Luke that made the boy's heart jump.

"Sure the big shipment is Thursday night?"

Again the name of Bray in what seemed to be a lengthy explanation. Caldwell talking, and out of his monotone two words leaped. "Fifty thousand."

"On the westbound?" Clay asked.

Dave missed the answer, but in another minute he caught a sentence from Steve, one indiscreetly high with jubilation.

"The James gang never held up but one at a time."

"Sh-h!" warned Caldwell, "Not so loud."

"You dead sure of Bray?" Luke inquired. ". . . guards on train."

Caldwell's grim answer was chill as ice. "How long would he live after he fooled us?"

There were more whisperings.

Abruptly Clay broke up the conference. "We better be going. No sense in making the kid suspicious."

Dave slipped back across the hay, lowered himself partway to the ground from the loft, and dropped upon his toes. He scudded across the meadow to the fringe of bushes along the creek, followed the brook to the willow clump, and from there ran to the house. He sauntered into the kitchen and hung up his hat on a nail.

"Hungry, I reckon," his mother said.

"Y'betcha!"

She began at once to prepare breakfast for him. He tilted back in a chair and read the Melrose *Democrat*.

Nobody could have guessed from his mother's greeting that he was the Benjamin of her heart. Jessie Tolt did not show her emotions. She was not demonstrative of her affection. Not for years had she kissed any of her sons. Mrs. Tolt was a strikingly handsome woman of fifty, dark, with black, long-lashed eyes. It was easy to see where the black Tolts got their looks. Nor could one have guessed how thoughts and emotions were churning in the brain back of the boy's impassive face. When Clay and Steve came into the house, his heels were hooked on the rungs of the chair and his eyes were glued to the newspaper.

"I see the *Democrat* claims Jim Sutter will get the nomination for sheriff," he mentioned.

"Looks like," Steve agreed. "He ain't as good a man as Evans. Few are. But he'll do well enough."

"Who's going to town this morning?" Mrs. Tolt asked.

"I reckon Dave's going," Clay answered.

"We're out of Arbuckle's. Get six-bits worth, Dave. Put it on the list, Steve."

The mother set a place and called her youngest son to breakfast. He pulled up a chair and sat down.

"I'm hungry enough to eat a mail-sack," he said.

"That stopped being news eighteen years ago, son," Mrs. Tolt reminded him with a smile.

They were a strange family, the Tolts. The father of the seven strapping sons of Jessie had come from Kentucky. He was a pioneer of the best type, honest, self-reliant, neighborly, religious. He came in a covered wagon, his wife Susan by his side. (At this time Jessie, his second wife, was in her cradle.) James had fought Indians, cleared land, built fences, planted corn, and raised cattle. Frontier life had been of the simplest. The first family of Tolt children, four sons and four daughters, saw the light of day first through the chinks of a log cabin. The naked earth served for a floor until puncheon could be substituted. A stick-and-dirt chimney with a rock back was used both for heating and cooking. An iron pot, a Dutch oven, a three-legged skillet, and a tea-kettle were the most important implements with which to cook. Furniture was home-made. Susan dipped her own candles and manufactured the household soap from a dye hopper. She did her own quilting and spinning.

Susan bore her husband a sturdy flock of children who grew up to be sober industrious citizens. The sons settled on places of their own, the daughters married young men of the neighborhood and reared families taught to obey the law and respect the rights of others. And in the fullness of time Susan was gathered to her reward.

In his loneliness steady James Tolt did the one reckless thing of his orderly life. He fell in love with and married wild Jessie LeMay. She was a splendid creature physically, a handsome deep-breasted daughter of the frontier. Nor had there ever been even a whisper against her morals. But there was in her a restless urge for life. She desired passionately to escape the dull routine of the pioneer wife. Rigorously she suppressed her longing and schooled herself to the inevitable. Yet, though she tried to be a docile mate to her husband, there must have been times when James Tolt wondered what manner of woman was this he was attempting to domesticate. He had seen her pace the cage of her married life with the savage fury of a tiger longing for the jungle.

All the repressed revolt in her found expression in the sons she brought into the world. There were seven of them, all tall and powerful. They grew up to be fine horsemen, crack shots, top hands with cows.

They were called the black Tolts because of the difference between them and their father's first family. The children of Susan were sandy of complexion and medium of height. Those of Jessie were all big and dark. The characteristics that stood out were those of the mother rather than the father. James Tolt was no weakling. It is possible that if he had lived longer he might have left a more definite imprint on the children of his second wife, these sons who could be so gay, so daring, so implacable, or so sullen. But he died three weeks before the birth of David, while Caldwell was not yet twelve. So they grew up on the untamed frontier with no check upon their undisciplined wills.

II

Dave Fixes It for Allan

Dave hitched up a team and started for town. What he had learned had changed his view about going. He wanted to get away by himself to think out this amazing thing he had discovered.

His brothers meant to rob the westbound Flyer next Thursday night. From Jack Bray, express messenger, they had found out that there was to be a big shipment of money. How Bray had become aware of this so far in advance did not matter. Probably word had been passed to him from the office. Anyhow, he knew.

That was not all. The plan was to rob the eastbound train too. The excited comment of Steve had told him this. *"The James gang never held up but one at a time."* Since both trains were to be robbed, it must be at the place where they met, at the town of Melrose toward which he was now driving. He would have to find out from someone, very casually, just when the trains arrived and left. Unless there had been a change in the schedule, the eastbound reached Melrose first and waited on a sidetrack for the Flyer. Maybe it would be better for him to ride into town tonight and see for himself. He could stay back in the shadows of some cottonwoods across the track and not be seen at all. Yes, that would be wiser. If he asked questions, perhaps someone might inconveniently remember it later.

From what Dave had overhead in the barn he could guess a great deal more than had been said. Twice last year and once this there had been train robberies within a hundred miles of the ranch. On each occasion his brothers had been absent from home for two or three days, perhaps longer. This had not been significant to him at the time. They were a wild and roistering crew and often did not show up for weeks. Perhaps they might be away buying or driving cattle. Perhaps they were at some trail-end town gambling and carousing. But his mind was satisfied now, beyond any shadow of doubt, that on these specific occasions they had been away robbing trains.

He knew the unsettled condition of the country. There had been within the past few years an increase of lawlessness. Several factors had contributed to cause this. One was the nearness of the Indian country, into which had poured many fugitives from justice and many of the poorer class of settlers who brought up their children in ignorance because of the lack of schools. Another was the opening of the country to homesteaders and the consequent break-up of the big ranches. Cattle had been trailed away in great droves. With them had gone many of the cowboys. Others had remained to take up land and farm. Still others, unable to give up the free life of the range for the more humdrum occupation of raising corn, lived in the chaparral and existed as cattle-rustlers and horse-thieves.

But Dave knew there was a wide gap between a rustler who sneaked out from cover to brand a slick ear and an outlaw daring enough to hold up a train. Not many even of the bad men in 'the nations' had hardihood enough for such a risky business. There could not be two such bands in the territory. His brothers, the black Tolts, would scorn to maverick, but it would be like them, if they crossed the borderline between honesty and crime, to aim high and wager their lives against large stakes. He was willing to bet anything that the express robbery at Painted Rock and the other two at Seven Oaks and Tie station had been their work.

The knowledge his eavesdropping had brought him both awed and thrilled Dave. He had been brought up carelessly, to accumulate lax views as to the law. But even to him it was shocking to learn of the flagrant transgressions of his brothers. He was disturbed, but he was even more impressed. All his life he had listened to stories of the James and the Younger boys. The exploits of the Daltons had come even more closely home to him, for he had ridden over the country where they had played hide-and-seek with such officers as Tilghman and Thomas and Madsen. His brother Dick Tolt had been killed in a gun duel with horse-thieves while he was deputy United States marshal. Both Caldwell and Clay had at one time or another been deputies and each of them had in the course of duty snuffed out lives. The point of view had been borne in on Dave that there was no impassable gulf between the hunter and the hunted. Cole Younger and Emmett Dalton were heroes to him just as much as was Bill Tilghman.

That his brothers meant to excel the Jesse James gang by holding up two trains at the same time made his pulses beat with excitement. Why not? The Tolts were better trailers and scouts, and just as good riders and shots as any of these older outlaws. There could be no question of their gameness. If they got into a tight, they would not try to kill their wounded companions as some of those wolves had done.

Now that he knew the plans of his brothers, Dave did not intend to be ignored with impunity. As yet he did not know what action he would take. Certainly he was not going to sit back with his hands folded while the rest of the black Tolts went into danger. But what could he actually do about it? He might, of course, show up at Melrose on Thursday night masked and armed with an ultimatum that if they went on with the affair they had to take him in with them. But that did not at all satisfy his vanity. What he wanted was to demonstrate to his brothers that he was as much of a man as they were. They had left him out of their plans. If he could find a way to force from them surprised respect because of some real *coup* pulled off—if he could make them admire him or get the laugh on them—there would be an end to that stay-at-home-with-mother stuff.

All very well to dream about. But how could he do it? He had to work within certain limits. Nothing that could hurt them was to be considered. He was devoted to them. They tremendously engaged his affection. Loyalty to them came first, far ahead of the urgent need to express his personal ego in some dramatic fashion that would amaze them.

In the pleasant midday sunshine he drove the buckboard through the suburbs of Melrose. A road shaded by cottonwoods turned at right angles to the left of the main thoroughfare. Into this he swung the pair of young bays. His whip flicked through the air and inspired a burst of speed that came to an end in front of a fence covered by crimson ramblers.

David tied the colts and passed through a gate into an old-fashioned garden of roses, phlox, sweet-williams, and other flowers. He jingled in his spurred, high-heeled boots down a walk bordered by jonquils.

A lad of his own age came clumping along the path to meet him. Both boys sang out jovial greetings. Allan Macdonald and young Tolt had been like Jonathan and that other David whose story has come down to us from Scripture. They had started to school together and learned the alphabet side by side. On roundups they had slept under the same tarp. Once they had gone up the trail as riders of the same outfit. Allan had dragged Dave out of the Cimarron when it was bankfull after a cloudburst. Not two weeks later, Dave had gone out to find his friend during a blizzard, had stumbled over him nearly frozen to death on Hell Roaring Creek, and had dragged him to a deserted cabin where they had waited until the storm was past. Their friendship was almost a proverb in the neighborhood.

"You darned old scalawag, so here's where you hang out," Dave grinned. "I sure enough caught you out this time."

"How about me catching you out?" Allan wanted to know.

A girl lived in the little house at the end of the path.

"Betcha I know what you're doing here, fellow. You been asking Ellen Owens to go with you to the dance Thursday night and she's been explaining how plumb sorry she is but she's going with a handsomer man."

"That ain't quite what she said. Seems she's being accompanied by a lopsided guy who butted in about last Christmas and asked her to go. I expect she'd give him the mitten if it wasn't for hurting his feelings. Wonder who he is. Fellow like that ought to be fed poison." Allan appeared to be innocently puzzled.

"Your information is all wrong, boy. Ellen musta been telling you about some of the lads she turned down. But stick around for a while. I'll fix it so as you can go with her."

Allen looked at him suspiciously. "Like sin, you will."

"Ellen in?"

"Yep."

"You trail back to the house in about ten minutes and you'll find you're elected to be her escort."

"You're loading me."

"No, sir. I can't go to the dance. Got to beg off with Ellen."

"Why can't you go?"

"Got a hen setting. I'll fix it for you. Drift along in a few minutes." Dave smiled derisively. "If I can't take her myself, I want to pick a substitute that's not dangerous."

Young Tolt flung up a hand in temporary farewell and moved on to the house. A girl opened the door to his knock. She was a vivid lass of golden blondeness. At sight of him Cherokee roses poured into her soft cheeks. Joy kicked up its heels in her sky-blue eyes before she decorously subdued the imp.

"You!" she cried in a voice low and melodious.

"Nobody else."

He held out his smooth brown hand and her little one was buried in it. After more blushes she rescued her fingers.

"Allan was just here," she said, to bridge a silence that might tell more of her feeling than words.

"I saw the old galoot. Trying to steal my girl, wasn't he?"

"I'm not your girl." Another tide of color swept her face. "He wanted me to go to the dance with him."

"That's what I came to see you about, Ellen. You better go with him."

She looked at him, astonished. "But I'm going with you, Dave."

"I can't go. Something has come up."

"What do you mean?"

"I just can't go. 'Course I'm awfully sorry. It's . . . business."

"Oh . . . business." Fire flashed in her eyes. What business could an eighteen-year-old boy have to keep him away from a frolic like the Ferguson dance? It was, of course, an excuse. He did not want to take her. "Very well, Mr. Tolt. I'll certainly excuse you . . . very gladly. I wouldn't interfere with your business for the world."

"Now, Ellen, you're not fair, honey—"

"Please don't use that word to me, sir," she flamed. "And what's the use of making so much fuss about it? You don't want to go with me. You're entirely free to take anyone else you like. It just happens I have a little business today myself, so if that's all you came to tell me—"

Allan arrived, and looked as though he wished he had not. He had heard the anger in her pulsing voice.

"I ain't figuring on taking someone else, Ellen. What I thought was that Allan here could take you in my place. I hate not to go, especially after I've invited you, but—"

She cut in bitterly. "That's so good of you, Mr. Tolt. I expect maybe I can get along without having to ask you to find an escort for me, though."

"If you'd be reasonable—" Dave protested.

The girl turned on Allan, her slim body quivering with rage. "So you came along to help him insult me, did you? I'm to be passed from one to another like a sack of meal! No, thank you. It's very kind of you to take pity on me, but I won't impose myself on your good-nature. Of course I'm very grateful. You understand that. I'm grateful that your friend asked me to go with him even if he did think better of it later. And I'm honored that after he dropped me, you were willing to pick me up. But I won't risk it, if you please. You might change your mind too."

The words flamed out of her in a torrent, but at the last her emotion betrayed her. A sob choked her throat. She turned and ran into the house, slamming the door after her.

The boys looked at each other sheepishly.

Allan was the first to speak.

"Well, you fixed it for me, didn't you?" he said.

Dave took off his dusty broad-brimmed hat and scratched his black poll. "I'll be doggoned if that don't beat the Dutch. What made her act thataway?"

His friend relieved himself of one blistering epithet, "Puddin' head!" and followed it by explanation. "How would you expect her to act? She thanked you proper, didn't she—and me too? Of all the lunkheads you take the cake, fellow. 'I ain't got time to take you myself like I promised, *honey,* an' if you don't like it, that's too bad, *honey,* but I got a friend here, *honey,* who—'"

"Shut your trap," Dave ordered, grinning ruefully.

"'—who must be a plumb idjit too, or he wouldn't be sticking around expecting me to fix it.' Boy, you ain't old enough to go gallin'. What you need is a nurse!"

"What I need is a drink! Let's hotfoot it to the Jerry Dunn and irrigate our throats. On the way you can tell me all about women."

Allan ignored the sarcasm. "I don't want a drink, and you don't either. Swallowing tarantula juice don't get you anywhere."

Tolt hooked an arm under his. "That's where

we're going anyhow, deacon. After you've finished with your talk on how to beau a young lady by one who knows, you can say a few well-chosen words on the evils of alcohol."

"I've yet to see anyone it did any good."

"Y'betcha! Take a drunkard's liver now and you'll find—"

"Oh, go to Mexico!"

"Every year an army of thirty thousand unfortunates, ruined by the demon rum—"

Allan gathered the reins of his cowpony from the ground and swung to the saddle. "See you later, fellow."

"At Jerry Dunn's."

Allan did not assent, but he knew that he would be there. It was born of his steady Scotch temperament that he must watch over his wild and reckless friend. He understood Dave because of the deep feeling he had for him. Young Tolt had qualities within him that warred with one another. He was the nicest kind of a boy, jolly, gay, and friendly, absolutely dependable as far as his grit and loyalty and generosity went. He would do to ride the river with. But Allan knew the other side of him too. Something stirred in him, roiled the bitter blood of the black Tolts, and all his sunny good-nature vanished. Anything was likely to happen then, no matter how desperate. As yet there was nothing evil in his record. But any day, given sufficient impulse, he might step across the line to lawlessness, as Allan suspected his brothers had already done.

Dave had always fascinated young Macdonald. The devil-may-care smile, so winning in its warmth; the swinging, panther-like grace, so suggestive of the untamed life of the chaparral; the dancing fire in the black eyes; no wonder Ellen's gaze (Allan had caught it at an unguarded moment when the girl thought there was none to see) followed him with that entranced look compound of adoration and dread.

He was such a superb young animal, Dave, with something sweet and endearing about him that drew Ellen's eyes as steel filings are drawn to a magnet. No girl had ever looked at Allan like that, least of all girls like Ellen Owens. He was too dependable, too curbed. A woman, Allan guessed, wanted to be thrilled by a man, to worry about him. She wanted her love to be full of despair and joy, to have it beating in her bosom like a bird against its cage. Nothing would be so deadly as to have it anchored to assurance. So he thought, sardonically, as he rode to the Jerry Dunn Saloon.

During the day there had not been many minutes when Dave had not been brooding over his problem. Knowing what he knew, how could he use the situation to establish himself with his brothers, to get the laugh on them, to make them acknowledge him a man? The question was still in his mind as he lurked in the shadows of the cottonwoods and observed the eastbound come roaring to a stop on the sidetrack. It was with him still when the Flyer drew into Melrose ten minutes later.

He watched the unloading of freight from the express car of the westbound. He saw the conductor pass into the telegraph office and later come out with the running-order slip in his hand. He noticed figures lounging to and fro on the station platform. Snatches of talk drifted to him. The agent was joshing the messenger about his girl. A crisp "All aboard" sounded. The wheels of the eastbound began to drone out the chant of the rails. The train disappeared into the night. Presently the Flyer too moved on its way. The tail light of the last car vanished around a curve.

Dave's eyes, burning bright, were fixed on the spot where he had last seen that lantern. For a wild idea had just been born in him. It was a crazy notion—absurd—impracticable. But it was tremendously exciting. His pulses tingled. Excitement drummed through his veins. Golly, if it could be done! If he could pull it off!

Suppose a fellow happened to be lucky. Could he do it then? Was it a one-man job? It never had been thought so. But then nobody had ever had the nerve to try it, as far as he had heard. That ought to make it easier. It would come as a surprise, like an unexpected clap of thunder.

Was it after all so crazy, when a fellow looked at it a second time? Someone had been the first settler in this country. Someone had taken up the first trail herd. Because a thing had not been done was no proof that it could not be. A fellow had to use his brains. The point was to work the thing out by gumption.

Dave swung to the saddle and rode back into the brush. Nobody had seen him. That was good. Nobody could say afterward that they had seen him hanging around watching the trains.

Already he had made up his mind to do it. He began to see, rather vaguely as yet, how the thing might be pulled off. If he could use finesse, so much the better. A dozen times on the way back to the ranch he stopped Calico and stared between the ears of the cowpony into the darkness. He was thinking in flashes, but with a close concentration on the project. His mind did not work in logical sequence, but it was wholly absorbed with the plan.

He could not use Calico, of course. If anybody should see the horse the color would be noted. An inconspicuous roan would be best . . . He had better board the train at Twin Buttes. That would just about give him time enough. He must leave before the Flyer reached Melrose. That would mean he must have another horse waiting for him at the point where he dropped from the train. Unless . . .

Dave slapped a hand against his shiny leather chaps. Sure. He would have Allan's boat ready under the bridge and he would not need a second horse. If he was careful there would be no evidence as to how he made his getaway, since he could step down to the boat on the big rocks that buttressed the bridge.

As far as he could see, there would be only two or three ticklish moments in the whole business. One of these, the most vital, was that of his meeting with Bray. If the express messenger suspected him, the enterprise would fall to pieces right there. He would have to work that out very carefully.

His brothers Luke and Steve were sitting on the porch of the house when he came up from the corral.

"Been out, kid?" Luke asked, cleaning out the bowl of his pipe with a knife-blade.

"Yep," Dave answered.

Steve grinned. "I'll bet her name's Ellen."

"Whose name?" Dave asked, a chip on his shoulder.

"The young lady our kid brother has been calling on."

"Shows what you know. I haven't been calling on any."

"Just out for the ride, eh?"

It occurred to Dave that the alibi his brother had offered was as good as any. He did not want to start any suspicion of what he had really been doing. That he would explain later, after he had shown them whether he was a kid or not. Therefore he withdrew, evidently with reluctance.

"More than one girl in this county, ain't there?"

Steve shook his head. "He's a wild young hellion, Luke, a regular heart-smasher. We gotta do something about this."

Dave snorted in disgust and passed into the house. After Thursday night they would lay off this funny business with him. They would be sore at him when they learned how he had fooled them, but he did not care anything about that. They could get over it, and they would never again talk as though he was a school kid.

During the next two days he made what few preparations were necessary. The most important was getting Allan's boat. He did that Wednesday night. There was no difficulty in slipping down to the river and getting the boat. He knew where the oarlocks were hidden in a huckleberry bush and the oars in a hollow gum log. Gently he pushed off from shore and drifted downstream. Occasionally he dipped an oar into the water to keep the boat from getting out of the current and into an eddy. When he came to the railroad bridge, after two hours of travel, he pulled in to the rocks at the foot of one of the abutments.

He hauled the boat up on the rocks and covered it with brush growing at the edge of the river.

Once or twice, when he stepped on the ground instead of a stone, deceived by the darkness, he carefully obliterated the footstep.

While he was still under the bridge he could hear the shrill whistle of the Flyer as it raced westward. Presently it went roaring across the bridge. Dave could feel the structure quiver beneath the weight of the train as it rushed along the rails.

Stepping on the rocks, Dave clambered to the track. He turned south, after tying sacking to his feet. For two miles he followed the track, stepping on the ties and not on the ballast between them. A trestle ran above a creek. From the end of a tie he lowered himself and dropped into the little stream.

He walked along the bed of the creek for fully half an hour as it wound toward the river. Not once did he leave the water during that time. All this might be unnecessary trouble, but Dave did not intend to leave any tracks for either bloodhounds or trailers to follow.

He came to a place where a horse was tied. With his pocket knife he cut loose the sacking on his feet. This he buried beneath a large rock deep under the water. From boulder to boulder he moved to the horse, then released the rein and swung to the saddle.

It was well past eleven o'clock when he opened the door of the room where he and Steve slept.

His brother must have been sleeping lightly, for he wakened. "I'd think you'd get caught up with gallin' onct in a while, kid," he complained. "What time is it?"

"You stick your wooden head in the pillow and go to sleep, fellow," Dave advised cavalierly.

III

A Note Is Left

The station agent at Twin Buttes was unloading fast freight from the express car of the Flyer when someone raised the cry of fire. From the open door of the station, smoke poured in a billowing cloud.

"The depot's on fire," shouted a brakeman.

By common consent everybody converged toward the scene of the fire. Even the express messenger, Jack Bray, taken by the excitement of the moment, left his post of duty and joined the stampede.

One unobserved dissenter did not offer himself as a flame-fighter. He slipped from the back door of the station, crouched under the shadow of the raised platform, and ran beside it as far as the express car. Just before he vanished into the car, he flung an empty coal-oil can beneath the truck.

Bray was absent from the express car less than a minute. He hurried back on the run. A messenger had explicit instructions never to leave his car unlocked. Just now he had a reason why he wanted to have a clean record for obeying the rules.

The others presently returned. They had extinguished the blaze.

"Nothing but a lot of papers I had jammed in

the stove," the agent explained. "Don't see how it started. Someone must have flung a lighted cigaroot in there. Even so, I don't see how the papers ever got out."

"Hmp!" the conductor grunted. "If you ask me, I'd say it was done on purpose. Some firebug. Prob'ly a kid. If I had him here I'll bet I'd warm him up good."

"There was a smell of coal oil," a brakeman added. "That's why the floor caught so quick. Tim's right. It was no accident."

"What would anyone set the depot on fire for?" a platform lounger asked. "That don't make sense to me."

"A firebug hasn't got any sense," the conductor said dogmatically. "Well, we got to roll along. All through, Bray?"

"Yes."

"All aboard!" the conductor sang out.

The wheels began to turn. Bray shut the door of the car and turned to set about his duties. He stopped, aghast, staring at a masked man who had emerged from behind the crates. In the hand of the man was a Colt's forty-four.

"Hoist 'em!" a voice ordered.

The arms of Bray went up.

"What do you want?" he quavered.

"Turn 'round."

He did so. A rope dropped over his head and tightened, fastening his arms close to the body.

Expert hands busied themselves for two minutes, at the end of which time he was trussed so that he could scarcely move a finger.

"W-what do you want?" Bray asked again.

"I want that fifty-thousand-dollar money shipment. Where is it?"

"You're wrong, friend. I haven't got—"

"Don't waste time, fellow." The masked man found keys in the hip pocket of the other's trousers. "Which key? Don't fool with me. I'm dangerous as a side-winder."

"The little key, after you get in. It's a combination lock to the safe."

"Open the safe." The robber loosened the rope sufficiently to allow the messenger the use of one hand.

Bray opened the safe, after which he was tied again and flung down on the floor. With the small key the bandit turned the lock of the inner door. He found a sealed package. His pocket-knife ripped off the cover. Inside were a flat parcel and a canvas sack, both of these also sealed. The knife tore into both of them. One contained greenbacks, the other ten-dollar gold pieces.

Into a gunnysack the outlaw flung both the bills and the gold. From his pocket he took a card, upon which some words had been roughly printed with a pencil. This he left on the shelf where the money shipment had been. He closed, but did not lock, the inner door.

"I reckon that'll be about all I want," he said.

"Did-did you get on at Twin Buttes?" Bray asked.

"Never mind where I got on. You'll know where I get off. Listen, fellow. I want the train stopped so the express car will be just this side of the big bridge near the bend. I'm going to open the door so you can see just where we are. Don't make any mistake—if you want to keep on living. I've got to gag you, but you can nod when the right time comes for me to pull the cord. Understand? No funny business, or—"

The voice of the masked man was harsh and the uncompleted threat a sinister one. Bray gulped once or twice. "I—I'll do my best," he promised.

"See you do."

The bandit opened the door of the car, gagged the messenger with a piece of sacking, and dragged him to his feet so that he could look out at the panorama rushing past them in the night.

The minutes dragged. At last the railroad man turned his head and nodded. The robber pulled the cord and lowered the bound man to the floor.

He stood in the doorway, the gunnysack in one hand. As the train slackened speed, he leaned forward, watching for the right time to jump. The express messenger had timed very accurately the distance required for the train to stop. When the robber flung the sack to the ground and followed it himself, the car was within fifty feet of the end of the bridge.

The man landed on his feet and was impelled forward three or four steps before he could stop. The roadbed beside the track was of cinder, but he took pains to rub out the sharp indentations of his heels. He turned and ran back. His groping fingers found the sack.

Already he could hear the train conductor demanding who had given the signal to halt the Flyer. A brakeman with a lighted lantern was swinging down from the steps of the third coach back of the express car. Still unseen, the masked man ran along the path to the end of the bridge. The engine was well out over the bridge and he could hear the voices of the engineer and fireman. As the bandit descended to the river, he saw the fireman craning out from the cab.

The outlaw swept aside the brush that covered the boat and eased it gently into the stream. He dropped the sack in the flat bottom and took the seat near the center. With an oar he pushed the boat noiselessly out from the bank. Without haste, without rippling the surface of the water by the least splash, he dipped the oars into the water and pulled easily against the current.

The night was dark enough to screen him except at a very close distance. He had no fear of immediate pursuit. The train crew would find Bray, release him, and listen to his story. Then the conductor would decide to go on to Melrose and flash the story over the wire to the division superintendent. Unless he had been seen by the fireman—and that was very unlikely, since the man was looking out from the lighted cab into the darkness—none of the crew would know how he had escaped. It might be that he and his companions were still lying in the brush beside the track. Undoubtedly the trainmen would be very uneasy in mind until they had got away from the scene.

After he had pulled upstream a quarter of a mile, the man in the boat tied the bandanna handkerchief used for a mask around a stone brought for the purpose and dropped it into the river. He grinned.

"About now," he murmured aloud, "the boys are enjoying a nice pleasant surprise." He chuckled as he put his back into the oars to get more speed. "Bet your boots Mr. Jack Bray is having a heck of a time satisfying them he did not throw them down. They'll be right suspicious, I reckon."

His surmise was correct.

The two older brothers were in the express car. The other three covered the crews of the trains. More than once a shot rang out as a warning to the passengers to attempt no resistance. Neither Caldwell nor Cole paid any attention to these. They were signals that all was well.

Caldwell glared at a slip of paper lying on the shelf in front of him. He picked it up and carried it to the light. Over his shoulder Cole too read the message.

> Fooled! Beat you to it by ten minutes. Better luck next time. When I see you, I'll explain how to rob a train.
>
> The Kid

What did it mean? Who was the kid? How did he know they were intending to hold up the Flyer at Melrose that night?

To that last question there was only one answer. Jack Bray had been false to them.

Caldwell ripped the mask from his face and turned on the man watching him with fear-filled eyes.

"So you threw us down?"

The voice of Caldwell Tolt was quiet, but the sound of it made the express messenger shiver.

"I swear to Heaven, Caldwell—"

"Didn't you know us better than that, you poor fool?"

"I didn't. Lemme tell you how it was. Listen. I been figuring it out. This fellow set fire to the depot at Twin Buttes. He musta hopped in here when I ran to see the fire and hid behind the crates. First I knew he had me covered. Then he tied and gagged me."

"You thought that old trick would work with us, eh? Why, the fellow gives it away in his note. He admits he knew we were going to rob the train. *Who told him?*"

Beads of perspiration stood on the forehead of the messenger. He was talking for his life, and he knew it. Presently, unless he could persuade this man he had not betrayed him, a crook of a finger would send a bullet crashing into his brain.

"You gotta believe me, Caldwell. It's the truth. I don't know any more than you do who he is. It's like I been telling you. He made me stop the train and let him get off at the bridge. Pulled the cord when I gave the word. As the train slowed up, he jumped."

"Says he was ten minutes ahead of us, Bray. *Who told him that?*"

"Listen, boys," the messenger pleaded, despair in his face. "I ain't a plumb idiot. I wouldn't throw you down and expect to talk you out of gunning me. It ain't reasonable. Look at it my way and—"

"Who told him? Answer our question." It was Cole this time, implacably harsh.

"I don't know. Maybe one of you boys talked, maybe—"

"Talked ourselves out of fifty thousand dollars?" Caldwell asked grimly. "Come clean, Bray. Who did you let into this? We want his name."

"I'd swear it on a stack of Bibles, boys!" Bray

cried. "I'm innocent. Don't kill me. I'll stick around. You can bump me off later if you ain't satisfied. I got a wife and three babies. Think. If I was double-crossing you, would I let my partner write a note to you like that? It would be like signing my own death-warrant."

That was true. It was a point that had already occurred to Caldwell. He could not quite believe that Bray was such a fool. Nor could he think the man bold enough to sell them out and stay to face the music. There was something mysterious about it. Yet the one fact that stood out was that nobody but Bray knew of their plan except themselves.

"Have you been drinking lately?" Caldwell asked.

"No. I never do drink. Boys, I've kept this under my hat. I've been a clam. It didn't get out through me. I'll take my oath on that."

"How did it get out? Who else knew we were going to hold up the Flyer tonight at Melrose? Tell me that."

"I don't know. I haven't got a notion who this fellow is."

"He signs himself the kid. Know anybody called that?"

"No, I don't."

Caldwell moved a step closer. "Give me his name. Tell me where he's taking that money."

"Don't!" shrieked Bray. "For God's sake, don't!"

"Last chance, fellow. Who is he?"

Caldwell's brown hand moved to the butt of his revolver.

The knees of the messenger knocked together. Cole had been watching him steadily. He lifted a restraining hand.

"Wait," he said to his brother. "I don't believe he threw us down, Caldwell. Let's give him a chance, anyhow. What say we take him with us and talk this over with the other boys?"

In Caldwell's mind, too, there was a doubt. Logically he could see no explanation except the one that Bray had double-crossed them. But some feeling not based on reason told him there was a mystery here not yet solved. He was no cold-blooded murderer. Swiftly he made a decision.

"All right. We'll take him with us. If we find he's been false, we can dry-gulch him some-where."

The reprieve was too much for the messenger. His legs buckled under him and he slid down in a faint.

The Tolts looked at him in disgust. They were not used to dealing with men whose nerves were so tricky. One virtue that the frontier breeds is courage.

"No sand in his craw." Cole commented. "He'd never have the pluck to play us a trick like that."

"No," his brother agreed. "Yet he did, looks like."

"We've got to be going."

"Yes."

Caldwell dragged the messenger to his feet. The man's eyes opened. From blankness they came to fear. He recollected where he was.

"You're going with us. Understand?"

"Yes. I—I want to go with you, Caldwell," Bray gulped.

"Do you?" Tolt's voice was harsh. "That's fine, since you're going, anyhow. If you make any break to get away, you'll be committing suicide. Don't forget that. Tumble out of here."

Ten minutes later the train robbers and their prisoner were moving rapidly down a main-traveled road. This they presently left, to push into the brush. After an hour of fast travel, they came to a rimrock, along which they moved in single file, sticking to the sandstone to obscure the trail. From this they descended to a creek and followed the bed of it for miles. One at a time they left the stream, at distances of seven or eight hundred yards apart. North, south, west, they went. He would be a good trailer who could follow the spoor of any one of them.

IV

The Dance at Ferguson's Ranch

Allan Macdonald rode up to the Ferguson Ranch about eight o'clock and tied his horse to the hitchrack. He could hear the squeak of the fiddles, the shrill voice of old Dunc Dagley calling a quadrille, and the shuffle of feet on the floor.

A group of lads hung around the door of the house, most of them young fellows who felt less awkward there when re-enforced by others than on the floor among the dancers. Allan joined them.

His gaze searched the room and found one of the two persons for whom he was looking. Dave Tolt was not present. Allan had half-expected to see him in spite of that setting hen which the boy had said would keep him away. But Ellen Owens was in one of the sets, dancing with Jim Nelson.

She was the best dancer in the settlement. In one's arms she was as light as a feather-down. Her winged feet moved to music as one who loved the rhythm of it. When Allan danced with her, he felt a strange sense of enchantment. She was no longer just a girl, with tiny freckles powdering an impudent little nose. There was glamour about her. She was the soul of poetry and music.

But tonight there was a difference. Ellen was gayer than usual. She talked and laughed more.

Because he knew her, just as he knew Dave Tolt, by the talisman of love, he guessed the reason for her animation, for the excited flush on her cheeks. She was defiantly intent on showing how happy she was. Watching her, Allan for the first time felt an odd sense of pity for her vulnerable youth. It would be so easy to wound her through the emotions. She quivered so with life, went forward to meet it so eagerly and joyously, that she laid herself open to injury. It came to young Macdonald, with a sure instinct, that there could be no happiness for her with such a man as Dave Tolt. If she followed his reckless steps, it would be only to find grief and sorrow at the end of the journey.

He did not ask to dance with her. In her mind he was associated tonight with the humiliation Dave had put upon her by his casual repudiation of the date they had made. She would not want to do a quadrille or a schottische with him, and it was like Allan not to press his attentions when not desired.

For half an hour he hung around, then abruptly left the house and walked across the yard to the hitchrack.

Jim Nelson called after him. "Where you going, Allan? Didn't someone tell you there's a dance at Ferguson's?"

Allan swung to the saddle. "I'm not dancing tonight. Got to see a fellow up the road."

He struck a trail through the brush that led him,

after several devious miles of travel, to the Tolt place.

From outside he called "Hello the house!" before he dismounted and clumped across the porch to the door. Jessie Tolt opened to his knock.

"Evening, Mrs. Tolt. Dave in?" he asked.

She looked surprised. "Have you forgotten it's the night of the Ferguson dance?"

"He ain't there—not when I left."

"He's getting his girl, don't you reckon?" Jessie Tolt smiled, the swift warm smile her son David had inherited. "Did you ever know him to stay away from a dance?"

"No, but—he kinda told me, Mrs. Tolt, he didn't allow to go to this one."

"Why?" she asked, surprised.

"Business, he said."

"What business has he got that would keep him away from any frolic, let alone a dance like this? Don't worry. He's probably there by this time—with Ellen Owens."

"No, ma'am. Ellen came with Jim Nelson."

"She did?"

"Yes, ma'am."

"Have they had any quarrel, Ellen and Dave? He told me last week he was going with her."

"They sorta had a misunderstanding," Allan admitted. He was sorry now that he had come. Certainly he did not intend to tell any tales out of school.

"What about?"

"Oh, I dunno." He laughed awkwardly. "You know how young folks are."

"Did she give Dave the mitten?"

"No, Mrs. Tolt. If you want to know how it is, I reckon you'll have to ask Dave himself."

"It's his fault. I'll guarantee that," she said promptly.

"Well, I'll be going along back. Thought maybe you knew where he was."

But Allan did not return to the Ferguson place, not for several hours at least. For him there would be no pleasure in going back to watch Ellen dancing with other men, knowing that she was being driven to gayety by a fever of pride and unhappiness. He rode home. But he did not go into the house, since he did not want to answer his mother's questions as to why he was not at the Ferguson dance. He left his horse saddled in the stable and lay down on the hay in the barn loft. His mind was not easy about Dave. He could find no reason sufficient for keeping him away from such a party, one that was an annual affair celebrated in the neighborhood.

Could it be another girl? He rejected the idea. Dave would not deliberately insult Ellen. There must be another reason, a potent one; and for the life of him Allan could not think of one important enough to satisfy him.

The thing was so disturbing that in the end he

rode back to the dance. Perhaps Dave had showed up after all. Very likely he was worrying about nothing.

In answer to his question one of the door loungers told him Dave had not been seen.

"That's funny too," the young fellow added, "for I never knew him miss a big blowout like this before."

"He musta broke a leg," another said with a grin.

"He musta broke two," a third corrected. "One busted leg wouldn't keep Dave away. Wonder what that boy's up to. Funny, there ain't a black Tolt here tonight."

"That's a fact," Jim Nelson agreed. He added amiably, "I'll bet they're raising Cain somewhere."

Herb Peterson raised another point of order. "Where you been yore own self, Allan? You come and go without shaking a hoof onct. Then you come back hours later. You've not been drinking, deacon. What's on yore mind?"

"I'm gonna join the church and quit dancing," Allan explained cheerfully.

"The hell you are! Think up another good one."

The sound of a horse's drumming hoofs was heard in the yard. A few moments later its rider appeared in the doorway.

"'Lo, Dave!" Nelson shouted at the newcomer. "Where in Mexico you been?"

Dave laughed. "You'd never guess. I was out

last night some late. Well, I took a li'l' snooze just before I started to the dance, and I'll be dadgummed if I didn't sleep till about half an hour ago."

Allan looked at him. The explanation had been given easily and lightly. Dave had not blinked an eye. But Allan did not believe a word of it.

In Cattleland dances occurred all too seldom. Pioneers came for many miles to lighten their drab lives on such festive occasions. The young men cantered up on cowponies. Whole families arrived in wagons. Babies were put to sleep in rows on the beds of the ranch-house. The dancing was fast and furious.

When the morning sun slanted over the willow bushes bordering Squaw Creek at the Ferguson place, the fiddles were still sawing and boot-heels cutting capers on the floor. Only a few of the more sedate had set out for home.

A man rode up to the ranch on a fly-bitten sorrel, trailed the bridle reins, and walked into the house. The man was Pete Evans, sheriff of the county. He circulated quietly among the guests, passed the time of day with one and another, asked a few questions so casually that he did not seem to listen to the answers.

Evans was an old cowman. He had in days past been up the trail to Abilene and Dodge and Ogallala. In the vernacular, he had for twenty years choused longhorns through the brush. Because he knew cows and their ways and cow-thieves and their ways he had been elected sheriff by honest citizens who trusted him. A tough, hard-bitten *hombre*, Pete Evans, one who would sleep on a cold trail many nights to get his man.

The quadrille caller's sing-song chant came to an end with an injunction to "take yore pardners you know where." Evans interrupted a rising hum of conversation to make an announcement. He stood on a bench close to the two fiddlers.

"Last night at Melrose the eastbound and the Flyer were held up and robbed."

The talk died down to give time to digest this astonishing news, then broke out again in a burst of eager questions and comment.

The sheriff stilled the hubbub. "I'm here to raise a posse to take the trail of the bandits," he explained. "I want you, Saunders—and you, Buck Pettis—and Bert Steelman—and Hank Wayne." His gaze traveled over the lifted faces and came to rest on that of Dave Tolt. "And you too—young Tolt."

"I'm not armed," Pettis protested.

"I know. Go home—all five of you—get well armed and mounted on good horses. Meet me at Webb's Corner inside of an hour." Evans had another word for Dave. "If any of your brothers are at home, boy, bring a couple of them with you."

Dave nodded, his eyes shining. The excitement in him was tinctured with mirth. It was natural enough the sheriff should want some black Tolts on his posse. They were good trailers and first-class fighting men. But under the circumstances —the knowledge of which was Dave's very secret possession—a posse of Tolts would be a joke on Evans too good not to enjoy. The lad could see his brothers, seriously solemn, riding diligently on their own trail to capture themselves.

The dance broke up. Ranchers stayed a little while to talk over the train robbery, then hitched up and drove home to get some sleep for themselves and their families.

Allan Macdonald rode home slowly. He was greatly disturbed. It was, of course, absurd to let his soul be drowned in dread with no sufficient evidence to cause such a depression. Why had he thought so instantly of Dave and his brothers? Very likely they had a perfect alibi. And yet . . .

Everything dovetailed to raise his suspicion. Dave had broken his engagement to take Ellen to the Ferguson Ranch dance. None of the Tolts had been at the frolic. Why had that imp of deviltry leaped to Dave's eye when Evans had named him for a place on the posse?

Just why had the sheriff picked Dave? There were older and more experienced men in the room, old-timers who had been tried and given proof of their fitness to cope with an emergency.

But Evans had passed over them to choose an untested boy. Had he a reason, one known only to himself? Evans was a shrewd man, very resourceful. He had made good as a law enforcer. If he had not positively declined a renomination, he would without doubt have been reëlected in November. Why, then, had he selected Dave? Allan wished he knew the answer to that question.

Remote streams of influence pour both before and after birth into the being of all of us. In Allan was a blend of the Scotch Presbyterian and the clan Highlander. One strain gave him solidity of character, the other loyalty and devotion. All his life he would walk the straight line of duty because of this inheritance. But in Dave were currents far less stable. He was a creature of unschooled impulse. It would be easy for him to go wrong, since his will to do right was not founded on principle.

Allen could not set about his daily work and let the problem alone. He had to make sure. He had to find out whether Dave had stepped outside the law so flagrantly.

There would be no use in going to his friend with a blunt question. Dave would give him that engaging and debonair smile as he evaded an answer. For if young Tolt was in the train robbery, he was not in it alone. Allan took that for granted. He could tell nothing without betraying his brothers.

Allan rode in to Melrose to get the details of the affair. No other subject of conversation was being talked on the streets. It was a confusing story. According to the train crew, one man had robbed the express car of the Flyer and had jumped from the train at the bridge. Later, the train had been held up again at Melrose.

This was not reasonable. One could not stretch coincidence so far as to think that two gangs would try to hold up the same train on the same night. The solitary bandit could not be playing a lone hand. He must be a member of the outfit that had worked at Melrose. But what was the sense of having him rob the train before his partners did the same thing? On the face of it this seemed absurd.

Allan could find no starting-point at Melrose. He rode along the track as far as the bridge at the bend, then sat in the saddle with his elbow on the horn and his chin resting on the fingers of his fist while he thought the thing over. Presently he swung down and gazed at the river below.

How had the lone bandit made his escape? It was possible that he had a horse waiting for him in the brush. That would be the obvious way. But a horse leaves a track that can be followed.

Macdonald put himself in the place of the robber. Why stop the train just at the bridge? Was there any reason for him to stop it here rather than somewhere else? No reason, unless . . .

The eyes of the boy grew quick with excitement. Of course. That must be why.

He descended on the rocks to the river. Underneath the bridge he found the marks in the sand where a boat had been drawn up to the rocks. Evidently it had been a flat-bottomed boat, a wide river tub much like his own. The fellow had launched the craft in the darkness, no doubt, and pulled either up or down stream.

Allan obliterated the marks of the boat and walked back to his horse. He made one mistake.

It did not occur to him that his own tracks would have any significance.

The affair was still a Chinese puzzle to Allan. What had stimulated the lone bandit to do the job? Why take all this trouble when his friends were waiting at Melrose to hold up the Flyer? Allan could see no reason or point in robbing the train twice.

There must have been some cause for doing so, but the motive was one he could not fathom.

Young Macdonald rode back to the ranch and ate his dinner in an unusual silence.

"What's ailing you?" his mother asked.

He roused himself. "Nothing. I was thinking about the train robbery. They say the bandits got fifty thousand dollars from the express car and about ten thousand from the passengers of the two trains."

"It'll bring them nae guid luck."

"No," Allan agreed. "Did Father leave word about mending the line fence?"

"He said for you to do it as soon as you came hame. Were you at the dance a' this time?"

"I rode into Melrose. Everybody is excited over the robbery. Sheriff Evans is out with a posse. Dave is with him."

"I hope the sheriff catches them and puts an end to sic doings. There are ower many folk like that in this part o' the country."

Allan assented, with mental reservations. If the outlaws were the men he had in mind, he did not want the sheriff to run them down.

For two days Allan thought of little else. Worry rode his shoulders while he worked. It lay down with him at night. Once he saw Dave. The posse had returned from an unsuccessful attempt to follow the trail of the gang that had held up the train. Allan had not been able to talk alone with his friend, but he sensed a new reserve in the manner of young Tolt.

Sunday morning he walked down to the river and sat down in his flat-bottomed boat. Nobody would disturb him here. He could think at leisure.

His gaze rested on the rope which fastened the bow, at first absently, his mind registering no conclusions. Presently his eyes fixed on the knot tied around a young willow. They grew live with interest. It was a knot unused in Cattleland. A sailor had taught it to him and to Dave. Probably nobody else in the neighborhood knew how to make it. Allan knew he had not made fast the boat with that knot.

He found it too complex to employ, but it was a favorite of Dave's. The use of it had become almost automatic with his friend.

Allan had been out on the river Wednesday morning. Now he found the boat made fast by Dave's reef knot. A weight as of lead pushed upon his heart. Dave had written his signature unwittingly, telling him that the train robbery was his work.

He no longer had any doubt that young Tolt had been the lone bandit who held up the express car. He had borrowed Allan's boat, hidden it under the bridge, and made his escape in it.

He must have pulled up the river in the darkness and at this point left with the money taken from the safe. Very likely one of his brothers had met him here; or possibly had waited for him under the bridge. On this detail Allan reserved judgment. According to the train crews there had been five masked men in the gang at Melrose. That accounted for all the black Tolts except Dave. Yet surely they would not have let him attempt so dangerous a thing alone. Perhaps they had taken in with them as a confederate somebody else, though that did not seem like them. A strong family tie bound them. They were sufficient to themselves. Outsiders were rarely invited to join them even in their harmless sprees.

Two of the second family of Tolts were married and had families, but even these bonds had not been able to break the fraternal solidarity.

The time element had to be considered. Dave would not have had time after pulling up the river from the bridge to ride back home before showing up at the dance. Had he buried the loot? Or had he turned it over to one of his brothers?

Allan tried to put himself in the place of Dave. The trouble was that he did not know the facts from which to make deductions. According to the story Bray had told the trainmen before his disappearance, a single bandit had robbed the express car. Had Bray told the truth? Very likely not. It looked as though he was one of the gang and had vanished with the others into the brush to avoid arrest. But if his tale was true and if the five masked men at Melrose were Tolts, then Dave must have cached the express shipment either before or after leaving the boat.

Where would he be likely to bury it?

V

Dave Declares Himself

Three of the black Tolts were talking together in the horse corral. Dave sauntered toward them from the house.

Cole called to him. "Wish you'd fork a bronc, kid, and run up the horses in the south pasture."

Dave showed no resentment at this summary disposal of him. He grinned, from an inner source of amusement. Presently they would change their tune.

"Haven't you fellows ridden enough lately? I'd think you'd stay lit for a spell." He drawled his question and his suggestion indolently.

Luke turned suspicious eyes on him. There was something unusual in the kid's manner, an assurance behind which lurked an odd jubilation. "What d'you mean?"

The boy looked as innocent as a cat which has just stolen the cream. "Must I mean something particular? You got a bad conscience, Luke?"

A little impatiently, Sam brushed the conversation aside. "Run along, Dave. We're talking business."

A week ago the youngest of the Tolts would have been sullen. He would have been hurt at being excluded from their confidence. Now he was gayly indifferent. This was the last time any of them would ever pull with him that go-off-and-play stuff.

"Where'll I run to?" he asked.

"Run and get the horses like Cole said."

Leisurely Dave climbed the corral fence, took a knife from his pocket, and began to whittle a stick. "I'll bet two bits I can put a name to that important business you're discussing."

"Meaning what?" Cole asked curtly.

"The holdup of the Flyer."

"What would we be talking about that for?" Luke snapped.

Dave's smile was bland. "Ain't everyone talking about it?"

"Nothing to us, is it?"

There was a just perceptible pause before Dave answered. "I reckon not, Luke, unless you were figuring on going after the reward."

"We weren't figuring on it," Cole said harshly. "We haven't lost any train robbers. Have you?"

"Me? No." Dave opened his eyes wide. "I'm only a kid, you know."

The black eyes of Cole fastened on him. Only a kid. The kid. A glimmer of an idea was reaching the outskirts of Cole Tolt's mind. It had not formulated itself yet, but presently it would.

"But if I was as old as you-all are, I'd go after

that six thousand dollars' reward. Six thousand isn't fifty thousand by a long way, still—"

Dave left the sentence suspended in air.

"We're obliged for your advice, bud," Sam said, with obvious sarcasm. "What's your idea about those broncs—that if you whittle long enough they'll come running up?"

"A lot of money—fifty thousand. Even if you had to split it four-five ways," Dave murmured aloud, as though to himself.

Three pairs of black eyes focused on him.

"What's in your noodle, kid?" Cole demanded roughly.

"Oh, I was kinda thinking. The robbers hid it, don't you reckon? Likely they would, until the hunt quiets down. If a fellow could find it—"

"You better forget that kind of talk, kid," Luke told him abruptly. "It doesn't get you anywhere."

"Doesn't it? You never can tell. I could do a lot with fifty thousand, if I am a kid . . . What do you reckon these fellows took Bray with them for? Or was that just a bluff, to fool the train crew? Maybe Bray was in cahoots with these birds."

"You're certainly smart as a whip," Sam said ironically. "By and by you'll figure out who the holdups were."

Dave sliced a long shaving from the stick in his hand. "Oh, I've got that figured out now," he drawled.

Cole's shining eyes were fixed intently on the boy. "Meaning who?"

The youngster returned his gaze, a gleam of a smile on his brown face. "Meaning the black Tolts."

Luke spoke, harshly, frowning at Dave. "What do you claim to know, kid?"

"Nothing," Sam cut in. "He's shooting off his mouth. We'll stop that kind of talk right here. There won't be any more of it."

Cole slid down from the fence where he had been sitting and moved toward Dave. From his coat pocket he took a slip of paper and handed it to the lad. "Ever see this before?"

Dave looked at what was written on the paper.

Fooled! Beat you to it by ten minutes. Better luck next time. When I see you I'll explain how to rob a train.

The Kid

The boy grinned. "Seems to me I have."

"You wrote it?"

"Maybe so."

Sam let out a startled exclamation. "You mean, Cole—"

"I mean that Dave robbed the train and took the express shipment."

The other two brothers stared at Dave, still unbelieving. For the moment astonishment robbed them of speech.

"Speak your piece, boy," Cole ordered curtly. "In a hurry. No more joshing."

The youngest brother told his story. The others listened without interruption until he had finished.

"So you were in the barn and heard us plan it?" Cole asked.

"Like I just told you. Yes."

"And you slipped into the car without Bray noticing it?"

"When he ran to see the fire."

"Then you threw down on him after the train started?"

"That was the way of it."

Luke broke in with a reminder. "I'd better get to the boys right off and let them know. On account of Bray."

"That's right," Cole agreed. "Slap a saddle on that claybank and hurry, for God's sake. If they bumped Bray off—"

Already Luke was running for the barn. Three minutes later he galloped down the road.

"You did fine," Sam told Dave bitterly. "I reckon you never thought of Bray, never figured we'd decide he'd thrown us down. You were so busy getting all swelled up on yourself, you left him to face the music. If the boys have shot him, you're to blame."

"Shot him!" Dave echoed, going white to the lips.

"Why not? Did you allow we'd sit down and let him go back on us? Don't you know us better than that? Bray had the narrowest escape of any fellow I ever knew. You just missed making your own brothers murderers. That's how smart you are. And all to show off, so you could throw a big chest and say, 'Look at me.'"

"That's true, Dave," Cole confirmed. "Why did you do it? Aren't you one of us? What's the idea?"

Filled with self-reproach, Dave blurted out his defense.

"How do you mean one of you? You treat me like I was a baby. You go around whispering, pulling off this and that, and never letting me in on any of it. All right. Have it your own way. Suits me if it does you. But I've served notice on you where I stand. I'm one of you or I ain't. Which is it? You got no right to leave me out and then kick because I play a lone hand."

"We left you out because we didn't want to get you into trouble," Cole explained.

"Right good of you. Well, I'm not in trouble. I'm about fifty thousand dollars out of trouble. I expect I'll start a bank maybe. Would any of you like to borrow money—on good security?"

Sam laughed. "He's got us where the wool's short, Cole. It's the doggondest piece of nerve I ever did see. But he's made his play, and it takes the pot. No use trying to keep him out any longer. He's like all the rest of the black Tolts—got hell in his neck. And that's all there's to it."

"Looks like," Cole agreed. "Where's the loot hidden, kid?"

"I'll lead you to it," Dave said promptly.

He did not care a jackstraw for the money. His brothers might have all or any part of it they wanted. What he wished was to be part of their fellowship. He felt like a young esquire who has won his spurs. Henceforth he was one of them.

But one fear still disturbed him. "Where's Bray now?" he asked. Then he answered his own question. "With Caldwell and Steve, I reckon. The boys won't . . . hurt him before Luke gets there, will they?"

"Hope not," Cole said. "Steve's some impulsive and Caldwell's a whole lot annoyed. We've been holding Bray to satisfy ourselves. Luke will be in time, I reckon."

Dave knew he would not be happy until he heard Bray was safe.

Sam could not keep his thoughts from the *coup* his young brother had pulled. It was an amazing thing to which he could not get his mind adjusted. They had thought they were setting a precedent in audacity by robbing two trains at the same time. But he had gone them one better by getting away with the express shipment single-handed. Nobody had ever done such a thing before—and Dave was only a kid. "Where have you got the stuff cached, boy? Is it in a safe place?" he asked.

"It's in that cabin on the island, the one Allan and I built to sleep in when we used to go camping," Dave answered. "I dug a hole in the dirt floor and buried it there."

"Nobody could have seen you there?"

"No. I worked without a light—dug the hole with an old axe we left there."

"Better get it right off, I reckon," Cole suggested. "We could make out we were fishing."

They saddled and rode across to the Macdonald place, taking with them fishing-poles, bait, and tackle.

Mrs. Macdonald came to the door when they hallooed the house. Allan was not at home, she explained, but of course they could take his boat. She asked Sam if the posse had found any track of the bandits.

"No, ma'am. I reckon they came over from the Nation. We won't ever hear any more about them, unless they break loose again. My notion is that they're on the dodge in the brush a hundred miles from here by now," he said.

The fishermen pulled across to the island and walked up the slope to the dugout the boys had built four or five years earlier.

"In that corner over there," Dave told them. "There's a covered box in the ground where Allan and I used to keep all sorts of things. We haven't used it since we were kids."

Dave got the axe and used it as a shovel to clear away the dirt.

"Ground's soft," Sam said, watching him. "You didn't tromp it down good."

"But I did," Dave denied. He was oppressed by a queer sense of defeat, a premonition that all was not well. He remembered that he had left the rusty axe outside, and he had found it leaning against the wall in a corner. And surely he had packed the earth tighter than this before he had left.

With his hand he scooped from the lid of the box the last of the loose mold. His brothers sat on their heels, close to the hole he had dug, their black eyes fixed on the box.

Dave lifted the top. He stared down, astonished and dismayed. The box was empty.

After his father, mother, and sisters had gone to sleep, Allan slipped out of his room by a window and soft-footed to the stable. In one of the stalls was a big horse with a roached mane. He saddled, then went to the oatbin and dived his arm deep into the grain. After a moment of rummaging he straightened and dragged out a gunnysack.

The contents of the sack were heavy. He tied with a second string the mouth and made the bag secure to the saddle. This done, he led the gelding down the road for a hundred yards before he mounted.

The thing he was going to do had to be done

secretly. Nobody must ever know it. In no way must it ever be brought home to him. For that reason he did not follow the road, but turned into the brush and cut across country. He traveled westward. So familiar was the terrain to him that he did not need the light of the stars to give a direction. He could have found his way in the blackest night.

He cut across the road again at Three Crossings and about half a mile beyond that point came to it again. Here he was forced to follow a beaten track, since barbed-wire fence ran along one side and a ledge dropped to the river on the other.

There was no reason why anyone should interfere with him. That was the least of his worries. But he did not want to be seen. He did not want anyone to be able to say that they had seen Allan Macdonald riding to or from Melrose on Sunday night.

His luck did not hold up. He met a man riding in the opposite direction. Allan kept going, hoping he had not been recognized. This would be too good to expect, since he had known the other rider at a glance. The man was Clem Howland.

A voice shouted to him. "Hey, young fellow! Stop! You—Macdonald!"

The last word brought Allan to halt. Since he had been identified, he must show no sign of concern. He twisted in the saddle and waited. Howland turned his horse and came back.

Clem Howland had a bad reputation. He was known to be a killer and suspected of being a rustler. Four months prior to this time he had capitalized his notoriety as a gunman by securing an appointment as deputy United States marshal, succeeding Clay Tolt, who had resigned.

Allan waited uneasily for the man to speak.

"Where you going this time o' night?" the deputy asked harshly.

The gorge of young Macdonald rose at the man's insulting manner. Howland was a bull-necked, gross-bodied man with cold, protruding eyes. Deterioration was written large on him. He had been very muscular and strong, but dissipation and slack living had taken their toll of his force. He was still one to fear, for he was a dead shot and had no scruple about taking human life. Most men even on the frontier would have walked a long way around Clem Howland rather than come into conflict with him.

Allan swallowed his anger. He wanted no trouble with the fellow. After all, he was only a boy and this bully held a notorious reputation as a gunman. Moreover, just now Allan wanted no doubts about him increased but rather allayed. The sack tied across the horn of his saddle made him vulnerable.

"Kinda driftin' around," Allan replied. "Some of the boys are frolicking in town tonight. Thought I'd sashay in and say 'Howdy?' to them."

"Funny time you're starting," Howland said offensively. "What boys?"

"Do you care when we start, Mr. Howland?" Allan asked.

"I said what boys," the man reiterated.

"Oh, I dunno. You know our crowd. I can't say for sure just who'll be there."

"Dave Tolt maybe—and Steve."

"I don't reckon so."

The deputy's gaze rested on the gunnysack. "What you got there?" he asked sharply.

Allan felt his muscles tighten. Already his nerves were taut. In the darkness he had shifted the quirt in his hand so that he held it about a foot from the loaded end. Now his fingers bit into the rawhide with a grip almost convulsive.

"A feed of oats," Allan replied. "No telling when I'll get home."

"So? Oats, eh?"

Howland leaned forward to put his hand on the sack. At the same time Allan touched his horse with a spur. The gelding went into the air, came down, and did a sidling dance. The deputy pressed closer.

"I gotta be going," Allan announced. "So-long. See you again."

He started to turn his horse, but was a fraction of a second too late. Howland caught the bridle rein.

"No, you don't!" he told the boy roughly. "I'll see what's in that sack."

Allan's quirt swept up and swiftly down. The loaded end struck the deputy marshal's head an inch above the temple. Even though the man's hat protected him to a certain extent, the blow fell with a force that was paralyzing. Howland swayed in the saddle, drooped heavily, and slid to the ground. The boy raised the quirt again and cut the horse across the flank. The cowpony bolted down the road.

Macdonald whirled his horse and put it to a canter. He wanted to get away from the spot as fast as he could.

Half an hour later, he rode into Melrose through the silent suburbs. He tied the horse to some bushes back of a barn. On foot he moved toward the single long business street. Presently he diverged, turning into an alley that ran parallel to the main thoroughfare. Down this he went gingerly, the sack on his back.

So far he had been lucky. Nobody had seen him since he had reached Melrose. From the Jerry Dunn saloon came a sound of drunken voices. Except for that there appeared to be no sign of life in the town.

He reached the building he wanted, the rear door of the express office. To the left of the door was a barred window, the irons about six inches apart. Swiftly Allan arranged the contents of the sack in such a way as to leave it as lean as possible. With a large stone he broke the lower right-hand pane of the window, tapping at the glass to leave as large a free space as possible. He picked up the sack, put one end through the opening, and thrust the bundle into the room. As soon as he heard it fall to the floor, he ran up the alley, dodged from it into Main Street, and raced along the road to the residence section.

Presently he reached his horse, swung to the saddle, and galloped out of town.

VI

An Arrest

News travels like wildfire through the brush country. Within a few hours remote ranches learned that someone had returned to the express company the fifty-thousand-dollar money shipment that had been stolen from the Flyer. This report was more astounding than the robbery itself. Why should anyone go to the trouble and danger of holding up a train if the proceeds were to be tossed back to the company through a window as casually as a bundle of old rags?

Another mysterious factor was the reappearance of Jack Bray. The story of the express messenger left a good deal to be explained. He said that he had been blindfolded, taken into the hills, kept under a close guard for three days, and at last had been released by the bandits. He could give no description of the outlaws, nor could he suggest any plausible reason for his abduction. The opinion of the officials was that he was concealing information, either because he was afraid to talk or because he had been in the conspiracy to steal the express shipment. But the most rigid investigation could not shake his tale.

Two men rode up to the Macdonald place the

day after the return of the money. One of them was Sheriff Evans, the other Clem Howland. They inquired for Allan.

The boy's mother said he was not at home. She was curious. "What do you want with him?" she asked.

"Want him to explain this express robbery," Howland blurted. He was furious at the humiliation of last night and he was quite willing to hurt the mother of the boy who had assaulted him.

"What do you mean?" Jean Macdonald asked. There was no alarm in her voice. She knew her son. He could not be implicated in so dreadful a business as this.

"Can't you hear? He and that Dave Tolt are in this holdup clear to their hocks. We want him."

"That's not true," the woman answered quietly, an edge of scorn in her manner. "It's silly to say such a thing. Allan is a good boy." She turned to the sheriff. "I'm surprised at you, Mr. Evans."

Pete Evans was disgusted with Howland. They had agreed to say nothing about their reason for wanting to see Allan until he was in their hands. "We think maybe he has found out something, Mrs. Macdonald, so we want to have a little talk with him," he answered.

"What could he have found out?"

"That's what we want to ask him," Evans evaded.

Howland took off his hat and showed a blood-stained bandage tied around his head. "That's what he did, yore good boy, when I started to arrest him last night—hit me unexpected with the loaded end of his quirt and then lit out. Where's he at? I aim to get him if I have to go to hell after him." The man spoke with savage venom.

"I don't believe it. I don't believe a word of it," the mother flung back. "Here he comes—with his father. Ask him anything you want to, Mr. Evans."

With an oath of rage Howland reached for his gun. The sheriff spoke, not loudly, but with sharp decision.

"Don't you, Clem! I've warned you. If you make a break, I'll drop you in your tracks."

"Hell! I'm gonna arrest him."

"You've said it. We'll arrest him. There won't be any gunplay. Understand?"

The two Macdonalds rode up to the officers. The father was a heavy-set man, strongly built, clear and steady of eye, an individual of poised force who stood out in a community of individualists.

"They say they want Allan for the express robbery, James. Isn't it silly?" the mother cried.

James Macdonald turned to the sheriff. "What nonsense is this, Mr. Evans?"

"We want to ask the boy some questions. We think he knows something."

"We know damn well he does!" Howland broke in vindictively. "And it doesn't matter how he answers them. He's going with me to the calaboose, and if he tries any tricks with me, I'll pump him full of lead. I'll show the young squirt whether he can knock me cold when I'm not looking."

"What does he mean, Allan?" the older Macdonald asked.

"I hit him with my quirt last night," Allan admitted.

"Because I'd caught him with the express loot and he knew I'd arrest him," the deputy marshal added triumphantly.

"That isn't true, Allan?" his father questioned.

"I didn't hold up the express car. I don't know who did," Allan replied.

"That's a lie! You and young Dave Tolt were in it with the other Tolts!" Howland screamed. "I'll put you in the pen if it's the last thing I ever do. Think you can fool with Clem Howland, do you? There can't any man alive do what you did to me. I'd ought to bump you off. If you was a day older, I would."

"First off, let's clear this thing up. There must be an explanation. You're making a mistake, Mr. Evans. Ask your questions and Allan will answer them." Macdonald spoke evenly, not raising his voice, but anxiety could be read in his tone.

"Slip your boots off, Allan, and lemme look at them," the sheriff said.

Allan drew off his boots and handed them to the officer. Evans turned them upside down and scrutinized carefully the soles and the heels. Jean

Macdonald watched him, with fascinated eyes. Fear rode her soul. She could not guess the object of this, beyond the fact that its objective was to get her boy into trouble.

"What's all this fash aboot, Mr. Evans?" she cried, her voice shrilling. "Do you think he's wearing someone else's boots?"

"Don't worry, Mother," Allan reassured. "They can't hurt me if I've done no harm, can they?"

With a forefinger Evans pointed out to the deputy marshal peculiarities of one of the boots. "Same one that made the tracks down by the bridge—square toe—hobnails in heel—run down on one side about the same way."

"Do you know anything about this, Allan?" his father demanded.

"I know nothing I can tell."

"What were you doing down at the bridge?" Evans asked.

"I haven't said I was down at any bridge."

"Yore boots say it for you mighty loud," Howland cried jubilantly. "Fellow, you went down there to get in the boat after you'd robbed the express car."

"No," Allan denied.

"And you got scared and took the money back last night. I caught you doing it."

"Did you see the money?" Allan parried.

"Y'betcha. In a sack. That's why you laid me out. One o' these days, if you don't get sent up for ten-twenty years I'll settle proper with you for that."

"Allan! Allan! This isn't true!" his mother wailed.

The boy smiled at her ruefully. "I've done nothing wrong, Mother. Don't forget that."

"From ten to twenty years, I'd say," Howland chortled.

"Where were you last night, Allan?" his father said.

"I'll tell you, Father, but I don't reckon I'll tell Mr. Howland. He'll twist against me whatever I say."

"Where were you during the Ferguson dance?" the sheriff asked.

"Part of the time I was there, part of the time I was in our barn."

"What were you doing in the barn?"

"Loafing. Just fooling around."

"Where was Dave Tolt?"

"I don't know."

"Where were his brothers?"

"I don't know."

"Were you with Dave or with any of his brothers?"

"I was with Dave at the dance for a while."

"When? At what hour?"

"I dunno exactly. Maybe about midnight, and after."

"Did you dance?"

"No."

"Did Dave dance?"

"I didn't see him. Maybe he did."

"Don't you usually dance?"

Allan squirmed mentally. "I didn't feel like dancing."

"Were you with Dave or any of his brothers during the evening any place except at the dance?"

"No."

"When were you down at the bridge?"

An answer seemed indicated to Allan. "The morning after the holdup. I rode out there after I heard the story in town."

"What made you go under the bridge?"

"I was just prowling around. I don't know why. Curious, I reckon. Same as anyone else."

"What did you expect to find under the bridge?" Evans asked.

"Nothing."

"Were you there the night before—to meet someone you expected was coming on the Flyer?"

"No, sir."

"Were you on the Flyer yourself—in the express car?"

"I was not."

"While you were away from the Ferguson dance—say from about eight o'clock till close to midnight—were you with anybody who can prove your story is true?"

Allan thought a moment. He might mention

Mrs. Tolt. But that would raise inquiries he did not care to start. No doubt they would come up, anyhow, but that would not be his fault. Certainly he did not want to be called as a witness to prove Dave was not at home if that was his friend's story.

"No."

"You expect us to believe that you left the dance and spent three-four hours in your barn, then went back to the dance?"

"I don't know whether you'll believe it, but it's the truth."

"Was someone with you at the barn?" the sheriff asked. It had occurred to him that there might be a girl in the boy's story.

Allan flushed. "No, sir."

"Were you in the house at any time? Did your father and mother know you were here?"

"No."

"What was the idea in staying out there alone?"

"I was worried about something. No need going into that."

"What's the use of all this beefing, Evans?" the deputy United States marshal broke in roughly. "He's going with me to town. I came to get him and I aim to take him." Savagely he added: "Dead or alive. I don't care which. He'd pack fine dead."

"That's no way to talk, Clem," the sheriff reproved. "He hasn't refused to go to town with us. We've got to take him. That's a fact. His answers aren't satisfactory. But there won't be any gunplays—not while I'm on the job."

"May I talk with Allan alone for a minute?" James Macdonald asked.

Simultaneously the sheriff said "Yes" and the deputy "No."

"Why not?" Evans added.

"Suits me," Howland assented with a sinister laugh. "If he makes a break, it'll be tough luck for him." He drew a forty-four and rested the barrel on the pommel of his saddle.

The Macdonalds moved aside a few steps.

"Oh, Allan lad, what have you been doing?" his mother cried.

The boy's blue eyes met hers steadily. "Nothing to be ashamed of, Mother."

"But this dreadful trouble—why has it come on us then?"

"It hasn't come on us yet, Jean," her husband answered quietly. "It won't—if Allan has done no wrong. No dodging, boy. Can you tell me that you don't know anything about these train robberies?"

The steady gaze of James Macdonald burned into the soul of his son. They demanded the truth, and nothing but the truth.

"I can tell you, Father, that I didn't know there was to be any robbery, that I had nothing to do with it, and that I didn't hear about it until Sheriff Evans told us himself at the dance."

"And that you don't know who did it?"

"I don't know who did it." Allan stressed ever so slightly the verb.

His father drew a deep breath of relief. "I believe you. I know you wouldn't lie to me. But your bare word won't be enough to clear you with others. You've got to come clean, lad. What was in that sack you had with you last night?"

"I can't tell you that," Allan said firmly.

"But you must. Howland thinks it was the money taken from the express car."

"I can't help what he thinks."

"Why did you hit him with your quirt?"

"He was insulting."

"He is an officer of the law and had a right to ask to see what you were carrying. Come, boy. Whom are you protecting?"

Allan did not answer.

"What are all these mysteries?" Jean cried impatiently. "Why weren't you at the dance like every other lad?"

"I wasn't having a good time, Mother, so I came away."

"Time's up," Howland announced. "We're riding now."

"Is my son under arrest?" James asked.

"Y'betcha," the marshal answered jubilantly.

Macdonald looked at Howland and spoke his mind. "Man, you give me a scunner. If you dared you would take pleasure in killing my boy. But I'll see you don't. I'm going to town with you."

He stepped into the house and returned a moment later with a rifle in his hands.

The deputy glowered at him. "Are you threatening me?" he demanded.

"I am not." Macdonald spoke to his son. "Kiss your mother, Allan, and get on your horse."

Jean clung to Allan, trying to keep back her sobs. "The Lord be good to you, my bairn," she crooned. "And bring you back safe to me."

She watched the four men ride down the road until a bend in it concealed them from her. Though she felt sure her son was not a train robber, her heart was a river of woe.

VII

'My Friends Are Honest Folk'

Sheriff Evans was convinced in his mind that the black Tolts had instigated and put through the holdup of the two trains at Melrose. Bray was probably an accessory to the crime. But it was one thing to be convinced of that and quite another to find any definite proof. Evans intended to do his duty, regardless of danger, but he knew better than to voice opinions about the complicity of the Tolts without evidence to back them. They were dangerous men, ready to fight at the drop of a hat.

He was not so sure about Allan Macdonald. The boy had a good reputation. Even though he was David Tolt's friend, he was no wild young scalawag. Still, facts could not be talked away. He had been at the scene of the crime, either at the time or soon after. The alibi he offered was too flimsy to credit. Late at night he had been discovered with the plunder and had knocked cold an officer bent on investigation.

What Evans could not understand was why he had taken the money back to the express office. It was not like Caldwell or Clay Tolt to leave the loot with another member of the gang. Possibly young Macdonald had quarreled with the others; maybe his conscience had troubled him to the point of restoration. But how did he happen to have control of the money to dispose of it?

From Allan he could get no satisfaction. The boy would not talk, other than to reiterate that he was innocent.

When Dave Tolt came to visit his friend, the sheriff invited him into his office and motioned him to a chair. Evans sat down and put his feet on the desk.

"Cigar?" he asked.

"Much obliged. I reckon not."

Dave's black eyes observed the officer warily. He knew Evans had not asked him in to discuss the price of cows.

The sheriff lit up and emptied his lungs of smoke.

"Your friend is in a jam, looks like," he said casually.

"I reckon he'll get out of it," Dave answered lightly. "No reason why he shouldn't, since he didn't have a thing to do with the holdup of the trains."

"Didn't he? Were you with him that night at the time of the holdups?"

"Wish I had been. Fact is, I fell asleep and 'most missed the dance!"

"Where?"

"At home."

"Your brothers there, too?"

"Part of the time. I quit trying to ride herd on those lads long ago."

"Too bad."

"What's too bad?"

"Too bad Allan wasn't with you and your brothers, then he would have had a real alibi." The sheriff's voice may faintly have suggested sarcasm, but Dave took no note of it.

"Yes, if he needed an alibi—which he don't." Dave grinned at the officer insolently. "You ain't figuring on arresting everybody in the territory who wasn't at the Ferguson dance, are you?"

"Not everybody."

"Because you'd have to put me in your calaboose too if that was your notion."

Between puffs Evans observed him through narrowed lids. "So I would, and of course that would be ridiculous."

"Allan is only a kid. Why don't you pick on a man?"

"I would, if I could find a man whose boot-tracks had been on the spot where the bandit left the Flyer and one carrying the stolen shipment back to the express office."

"Why would Allan take the money back if he stole it?"

"I don't know. You're better acquainted with him than I am. Could you give me a reason?"

"No, sir, I couldn't. My idea is that the money

never was stolen, but had been mislaid carelessly somewhere. Now it has been found, the fellow responsible for losing it allows he'd better keep on passing the buck or he'll lose his job. How does that sound to you?"

"It doesn't sound reasonable."

"Does it sound reasonable that a fellow would risk his life to get all that *dinero* and then give it back to the company?"

"Not reasonable, but you can't buck facts. He brought the money back."

"Maybe he found it hanging to a tree," Dave suggested gayly. "You've heard about Santa Claus and Christmas trees likely."

The eyes of the sheriff reflected a new idea, one just born in his mind. Though he looked at Dave intently, the boy knew he was seeing something else.

If Allan had somehow hit on the cache and found the money, having had nothing whatever to do with the robbery, he might decide that the best way to get rid of the stolen plunder was to slip it quietly back to the express company. That would be a reasonable course for him to follow, provided he had cause for not notifying the officers and making the whole thing public. What urge would be sufficient? The sheriff could think offhand of two. He might move secretly because he was afraid the bandits would revenge themselves upon him. Or he might keep himself out of it to avoid questions the answers to which would point to his friends.

"You think Allan just happened to find the money?" Evans said at last.

"Me? No, I don't think he ever had it," Dave replied innocently.

"Then why wouldn't he let Clem Howland look at what was in his sack?"

"That bully puss fellow Howland! You'd ought to know, sheriff, that Allan wouldn't let that bird run on him. Where was Howland the night of the robbery? That's a question worth asking."

"I wouldn't ask it too loud, Dave," the officer advised significantly.

"Because he's a killer, I reckon." The boy's eyes gleamed. "Well, I'm gonna start asking it from right damn now."

"No use hunting trouble."

"And no use ducking it. Clem has done considerable talking. So I've heard. About where the Tolts were the night of the dance, for instance. When I see him, I'll ask Mr. Howland, deputy United States marshal, where he was roosting about that time."

"Better leave that to Caldwell and Clay, son."

"Oh, I don't know." Dave's devil-may-care smile flashed out. "I'm wearing man-size boots my own self, Mr. Sheriff, even if they don't fit any tracks you found around the bridge."

Evans lifted his shoulders in a shrug. "All right.

Have it your own way. Want to see Macdonald now?"

"I'd be obliged."

The sheriff rose. "I've no objections. Maybe you can get him to tell what he knows. Tell him if he'll talk and tell the truth, he'll maybe get his tail out of a crack."

His suggestion was apparently as careless as young Tolt's answer, but the eyes of the two met and were stark.

"Sure. I'll advise him to come clean."

"I felt certain you would."

"Y'betcha. I'll talk to him like a Dutch uncle and tell him to 'fess up what young lady he was going to see when Clem got on the prod."

Dave followed the sheriff down the corridor. At sight of his friend he sang out a greeting.

" 'Lo, deacon! You doggoned old buzzard-head, what you doing in the calaboose? I'm surprised at you, boy—going off robbing trains soon as I lift my eyes off'n you. Whyfor have you been trailing with me all these years?"

Allan did not respond in kind to this levity. He looked at Dave with no smile in his serious eyes. "I haven't robbed any trains," he said quietly.

"Anyhow, you knocked cold that decent, law-abiding citizen, Clem Howland. It sure made me feel sad to hear that."

"You boys can have ten minutes," Evans said. "I'll be back at the end of that time."

As soon as the two were alone, Dave plumped out a question.

"What have they got on you outside of guesses?"

Allan mentioned three things, his absence from the dance, the footprints at the bridge, and his meeting with Howland.

"Don't any one of the three amount to a thing," Dave commented. "You got a right to stay away from a dance if you feel like it. The tracks at the bridge ain't so good, but your story is reasonable. And, if I've got the right of it, Howland didn't get to see what was inside the sack before he went by-by."

"No, he didn't."

"You're riding high, wide, and handsome then, unless they dig up more evidence against you." A flash of white teeth showed in the brown face of young Tolt in an audacious grin. "To think I've been so close to a train robber all these years, sleeping under the same tarp and eating from the same chuckwagon, and me never guessing it."

Allan's blue eyes rested steadily on those of Dave. "Meaning who?" he asked.

"Excuse me. I forgot. You claim you didn't do it."

"No, I didn't do it. Did you?"

"Me? Little Davy Tolt?" Again the boy's smile broke vividly. "Oh! You're loading me. I thought you meant it."

"The sheriff thinks you and your brothers were in this."

"Does he say he thinks so?" Dave asked.

"No. And he won't say so unless he gets more on you."

"Fine. You can't call down a man for what he thinks if he keeps his thoughts under his own hat. I hear Clem Howland thinks and talks too. And that's not supposed to be safe."

Quickly Allan flashed a look at him. "You're not looking for trouble with that killer, are you?"

"No. I never look for trouble. But I'd say—just as an offhand opinion—that it'll be looking for you soon as you're out of here. Howland is a mighty vain proposition. He won't take it kindly that everybody knows you put him to sleep when he started to arrest you."

"I can't help that. I had to stop him from looking in that sack."

"You had the loot in it, eh?"

"Yes."

"Taking it to the express office?"

"Yes."

"Why?"

The eyes of the two boys clashed.

"Because I'm an honest man. I don't hold with robbery."

"Upsetting some other fellow's apple-cart. That the idea?"

"If you want to put it that way."

"What beats me is how you ever got hold of

the money, you being an honest man who don't uphold robbery. Did these holdups bring it to you because they had repented and ask you to tote it back to the company for them?"

"No, that wasn't the way of it. I found where they had cached the stuff and dug it up."

"Howcome you to find the cache?"

"I used my brains."

"Brains or luck, one," Dave amended. "Spill your story."

"First off, I figured how the fellow who robbed the express car made his getaway. Why did he stop the train at the bridge instead of in the thick bush half a mile east of there? It wouldn't be half as easy to keep a horse hidden near the bridge. The answer jumped right out at me. He wasn't using a horse, but a boat."

Dave looked with a new respect at this tall, spare, berry-brown lad. Allan had always been his follower. Now some arresting quality of strength held the eye. Macdonald had found himself. It was a fair guess that he would stand on his own feet henceforth, a cool, competent personality in his own right.

"So he used a boat?" Dave murmured warily.

"He used *my* boat. I didn't find that out until Sunday morning."

"My! Two whole days wasted. What makes you think the fellow used your boat?" The black eyes of Tolt were like rapier points. "Did he leave a note in it sorta explaining why he'd borrowed your boat?"

"He didn't write a note, but he told me just as plainly who he was as if he had."

Once more the two young fellows measured looks.

"Now I wonder how," Dave said in a low voice.

"He tied the boat to a sapling with a reef knot."

Again Dave appraised his friend with that look of searching respect. "By jacks, that was careless, wasn't it?" he said gently.

"Some careless."

"Unless, of course, someone else borrowed your boat to go fishing. Almost anyone. Me, for instance."

"You didn't, did you?"

"I don't recollect that I did. Well, up to date that was sure fine deteckative work. Don't let me interrupt your story. You've got me all excited. How did you find the jack—the *dinero*—the loot—the hidden treasure?"

"I made up my mind who the bandit was. Then I put myself in his place and figured what I'd do under the same circumstances."

"I reckon we'll have to say brains, not luck," Dave conceded. "But even so, I don't see how you could put your finger on the spot. He might have hidden the stuff in 'steen thousand places.

Maybe he'd taken it along with him to the Nation, if that's where the fellow lives."

"He doesn't. He lives near here. I happened to know he didn't take it home with him, because he didn't go home right away. From our place he went to the Ferguson dance."

Dave's face expressed the proper bewilderment, followed by naïve surprise. "You're not telling me that it was Sheriff Evans himself?"

"No, I'm not. I don't intend to name him."

"I'm plumb disappointed," Dave said ironically. "So you put yourself in this bird's place and walked right to his cache."

"Not right away. I didn't work it out till afternoon. Fact is, I got in the boat and went down to the bridge. On the way back an idea came to me. Might be right or might be wrong. Anyhow, it did no harm to make sure. I pulled in to our old shack and took a look at the box where we used to cache things when we were kids. There it was, a sack of money, gold and greenbacks."

"Boy, you're certainly smart as a whip. I'd bet the gent who hid it was annoyed when he found it gone."

"I shouldn't wonder."

"Now all you have to do is to tell Evans who you think this guy is."

Allan flushed angrily. "I'm not telling Evans that."

"No? Why not?"

"Because the man was my friend."

"Oh, he *was* your friend. Ain't he your friend now?"

Each of them looked frostily into the eyes of the other. Yet back of the challenge in Allan's gaze was an appeal.

"I'm not sure," young Macdonald said steadily. "That's what I'm going to find out one of these days. My friends are honest folk. I don't trail with outlaws. It's up to him, not me. If he goes straight, I'll ride to the end of the road with him, but if he follows a crooked trail, I reckon we'll come to the parting of the ways."

Dave reddened. This was plain talk, and no answer could be made to it on its merits. Tolt's irritation found expression in a gibe of annoyance.

"I sure enough was right when I nicknamed you deacon," he flung out.

"Maybe so," Allan replied stiffly. "I don't aim to call wrong right, if that's what you mean."

"You better join the church and be a preacher," Dave jeered. "You're too doggone good for a sinful brand like me."

"If that's the way you feel about it, 'nough said," Allan retorted gruffly.

Evans appeared at the end of the corridor. "Time's up, boys."

Without offering to shake hands through the bars, Dave turned and walked down the passage. He was angry at Allan for his uncompromising ultimatum, but he was annoyed at himself too. The talk had not followed the course he had expected. The last thing Dave wanted was to break with his friend. And that was what he had done.

After a week in jail, Allan was released by Sheriff Evans for lack of evidence. It was that officer's opinion that the boy was not guilty of complicity in the robbery itself, but was concealing material evidence. The suggestion offered by Dave Tolt, that his friend had found the treasure hanging on a Christmas tree, might not be literally true and yet contain the germ of truth. The only reasonable explanation of the return of the shipment was that an innocent party had found it.

But this was only a guess, and no amount of grilling had any perceptible effect on the Scotch granite of Macdonald's resolution. He would tell only what he wanted to tell and no more.

Before Evans freed him, he gave his prisoner a word of advice. "Lie low, boy. Stay away from Melrose. Clem Howland has been doing a good deal of drinking and he has made threats. No use tempting Providence. That fellow is a bad *hombre* with a gun."

Allan thanked him, but he made no promises. He intended to avoid the deputy marshal if he could, but he would not go into hiding because of him. If there was any trouble, it would not be of his seeking.

Release from prison did not bring to Allan any joy. As he saw it, he had done no wrong. He could do nothing else but return the money and at the same time protect Dave. Yet he had lost his friend and become an object of suspicion in the neighborhood. There was in the manner of those he met a reserve new to his experience. A barrier had been built between them. They were honest settlers. He was outside the law, a suspect whose guilt could not quite be proved. Not even with his parents, who were convinced of his innocence, could he escape a certain constraint.

Before Allan had walked a hundred yards from the jail, he had been shown where he stood. He came face to face with Mrs. Owens and Ellen. They had been downtown and were returning home with a market basket of groceries and other supplies.

Involuntarily Allan slackened his pace to speak to them, but he saw at once he was to be rebuffed. The face of Mrs. Owens set. She looked full in his eyes and passed without recognition. Pink flooded Ellen's cheeks. Her embarrassed gaze fluttered to the ground.

Notice had been given that no suspected bandit could consider themselves friends of the Owens family. Allan took it hard, though he spoke of his hurt to nobody. A week later, he heard that Ellen had been to a church social with Dave Tolt. That was the justice of the world, he thought sardonically. Dave had robbed a train and was an acceptable suitor; he had tried to right the wrong and was held an outcast.

For weeks Allan rode the range. He had no desire to go to town or to mingle with people. With bitter stoicism he was facing the unkindness of a world which he felt was against him.

James Macdonald sprained an ankle stepping accidentally from the porch on a dark night. He looked at his swollen foot next morning and decided regretfully that he would have to keep his weight off it for a few days.

"You'll have to go to town, Allan, and arrange about that shipment of three-year-olds. Tell Magee we can throw in a hundred prime stuff and find out just when he wants them delivered." James looked around, to make sure his wife was not in the room, then lowered his voice to add: "Clem Howland has been away in the Cross Timbers country for couple o' weeks, or I wouldn't ask you to go, son."

Allan made no comment, but before he left for town he cleaned and oiled his forty-four. Word had reached him a few hours before that the deputy marshal was back in Melrose.

At the Longhorn Corral, Allan met Jim Nelson. The young man was saddling his horse preparatory to leaving town. Very casually Jim dropped information.

"Clem Howland is in town."

Before Allan answered, he slipped the bridle from the head of his pony. "I'm not looking for Clem Howland," he said quietly.

"Claims he's looking for you. All full of war talk. Can't get over it that you made him look like a fool that night."

Allan said nothing. Jim was a good friend of his. He could not quite let the matter drop there.

"Maybe I could go uptown and do yore business for you," he suggested.

"Maybe I could do it myself," Allan told him evenly.

"That bird is poison. You know that. No sense in making yoreself a target for him."

"Do you want me to run away from him?"

"I'd ride 'round him if it was me."

"What I've been doing for a month, Jim. If he wants a showdown, I reckon he'll have to have it."

Allan walked up Main Street from the corral, but not until he had stopped in an empty stall to make sure the revolver thrust between the front of his trousers and shirt would slip out easily.

Coming out of Kinnear's New York Store, he met Dave Tolt and Ellen Owens entering. The meeting was entirely unexpected. Ellen gave a little gasp, hesitated, made as though to speak, then passed inside. Allan set his jaw and moved on his way.

A moment later he heard the swish of skirts. A soft voice called his name. He turned. Ellen looked up at him, face flushed, eyes shy.

"I don't believe a word of it—not a word of it. But Mother . . ."

A trumpet blew a joyful paean in his heart. He felt tears scorch his eyeballs. "I'm obliged," he stammered. And then, in a burst of gratitude, "Bless you."

She was gone, swift as she had come, but she left behind one whose lifted soul sang as he walked down the dingy street of false fronts. Ellen believed in him. That was the best news he had heard in many a day. Secretly she was his friend, perhaps openly. For all her gentleness she was frank. It was probable that Mrs. Owens knew what she thought and that only parental discipline held her from overt expression of her conviction. That courage had been necessary for her to tell him, even to speak to him at all after she had been forbidden to do so, he understood without explanation. What happened now did not matter. Ellen knew he was no thief.

He went to the Cattlemen's House to look for Magee, but did not find him there. The landlady told him the drover was uptown, probably at the Jerry Dunn Saloon. "He spends most of his time there," she said dryly.

A man hailed him, Tom Lomax, an old settler who lived ten miles north of the Macdonalds.

"Boy, better light a shuck outa town. Clem Howland is on the prod."

The reiteration of this was disconcerting. Allan felt a momentary fluttering of the heart, but no fear found expression in his steady light-blue eyes.

"So I've been told," he said.

"Fork yore bronc, then, and git out."

"I've got business to finish first."

"Smoking Moses! What's eating you, Allan? The most important business you got is to save yore fool hide."

"I won't bother Howland if he doesn't bother me."

"Bother you! Don't you know he's a killer with seven notches on his gun? Claims seven his own self. You want to be number eight?"

"No. But I'm not going to spend my life running away from him."

Lomax argued with him in vain. Allan left him still protesting. The young man headed for the Jerry Dunn Saloon. He went warily, watching every window and every street-corner. That his enemy would shoot without warning he did not need to be told.

The chances were that Howland did not know he was in town. If not, he would likely get an even break. At least on the surface. Allan was no expert with a six-gun, not as compared with the deputy marshal. He was a fair shot, but not an unusually fast one. As the boy figured it, he would have an outside chance if he was lucky.

He did not know whether he was frightened or not. Probably he was. His heart was behaving queerly. It seemed to have dropped out of place, with a heavy cold weight pressing upon it. Yet, as far as he could judge, his nerves were quite steady and his muscles under control. He was nervously excited, but his experience told him that as soon as he faced actual danger he would be cool and would do what had to be done with the maximum of efficiency at his command. It would be soon now, he thought. All right. The sooner the better, since it had to be.

VIII

Three Guns Blaze

There was a poker game going at the Jerry Dunn. It had started the night before as a piker's game, but in the course of hours the stakes had increased and the small fry had sifted out. Five men sat around the table now. Two of them had great piles of chips in front of them, stacks of blues and yellows as well as whites. The others had not fared as well.

Cigar stubs and ashes littered the floor near the poker players. In the air was the stale reek of whiskey. Scattered decks of cards, flung away by irritated losers, were all over the place.

Curt Magee's broad back was turned to Allan. Next to him was a cattle-buyer from Kansas City. The third man was a big red-faced fellow unknown to Macdonald. His neighbor on the left, sitting against the wall where nobody could approach him without being seen, was the deputy United States marshal Howland. The fifth gambler looked like a tinhorn professional, to judge by his pallid, immobile face, his flashy clothes, and his long white fingers. Most of the chips were in front of him and the Kansas City cattlebuyer.

Allan did not interrupt the game. He spoke to the bartender. "Like to speak to Magee a minute. Mind asking him to step forward, Tim?"

The man in the white apron leaned across the bar and whispered hoarsely. "No place for you, young fellow. Clem has done made his brags. He's been losing all night an' he's ugly as sin. Being down to the blanket don't set well on him. Hit your saddle on the run an' light out."

"Tell Magee I won't keep him but a minute."

Tim's glance flickered anxiously toward the poker table. At any moment Howland might look up.

"Say, kid, listen. Pull your freight an' keep going like the heel flies were after you. He's on the hook today. You'd be duck soup for Clem. I don't want no trouble here. Chassé along."

"I will, soon as I've finished my business with Magee."

The voice of Tim grew plaintively persuasive. "Dadburn it, fellow, have some sense. He'll fix your clock sure if he sees you. Don't stick around an' try to run a sandy."

Running the few chips left him through his fingers, Howland scanned the hand that had been dealt him and flung the cards down with a curse. He looked up, an ugly look of malice on his face. His cold blue protruding eyes widened in astonishment. He had seen and recognized Allan. The intent to kill now crystallized instantly in his mind.

His face became venomous. The lips were a thin line, cruel as a steel trap. Rising, he seemed to weave slightly from side to side. His right hand crept slowly toward the pistol butt at his side.

It was astonishing how quickly the sense of impending tragedy propelled bystanders to spasmodic action. Magee's fat bulk dived for the side door. The cattle-buyer went under the table. The tinhorn scudded for a window and took the hurdle in championship form. A cowboy sleeping off a drunk woke up with a yelp of dismay and flung himself through the swing doors. Yet not a word had been spoken either by the marshal or by the boy in front of the bar.

Howland came around the table. He pushed chairs aside with his legs as they got in his way, but he did not lift his shallow eyes from the young fellow he intended to kill. As yet he had not drawn his revolver. No need to hurry. He could beat this amateur to the draw any time he chose. First he wanted to devil him into making a move.

"Well, well!" he jeered, "so here we are."

Allan said nothing. He watched him intently, weight on the balls of his feet, slim body catlike in its lithe and tense alertness. He might be beaten to the draw, but it would not be because he was not ready.

"Talked yourself out of the calaboose, eh? Evans is sure easy. Then you came here to kill me,

I reckon. Want the witness against you bumped off so he can't testify. You're certainly one blood-thirsty young ruffian. Well, Mr. Train Robber, it won't be thataway today."

The side door of the Jerry Dunn opened and somebody came into the big room. Neither Allan nor his enemy knew who it was. Their eyes were fastened unwinkingly one to the other.

The voice of the killer flowed on evenly. He was working himself up to murder. Epithets dripped scabrously from his lips, foul phrases dragged out of the cesspool that was his mind. He cursed Allan and his generations, his associates and companions. So he came at last to the black Tolts.

Still Allan made no answer. His eyes were pinpoints of light—watching, watching for the signal he knew would come. That he had a chance he knew. Howland underestimated him, and the marshal was launched on a tide of abuse that reacted on himself and left Allan cold. One swept by passion is at a disadvantage in swift gunplay.

Riding a big wave of anticipatory triumph, the marshal poured forth fluent and blistering maledictions on the Tolts.

"Figured they'd save you, I reckon," he sneered. "Allowed I was scared of them an' would lay off'n you because you're in their gang. Listen. There ain't Tolts enough in this county to bluff me. If they think so I'll be waiting at the gate for them."

Howland stopped abruptly. He had finished talking.

In that split second before the guns roared, a voice lifted itself. "One of those no-account Tolts present," it said, almost indifferently.

Both the gunman and Allan turned. It was Dave Tolt who had come in by the side door. He stood in the shadow close to the piano, the darkest corner of the room, then moved forward a step or two with the undulating panther-like grace that was his. His shining black eyes were cold as agates, but the life in them belied the slow taunting drawl with which he had spoken.

The killer was taken aback. He had a slow mind, in spite of the swift muscular coordination. The presence of this boy as an individual did not disturb him. But what lay back of it? Was he trapped? Were the Tolts here in force to destroy him? Like a fool, he had spilled a lot of drunken talk. Was the day of retribution at hand?

"You had a few remarks to make about us Tolts," Dave said, almost gently. "Do they stand?"

"You trying to bluff me?" roared the marshal.

"Why, no! Would that be any use? You'd be waiting at the gate, wouldn't you, since there ain't enough Tolts in the county to bluff you?"

The rage in Howland's mind boiled up and flowed out like a flood of lava. It swept him away with it.

As the barrel of his revolver lifted, a curious thing happened. Creeping along the floor to get out of the line of fire, the cattle-buyer's shoulder brushed against a window-blind and sent it up like a rocket. The light of the sun poured blindingly through the glass into the face of the marshal.

Two revolver shots rang out simultaneously, a third a fraction of a second later. Howland tottered and collapsed. He lay on the floor, weapon in hand. His body heaved convulsively and then lay still.

Dave moved forward cautiously, his gun trained on the prostrate figure.

"Look out!" Allan warned.

"He ain't playin' 'possum. He's dead," Tolt said coolly.

Tim's face, from which the blood had washed, appeared above the bar. "Who got him?" he quavered.

"I got him," Dave said quietly. "Maybe Allan did too."

The bartender was escaping from his fright. There was not going to be any more shooting.

"No regrets, I reckon," he said. "Clem had it due a long time. He was a sure-enough bad man."

A few moments before, nobody had been in sight but the two boys and the deputy marshal. Now through all the doors and windows people were pouring into the room.

"Way for Doctor Marshall," someone called.

The doctor was a stout little man who both worked and played hard. He covered the country on horseback or in his buckboard for fifty miles to attend to the sick and in his off hours could be seen at the gaming-table.

One long look was enough for him, but he supplemented this by an examination before he pronounced a verdict in one word.

"Dead."

Sheriff Evans came into the room. "Who killed him?" he asked.

"I reckon I did," Dave said.

"I shot too," Allan supplemented.

The cattle-buyer spoke up. "Soon as he saw this kid, young Macdonald or whatever his name is, Howland started to run on him. He was aiming to kill him. Then this other kid came in, and seems he turned to kill him instead. I claim it's not important who killed the fellow just so somebody did."

"Two bullets hit him," the doctor announced. "One in the left shoulder, the other in or close to the heart. It was the last one that killed him."

"The one in the heart is mine," Dave said. "You can call it last, but it was first. Howland and I shot together, Allan a moment later. From where Allan stood the one in the shoulder must be the bullet he fired. Clem had swung round so his side was toward Allan."

"That's right," assented young Macdonald.

"Did you boys come in here to kill him?" Evans asked.

"I came in to see Curt Magee about a shipment of cattle," Allan answered.

Tim supported him. "That's what he told me, sheriff. He wanted me to get Magee without disturbing the game. Then Clem saw him and started to make trouble."

"How did you get into it, Dave?" the officer wanted to know.

"When I sashayed in here, this fellow Howland was cussing out the Tolts. I asked him whyfor, and he came a-fogging."

"Did you ask him that question you said you were going to, about where he was roosting at the time of the robbery?"

"No, Sheriff. He didn't give me a chance. All I asked him was if he meant all the mean things he was saying about the Tolts. He claimed he did. I gave him a chance to back water. He chose to draw his cutter instead."

"All I want is to get the right of it, Dave. He's been doing too much talking. I grant you that. But he was a law officer and I've got to ask questions."

"Go ahead. Ask a whole mess of 'em. He was one hell of a law officer. If a man is a bully and a killer, a badge won't protect him, will it?"

"Good riddance," someone spat out.

"Y'betcha," Dave drawled, a sardonic gleam in

his eye. "I'm a peaceable citizen like all my family, but I aim to protect my good name when a scalawag blackens it. Any objections, sheriff?"

"Have I mentioned any?"

"No, come to think of it, you haven't. Well, you know where to get me if you want me."

Dave strolled out of the Jerry Dunn, mounted a long-barreled, heavy-quartered sorrel with a hook nose, and loped down the street.

The last houses of the little town dribbled behind him as he rode. The highway dipped down from the mesa. At the summit he dragged the sorrel to a halt. Two horsemen were coming up the hill. They were his brothers Caldwell and Steve.

"Headed for home?" Caldwell asked as they drew up beside him.

"I was. Wanted to see you about something."

"Been robbing some more trains?" Steve asked, an edge of sarcasm to his voice. Since the money had vanished from the cache, he had carried a chip on his shoulder toward the youngest of the Tolts.

"No. Ten minutes ago I bumped off Clem Howland."

Steve gasped. "You—what?"

"He was shooting off his mouth about the Tolts. I called for a showdown and he came a-foggin'."

"You killed Clem Howland?" Caldwell asked incredulously.

The boy's pulse was drumming with excitement,

but he answered impassively. "He'll never be any deader."

"Tell us about it," Caldwell said quietly. His dark, immobile face registered none of the amazement he felt.

Dave told the story.

"He was fixing to kill Allan when you took a hand?" Steve queried.

"He was getting all steamed up for it. Figured Allan was a kid who didn't have a chance. I'll say this. Allan never batted an eye. He stood there mighty cool and watchful. And when the time came he was right there."

"We'd better ride in and see Evans," Caldwell decided.

"I've seen him. It's all right with him, I reckon."

"It's got to be all right with everyone. Howland had it coming. But we don't want to act like we're on the dodge about it," the oldest brother said.

They rode into town three abreast, the sorrel with the hooked nose flanked by the cowponies of the other two Tolts.

Allan did not show the same insouciance as Dave Tolt about the tragedy which had just occurred. The deputy marshal had been a killer, cold-blooded and callous. At the moment of his taking-off he had been intent on murdering him. No personal pity for the man moved the young fellow. But to snuff out a human life is a dreadful thing. The shock of it sapped his strength. He felt suddenly sick and weak. If he had not actually killed Clem Howland, the intent of it had been in his mind.

"Clem's bullet went through this window-pane here," the sheriff said. "Mighty careless of Clem, I'd say, to let himself get where the sun was in his eyes. Not like him either. He usually fixed it so he got the breaks."

"I did that," the cattle-buyer from Kansas City explained.

"You did what?"

"I brushed against the blind as I was passing and when it jumped up the sun poured in."

"Right into Clem's eyes, so that he couldn't see," Evans nodded. "Explains why he missed young Tolt. The boys owe you the drinks, Mr. Johnson."

"They don't owe me a thing," the Kansas City man said with a nervous laugh. "I was worrying about B. J. Johnson—trying to get him out of the line of fire. By plumb accident I let the blind up. But I'm sure glad I did it." He flared to a sudden weak indignation. "He was a bad man if I ever saw one—had a mean eye. Soon as he saw this kid Macdonald, he set out to run on him so he could kill him. He got what he deserved, Mr. Sheriff."

This drew forth a chorus of approval. Not a few of those present had sidestepped Howland on more than one occasion and were glad to have him rubbed out. He had been a menace.

The three Tolts arrived just as the body of Howland was being carried from the Jerry Dunn. Caldwell walked up to the sheriff.

"Dave has been telling me of the service he has just done this community," he said hardily.

"That seems to be the popular way of looking at it, Caldwell," admitted Evans.

"Is it going to be the official way?" came promptly the blunt demand of Caldwell.

"I can't see how the boys are to blame, either one of them. Howland started the trouble. He was running on Macdonald when Dave came in. Both Tim and Mr. Johnson feel sure he meant to kill him. Probably he would have done it if Dave hadn't interrupted. The boys got the breaks when the blind went up. I'm glad they did."

"What blind?" Steve asked.

Evans explained how the sun had blinded the killer at the critical moment.

"Clem had been doing too much talking," Caldwell said. "I'll say now that I was coming to town to ask him to explain some remarks he had made. The boys beat me to it by about half an hour."

"It's a case of everybody being satisfied," Tim said. "No complaints. That fellow had me buffaloed and I'm right pleased that he's been bumped off. Drinks on the house."

While the others trooped forward to the bar, Allan slipped from the room. He did not care to celebrate the death of even an enemy. But for God's mercy they might have been carrying his body out of the saloon a few minutes ago instead of that of Clem Howland.

How had it happened that Dave Tolt had walked in by the side door just in the nick of time? Dave had all the daredevil courage of the black Tolts. Had he walked in out of sheer bravado to demand an accounting with the marshal for what he had been saying about the Tolts? Or had he known Allan was in the place and come in to help protect him against the vengeance of Howland? Either guess was tenable. Not once had Dave spoken directly to Allan or even looked at him, but Macdonald believed that his former friend had been moved by an urge to save him from the gunman. That would be like Dave, to risk his life for him and yet pretend scornfully that he had moved solely on his own account.

Allan had been walking down Main Street toward the Longhorn Corral. He meant to get his horse, ride back uptown, and have a business talk with Magee.

From a side street light, swift footsteps moved toward him. He heard his name called in a voice with knots of fear in it. Ellen's eyes, terror-filled, winged an appeal to him.

"Dave's all right," he told her.

"I heard—someone said—"

She stopped. Her slender figure swayed a little. In her face was no color.

"No. It's all right. He wasn't hurt."

"I heard a man was killed—and—and Dave's name came up."

"Marshal Howland was killed, not Dave. Shall I tell you about it?"

"Please."

He told her the story, from the angle he knew would do most to take the sting from the fact that Dave had killed a man. The boy had interfered to save him, he said, had deflected Howland's attention in the nick of time, with the utmost coolness, and had faced death to give Allan a chance. The boy stressed the point that both of them had shot the marshal, and that Dave was no more responsible for his death than he.

Slowly the color washed back into her face. Her shy eyes gave Allan gratitude.

"It's dreadful, isn't it?" she said. "But you couldn't help it, either you or Dave. He was a terrible man."

"Howland had made up his mind to get me. We'd had a little difficulty and I just happened to get the best of it. He was very vain, and he couldn't stand it. I kept away from him—haven't been to town for a month. But we had to meet sometime."

"Yes," she admitted absently.

Embarrassment had succeeded terror. A pink

wave was beating into her soft cheeks. She had given herself away to Allan. She had betrayed her deep interest in Dave. A sense of shame whipped her. Nice girls did not let their emotions betray them. They concealed their feelings about boys even from themselves. She must be a brazen creature.

"I—was afraid—for both of you," she faltered.

He tried to lift her out of her distress. "Sure enough. You're that kind-hearted. Well, we're all right, both of us." His voice was cheerful and matter-of-fact. It told her that she had shown only a proper interest in her friends, and it appropriated for himself fifty per cent of her anxiety.

"You'll be pals again now, won't you?" she said.

His face hardened. "I don't know."

"I wish you would. A friendship like yours ought never to be broken."

He made no answer. What was there to say? He could not tell her the real cause of the division between him and Dave, that they had chosen diverging roads of life to follow, that there could be no trust and faith to tie together the hearts of an honest man and a criminal. Nor could he defend himself without accusing Dave. He must let her think the fault was his.

"Dave feels awfully bad about it," she pleaded.

"Does he?"

Allan's stiffness repelled her. She had done her

best. Probably it was his Scotch dourness that stood in the way. She tried again, gently.

"Don't be stubborn, Allan," she coaxed.

"I'm the way I am," was all he found to say.

"I'd think that now, after he had done this for you—"

"I'll go see him," he promised.

"Tell him you're sorry, if you've done anything you shouldn't."

He looked at her strangely. No doubt she thought her handsome faunlike lover must be wholly in the right. She loved him, not for what he was, but for what she thought he was.

Allan carried away a heavy heart, not wholly on his own account. Her golden youth was caught in a current headed swiftly toward the rapids of tragedy. The pain of it caught him by the throat. Her childish soul looked through rose-colored windows on eternal Spring. The slender limbs carried her so swiftly and so eagerly to joyous life, and there could be nothing but disillusion ahead. For Dave had set his feet, gayly and intrepidly, on a crooked trail that must lead to disaster. Ellen was the last woman in the world to travel happily such a path with him.

Allan's attempt at a reconciliation got nowhere. Both the boys longed to renew their old carefree friendship, but the awkward embarrassment of shy youth defeated their desire. Dave denied flippantly that he had come into the Jerry Dunn with any thought of helping Allan. Macdonald accepted this explanation because he did not know how to break through it to the truth.

A deeper cause frustrated a renewal of the comradeship. The basis for it was gone. There was now no common ground of trust between them. Six months ago there had been nothing they could not discuss. Now there were barriers up they could not tear down, closed rooms in their lives they could not enter together.

For already the black Tolts were planning an enterprise just as lawless and far more desperate than that of holding up two trains at the same time. Caldwell and Cole were away scouting. They were taking their time and covering a good deal of territory. There was to be no mistake on account of inaccurate information. Every detail had to be worked out carefully.

Dave was a full-fledged partner now. There had been no argument about that. His brothers had taken him in as a matter of course. The boy's vanity, his loyalty to the family, the love of adventure so pronounced in his make-up, a perverted sense of romance born of his participation in an affair so secret and so dangerous, had easily outweighed the moral precepts taught him at school and Sunday School. He had never had a rule of life grounded on principle. It was not difficult for him to cross permanently the line which marks the distinction between an honest man and an outlaw.

Ellen realized the change in him and it distressed her. He was not so gay and boyish, not interested so much in the frolics of the neighborhood. Jim Nelson was getting up a hay ride. Dave decided they had better not count on him.

The girl had escaped such a little way from childhood that it was easy for her to put herself in the wrong. Had she offended him in some way? Was he just tired of her? Had he found another girl? She could find no such specific reasons for his moodiness. Indeed, he was a more demanding lover than before. It was as though he had of a sudden grown up and put away childish things. His shyness was gone. He wanted her. Why couldn't they be married . . . now?

Ellen opened her blue eyes wide. "But, Dave, we couldn't. I'm too young. Mother wouldn't let us, even if . . ."

She did not tell him that she was a little afraid of him in this mood. The boy she had learned to love was full of gay laughter. He had not been so moody, so . . . queer. Was it just a fancy that she seemed to catch glimpses of some dark shadow hanging over him?

"Why wouldn't she let us? Anyhow, it's not your mother I want to marry. We could slip away to Weston and get married without any fuss."

The girl was shocked. In her generation young

people obeyed their parents. Those who did not were bad.

"When you say such things I'm scared of you," she told him. "I won't listen to such talk, Dave. I'm surprised at you."

"All right. If you won't, you won't," he said sulkily. "How old do we have to be to suit your mother?"

"I don't know."

She did not tell him that her mother had of late been warning her not to see so much of him. Mrs. Owens had become alarmed. He was no longer just a nice boy. He had killed a man. No doubt there had been plenty of justification, but this did not alter the fact. She had made up her mind firmly that Ellen must gradually break with him. It was not only the killing. There were persistent rumors that the black Tolts were not the innocent cattlemen they appeared to be. It was unfortunate that Mr. Owens had rather intimate business relations with them. She did not want to offend the family. Still . . .

In secret Ellen wept because of the knot she did not know how to unravel. From a simple happy affair life had become unkind and complicated. She did not any longer wake up in the morning smiling in the sunlit bedroom at the prospect of possible pleasant contacts that might flutter the heart agreeably. Everything had gone awry. She did not lie awake after the candle had been snuffed to remember with a warm glow that Dave had said this and she had said that. She recalled instead that in parting Dave had flung out a bitter taunt and that at supper Mother had been so sarcastic that tears had sprung to her eyes. Everybody was horrid.

Well, not everybody. Her father was just the same. But it was not much help to have him pat her on the shoulder, pinch her cheek, and tell her to be a good girl and do as her mother said. It seemed to her that she got more considerate understanding from Allan than anybody else. They met rarely, and then only for a few moments at a time. It was not anything in particular he said that comforted her. Rather it was the impression she gained that she could rely on his sympathy no matter what happened.

She awakened one night from a dream so vivid that she sat up in bed and shivered with excitement. The background of the dream was a little vague. She had been wandering around, lost, on a snow-covered prairie. Wolves howled. Stumbling through the drifts, she found herself on a little hill. The wolves surrounded her, howling and snarling. One and another made little heaps at her. Then Allan was there, an arm about her shoulders, a revolver in his hand. He fired, again and again. She was no longer afraid. The wolves had vanished. Nothing in the world could hurt her with him there.

That was a curious dream, she thought, for of course it ought to have been Dave who had come to the rescue. Yet it was so natural for Allan to be the man. He was like that, so sure and dependable. Dave was never that. Her fancy did not find in him a refuge against danger or a help in time of trouble. She had noticed that he did not feel interested in her difficulties. They annoyed him. He wanted her to be gay and happy with him.

Meeting Allan on the street one day, she had news for him.

"Sheriff Evans was at the house yesterday," she told him eagerly. "Mother asked him about you, and he said he was sure you had nothing to do with the express robbery. He said you were shielding someone. He didn't say who."

"I can't get that fool notion out of his head," Allan said.

"I don't suppose there was anything in that gunnysack but oats," she said reflectively.

"What else could there have been, since I'm innocent?"

"Anyway, Mother feels differently about you. She said she always liked you and had thought you a good boy."

He flushed with pleasure. A door had opened for him, one he had thought closed forever.

"I'm glad," he said.

She slanted a smiling look at him. "You *are* a good boy, aren't you?"

"One of the best," he claimed boldly. "I'm such a good influence you ought to see more of me."

"Where?" she asked. "And when?"

"At your house, 'most any evening. Tonight would be a good time. It comes before tomorrow night."

Allan spoke with an assurance that had never been his before. He had always been afraid of her. She was so pretty and so dainty that he had been oppressed by a sense of unworthiness. But now he had an odd feeling that barriers had been brushed aside. She was more than a lovely girl whom he reverenced from afar. She was Ellen Owens, his friend, who grinned at him encouragement, wrinkling the piquant little nose with the powdered freckles. How the change had come about he did not know. But there it was.

"If you're quite sure you want to come," she demurred. "Good boys are so scarce. Maybe you ought to go see Nellie Ross instead. I think it would please her."

Allan blushed. He was aware that Nellie had cast come-hither eyes at him, and the fact had embarrassed him.

"I'm pleasing myself tonight," he explained.

"As well as giving me a treat," she murmured.

"Go ahead. Laugh at me. I don't mind."

"I wouldn't dare laugh at so good an influence. Wouldn't it be almost—wicked?"

"Don't mind me. Have a good time."

She gave him a parting shot as she left. "Father will be home to talk with you while Mother and I are out at the prayer meeting."

"That will be nice."

"And you can be a good influence over him too. We ought to spread it over the whole family far as it will go."

"What about the folks at the prayer meeting? Maybe they need me too. I ought to go with you and your mother, don't you reckon?"

Her eyes danced. She nodded at him. "You're getting along."

With which she departed. He could hear her quick footsteps go pitter-patter down the sidewalk.

IX

Ellen Says 'No'

The robbery of the express car had been a crime, wholly outside the law. The shooting of Howland was defensible, considered by the community an affair to be applauded rather than censured. Yet the effect of the latter was more decisive upon Dave Tolt than the former. The holdup of Bray had been a piece of boyish folly, done out of bravado. Dave regarded it as an adventure. The money had been returned to its owners. Nobody had been injured. He had got a great thrill out of doing something that never had been done before. The moral guilt of it scarcely touched him.

But the killing of Howland had been done publicly and had been widely discussed. In the eyes of his little world Dave observed a new respect that was almost deference. He saw it in store clerks, in lads with whom he had been used to frolic, in the awed regard of women. He had killed a noted gunman in a duel. The fact set him apart from the other youths of the neighborhood. The crook of his finger had made him a personality. His vanity sunned itself.

He craved more excitement. The activities of Cattleland seemed to him humdrum. Within the next few months he had crowded enough daredeviltry to startle the country.

The black Tolts rode far on their raids. They robbed a train in Kansas, a stage in the Nation, and a bank in Texas. Out of the profits Cole and Luke took a trip to California. They dropped off in Arizona on the way home and attempted to hold up the Pacific Coast Limited. An express messenger fought it out with them and drove them away, but not until the fireman of the train had been killed. Cole was wounded, captured, and tried. He was given a twenty-year sentence.

Caldwell and Steve entrained for Tucson. They joined Luke in the Rincon Mountains, watched their chance, and rescued Cole while he was being taken on a stage to the state penitentiary. Two weeks later, the four brothers reached home. They went on the dodge and lived in the chaparral.

By this time the whole Territory was aroused. Posses scoured the brush. United States deputy marshals, famous for their skill as trailers and their nerve as fighters, took up the hunt for the fugitives. Dave was seized while visiting his mother one night. He was held in jail for a month and then released for lack of evidence.

Reckless though the Tolts were, it became apparent that they could not elude their pursuers forever. With such men as Bill Tilghman, Heck Thomas, and Chris Madsen on their trail, it could be only a question of time until they were taken or killed. They would go the way of the Bass, the James, and the Dalton gangs. Better to quit in the heyday of their success, they decided. A dozen friendly ranchmen, a score of rustlers, kept them apprised of the movements of the officers, but eventually one of these, tempted by the large reward, would sell them out.

The Tolts made up their minds to pull off one big *coup* before they stopped. They had made a record by holding up two trains at once. They would rob two banks simultaneously. Only the Daltons had ever attempted so daring a feat, and the venture had brought death and disaster to them. They had been too careless, and they had had bad luck.

"Bad judgment too," Caldwell said. "It was a fool business for Bob and Emmett Dalton to wear false beards. Might as well have advertised they had come bank-robbing. Right away they were under suspicion. We'll ride in quietly like any other ranchmen, two in each party, tie our horses, and do the jobs in about five minutes. Before the word is passed around, we'll be riding hell-for-leather out of town."

"Sure. Use our noodles." Sam agreed. "That's what ruined the James outfit at Northfield. They didn't cover the bank clerks proper and had to go to shooting."

"The whole idea was crazy," Cole added. "Whoever planned it was a lunkhead. Think of trying to make a getaway across Minnesota, Iowa, and Missouri, three thickly settled farming states."

"We take horses for relays, don't we?" Steve asked.

"Yes. Leave remounts in the chaparral on the river flats south of Folsom," Caldwell explained. " 'Course we'll travel at night. If we're lucky, nobody will see us from the time we leave here until we get near Burke City."

"And after the cleanup we'll slide out one at a time for Oregon," Sam said. He produced a bottle and lifted it. "Here's to luck, boys."

The Tolts did not all leave at once. Cole and Sam dropped out of sight a couple of days before the others. They gave out that they were going to Fort Worth to buy a registered bull.

The evening before the start, Dave rode to Melrose to see Ellen. He did not call at the front door and ask for her. Mrs. Owens had long since served notice on him that he was not welcome. Instead, he waited until the lights went out and threw a handful of gravel at Ellen's window.

The girl came to the window and looked down. A full moon rode the heavens and the light haloed her golden head.

"Is it you, Dave?" she called down in a whisper.

He stepped out from the lilac bushes. "Come down. I want to see you."

"How can I do that? If Mother saw me—"

"She won't see you. Doesn't she sleep on the other side of the house?"

"Yes, but—"

"I've got to see you. It's important."

"Don't you see I can't, Dave? Not tonight. But tomorrow—"

"Tomorrow I won't be here."

He looked up at her, his eyes hungry with love. And her heart, as had happened many times before, sent a hot glow through her bosom for the handsome scamp. He was so engaging, so appealing. How could a girl help loving him? His recklessness, his reputation for wildness, might send qualms of dread through her when she thought of him as a husband, but they lent him glamour as a lover.

"Where are you going?" she asked, still in a low voice.

"Never mind where I'm going. Come down and see me."

"I'm not—dressed."

"Dress then—and hurry. I can't wait." He spoke imperatively.

She knew it would be indiscreet to do as he wished. The conventions which bound girls on the frontier were just as rigid as those elsewhere, but not always the same. Ellen was a good girl, careful of her reputation. If she should be seen with him at that time of night outside the house . . .

He smiled—the warm endearing smile she could not resist.

"I'll come," she whispered.

Presently the front door opened and she stole from the house. He drew her into the shadows of the lilacs.

"What do you want?" she asked tremulously.

He held her close. He kissed the apple-blossom cheeks and the soft throat in which a pulse of excitement throbbed. He kissed the scarlet mouth so like a misty rose in the half-light of night.

For a moment she clung to him, a rapt young creature with an emotion primitive and passionate fluttering in her bosom. Then she pushed him from her, resolutely, with her small clenched fists.

"I can't stay. What is it? What do you want to tell me?"

"I'm going away. Not for long. I'll be back soon. But after that I'm going for good. I want you to come and join me."

She looked at him, her brows knitted to a little frown. "I don't understand. Where are you going? And why should I come to you? Do you mean—?"

"I mean come and marry me, of course. What else would I mean?"

"Yes, but—Why couldn't we be married here? If Mother would let us. But she won't."

"We couldn't. You've got to do as I say." He

knew from the quick rise and fall of her small immature bosom that he was frightening her. "I'll be your husband, and I'll look after you. If you love me, you'll come."

"But why do you have to go? You make me afraid, Davy. Is—is something wrong? Are you in trouble? Have you done something?" Her voice shook a little.

"No. I'm just . . . going. You'll have to trust me. Don't you know I love you?"

"Yes, but—can't you trust me too? I don't want our love to be—like a coyote slipping through the brush—sly and secret. Oh, Davy! You don't either, do you?"

He cherished her cleanness and her sweetness, the quality in her that was flower-like and precious. But because he had no just answer to her question, he was irritated.

"A man has got to be the head of the house, not a woman," he told her. "He's got to have the say-so, and she's got to let him be the judge."

Ellen was not so sure of that. She had noticed that her father and mother talked over important matters and came to joint decisions. But she did not care to argue it. Her mind fastened to the issue. He was not her husband, but her lover. It was unfair that he should claim rights not yet his, granted they were rights at all. A flash of anger blazed in her. He was thinking of himself and not of her. Of late she had noticed that so often.

"You're not my husband, Dave Tolt. Since you're not, I've got to do as my father and my mother tell me. I won't do anything like that—run away and disgrace them and make them unhappy. I don't seem to know you any more. You don't act like—like—"

The resentment died down, subdued by a sense of hopelessness. She choked down a sob in her throat.

Dave caught her by the shoulders, almost violently. "I'm going to marry you in spite of hell and high water."

There was something dauntless in the steady regard of the girl. She had character.

"Never as long as I live unless you settle down and be good," she said quietly.

He felt the chill of defeat. In his heart he knew it was fair enough. She had given him his choice long ago. He had refused to be warned.

"I can't be a Sunday-School boy like Allan Macdonald," he protested. "I've got to be like I am. Can't you see that? But if you'd come and marry me I could be good. For you, I could, Ellen. I'd quit helling around then."

"Quit first," she insisted, though the lover in her clamored to surrender to his promise. "I know you're doing something wrong, Dave—whatever it is. Don't you see I've got to *know* you're good? I can't marry you and hope you will be."

"I'll see you when I come back. Then I'll

promise you to be like you want me to be. Don't throw me down, Ellen."

"I won't throw you down. You've been throwing yourself and me down, Dave. I'd think you'd see that . . . Goodnight."

She turned and ran swiftly into the house.

Dave cut through the brush to Willow Crossing. He followed no trail. A hundred times he deviated, circling to right or left to miss a tangle of bushes or a bluff that barred the way. But no matter how he twisted and turned, the white-splashed nose of his roan always pointed due north after the obstruction had been passed. The boy had that sixth sense of direction which comes to those who live in the saddle in open country.

As soon as he struck Buck Creek, he swung up it along a cattle trail through the fringe of brush bordering the stream. He did not push his mount, for he had plenty of time. His appointment was for eleven-thirty, and even if he loitered he would have half an hour to spare.

At Willow Crossing he tied to a sapling and lay down in a bank of ferns. He did not sleep. Thoughts trooped too actively through his mind for that.

This would be a big haul, if they pulled it off all right, the richest one the Tolts had ever made. Burke City was a busy trail-end town. Both of the banks must be bulging with money, for here cattle-drivers and buyers met to transfer the herds of longhorns that had been prodded up from the south. . . . After this raid they would quit. Bag and baggage the black Tolts would move out to Eastern Oregon and settle there. They would change their names. Land they had already bought. Caldwell had gone out and made a preliminary payment. Already money enough had been cached to stock their new range with graded cattle. Their mother would stay to sell out the holdings here and later would slip away to Oregon to join them. . . . He could not tell Ellen how they had got so much money together. If he did, she would not marry him. But after this one big job they were tackling now he would run straight. . . . Even a fool could have seen that the outlaw days of the Tolts were nearing an end. It was quit, or be rubbed out. After the Texas bank robbery they had just shaved disaster when a posse under Bill Tilghman and Heck Thomas had crowded them into a blind gulch. Only a sudden hailstorm had given the fugitives a chance to slip through the cordon. If captured, Cole would be sent to the Arizona penitentiary and Luke would be taken to Tucson, tried and convicted. During the holdup of the Kansas Western Flyer, Steve's mask had slipped. The train crew could identify him. The sooner they all vanished into the distant West, the better. . . .

Ellen was so sweet and gentle that he had not

realized until tonight how firm she could be. He had to make her see it his way. Until lately he had taken it for granted that she was his girl and would some day marry him. Maybe he had been too sure of her and had shown it. Girls like to keep a man guessing. Well, Ellen had him guessing now. She had put an ache in his heart tonight. . . . He hoped the Burke City business would go slick. Nobody had been killed on any of the raids in which he had taken a part. Better not think about that . . .

The hoof of a horse struck a stone. Dave sat up and listened. He heard a voice, low and guarded, the swishing of willow shoots as horse brushed through a thicket, the creaking of saddle leather. A bunch of cowponies appeared in the open, vague shapes growing definite in the uncertain light as they moved closer. Riders followed. He recog-nized his brother Steve.

"H'lo!" the boy called.

Steve answered. "H'lo, Dave! Beat us here, did you?"

Caldwell joined them. "We'll push up the creek a ways before we strike into the shinnery. You better stay in the drag with Luke, Dave. Watch out for that Black Diamond colt. He's wild and wants to bolt. When we get farther from home he'll settle down."

All night they traveled. Before dawn they picketed six horses in the lush grass of a small meadow hidden in the hills. The animals had been well watered. Not until the sun was far up did the raiders stop for breakfast and to conceal themselves from any chance wanderer in the hills. In the evening, after another five or six hours of steady going, six more ponies were picketed. There was a risk in leaving the horses. Somebody might stumble on them. But in this sparsely settled section, miles from any habitation, the chances were that nobody would come into the rock-girt park where the J T mounts were left.

After that, with no remuda to guard, the brothers rode faster. They dropped down from the hills into a country where farmers had begun to settle. Here and there in the gray light of early morning they could see the shacks of the homesteaders.

"Hoemen growing right numerous," Luke commented. "Soon this country won't be fit for a cowman to live in."

"Well, I reckon I can name about six cowmen who're allowing to light out from it mighty soon," Steve replied.

As the sun came up the party separated. Dave rode with Caldwell. They followed the other two after the expiration of half an hour.

The road circled down into a valley in leisurely fashion to get an easy grade. Settlers were more numerous here. The crops looked more promising.

Apparently land produced well. The farms had windmills and good barns. More frame and fewer sod houses were to be seen. This was territory contiguous to Burke City. To the east of the town farmers had taken up most of the acreage and were cultivating a good deal of it. West of Burke City was still open country. From that direction came the trail herds into the long dusty main street.

Caldwell and Dave rode into town. A hundred such men might have been seen in Burke City that day—gaunt brown riders of the plains, dust-covered and sun-baked, in jeans and high-heeled boots and old flopping hats. One could guess they had traveled far, for they had apparently grown careless of appearances. They lounged in the saddle seats and the slickers tied to the thongs beside the horns hung down over the right legs of the men. To the glance of an observer it was not manifest that rifles were concealed beneath those slickers.

Burke City hummed with life. A wagon drawn by three yoke of swaying oxen rolled slowly toward the Elephant Corral. A mule-skinner cracked his long whip expertly around the ears of his charges while a blistering vocabulary crackled above them in earnest invective. Cow-ponies were tied to hitchracks in front of saloons and gambling-houses. Rollicking punchers teetered down the sidewalks in their high-heeled boots.

"Live town," Caldwell commented. "Plenty of money here this time of year. We ought to do fine."

"Looks like," Dave agreed.

The eyes of the boy were registering impressions. He had never been here before, but in its general appearance it was a twin brother to any trail-end town he had seen. They all had a strong family resemblance. Dusty street, false store fronts, billiard-halls, saloons, gambling-houses, barber shops called tonsorial parlors, dance-halls, blacksmith shops, New York Emporium, restaurants, and in the outskirts corrals and shipping-pens.

Civic pride had found expression in the two new bank buildings. They were of brick, on diagonal corners of Twelfth and Front Streets. Above the banks were offices occupied by lawyers and doctors. The Drovers' and Cattlemen's Bank was housed in a two-story edifice, but the Burke City National home towered to three full stories. Residents of the town regarded it as the last architectural word, a skyscraper prophetic of the city's future.

The horses of the brothers moved at a walk. Dave noticed that alleys ran alongside the bank buildings and intersected other alleys in the rear. Some large cottonwoods occupied a pair of vacant lots north of the Drovers' and Cattlemen's.

"How would it do to leave the horses under the

cottonwoods while we do the job?" Dave asked.

"Just what I was thinking," Caldwell agreed. "It will be your job to stay with them."

"If I had my ruthers I'd go in with the rest of you."

"It'll be like I say, boy," the older brother answered.

The two horses walked down the street through the business section to the Alamo Corral. A few cowboys were playing poker on a blanket in one of the stalls. Cole was among them.

He looked up at his brothers indifferently without a sign of recognition.

"Just got in?" a freckle-faced puncher asked.

"Yes," Caldwell answered.

"Come far?"

"Quite a ways. From Lampasas County."

"Some trip, Mr. Texas Man. Your stuff come through good?"

"Fine. We drove easy and the stock put on flesh."

Cole spoke, looking up at Caldwell from the cards he had been studying. His voice had the casualness of one who makes talk for no particular reason. "Knew a fellow went to Lampasas last year. So I heard. Name, Stumpy Daggett. Got into a difficulty an' lit out sudden. When last seen his bronc was raisin' dust a-plenty."

"Never met him," Caldwell answered briefly.

But the brothers had looked at each other, had

asked and answered silent questions satisfactorily. Both of them knew now that all was ready and that the arrangements last decided upon still held. Since every detail had been carefully worked out, it would not be necessary to meet again for further discussion.

"You didn't miss a thing, friend." Cole went on casually, as he flung down his cards. "Stumpy claimed he was a bull rattler, one of these lead-pumpers always ready to cut loose his dog. Myself, I never noticed it."

Caldwell and Dave moved away.

"Could you lend me the loan of a sharp knife, mister?" a voice asked. "I lost mine through a hole in my pocket."

Luke was sitting tailor fashion on the ground, ostensibly busy with a saddle strap.

"Sure, stranger," Caldwell replied, and handed him a knife.

"I was sitting the buck last night when this cinch busted on me. It didn't do me a mite of good to grab the apple. The wall-eyed sunfisher I had forked sent me up to get a good look at the country before I hit the dust," Luke explained.

"Too bad," Caldwell sympathized. "No harm done, though?"

The glances of the two fastened, each upon the other, for a brief moment. Again an exchange of wordless information.

"Not a bit, except to my feelings."

"Never was a horse that couldn't be rode.
Never was a rider couldn't be throwed,"

Dave quoted, grinning.

"You're damn shouting, young fellow."

"Reckon I'll drift uptown for a while." Caldwell said to Dave. "Want to come along?"

"I better stick around here and water the broncs first," Dave decided, as was according to the program mapped out. "See you later, say in the Last Chance."

"Good enough."

Caldwell strolled out of the corral gate and turned in the direction of the business section of the town. Dave wandered back to the card-players. He had nothing to do, except to make sure that no inquisitive busybody meddled with the rifles beneath the slickers.

He watched a hand dealt and played, then ventured an observation.

"Funny thing about this town," he said. "I noticed the main street is Twelfth. I got to kinda wondering where First Street is."

One of the corral wranglers grinned. "It's 'way out on the prairie. Fact is, it ain't been laid out yet. The guy that surveyed the burg figured it would sound bigger if he began at Tenth."

"There's a wide place in the road up in Kansas that has got two streets," a cowpuncher volunteered. "One of 'em is called Fifth Avenue an' the other Thirty-Eighth Street. Kinda New-Yorky. I reckon First Street must be somewheres in Colorado."

Later, when reminiscences were in order and there was reflected glory in having even met any of the black Tolts prior to the bank robberies, some of the men in the corral claimed that they noticed the great resemblance these strangers bore to one another. It would not have been surprising if they had, since the strong brown faces, so marked of bone, so keen and hard, were far from a common type. But if so, none of those lounging in the Alamo mentioned it till afterward. Certainly nobody had a suspicion of the grim errand upon which they had come to town.

X

The Battle

Nor was there any suspicion when three groups of mounted men, each composed of two, converged toward Twelfth and Front Streets an hour and a half later. Burke City was a hitchrack town. Riders were as common as fleas on a flopeared hound. Nobody ever looked twice at a cowboy unless he was on a tear.

At a casual glance nothing distinguished these dusty horsemen from scores of trail-drivers moving up and down the wide thoroughfare. They were big, rangy, rawboned fellows, but so were most of the Texans who had come up with the herds. If there was a cold, unsmiling grimness in their dark faces nobody paid the least attention to it.

Burke City lay in a coma of midday sunshine. A peaceful languor had settled over the place. Only the restaurants were busy. Most of the punchers were out at the camps sitting cross-legged at the tail of their chuck-wagons with a tin plate and cup in front of them. About this time of day the town went into apparent siesta.

Beneath the two cottonwoods near Twelfth and Front the six riders met. They lost no time, wasted no words. From a saddlebag Caldwell took two gunnysacks. One he handed to Cole. Dave gathered the reins of the bridles. He was to wait with the horses.

The other five walked north. Caldwell and Sam went into the Drovers' and Cattlemen's Bank, Luke, Cole, and Steve into the Burke City National.

Dave knew he had been left in charge of the horses because Caldwell considered it the safest assignment. Maybe it was, but certainly it could not be called one restful to the mind. From the moment when his brothers vanished through the front doors of the banks he was in a fever of excitement. No sound reached him from within the buildings. That meant all was going well. But how time dragged! They had not been gone two minutes, but it seemed like an hour.

A voice, harsh and domineering, hailed him from the street. "Here you, fellow, get those broncs away from there."

Dave turned. He saw a man, large and heavy-set, moving toward him, authority in every line of him. It came to the boy, instantly, that this must be Guy Reed, the notorious marshal of the town. He had been chosen because of his reputation as a killer, just as many officers of the cowtowns were selected, on the theory that his skill with weapons and the fear inspired by his name would be assets in helping him to cope with the professional gamblers of the place and the tough cowboys who came up the trail.

"I reckon I don't get you," Dave answered, with a placating smile. The last thing in the world he wanted was to start trouble now.

"Get me!" the marshal roared. "Well, you'll get me, and damn quick. That's a park, where you're at. Understand? It's for town folks. You'll find corrals in this town, fellow."

There were two benches beneath the trees. By courtesy the place might be called a park, if one used his imagination a good deal.

"Sorry," the horse wrangler said. "We didn't know. The boys are getting money from the bank. They'll be out in a minute, then we'll shove along."

"You'll shove along now. See that sign over there? Read it, if you know how."

Dave read. "Please do not tie horses within a block of the banks," was printed on a board.

"Didn't see it," the boy explained. "If we had—"

"Well, you see it now. Pull your freight with that bunch of broomtails."

Reed's manner was overbearing, his eyes fishy and opaque as lead, fixed in their stare, without any life in them.

Dave played for time. He could not move the horses, since his brothers would come in a hurry when they came. Mounts a block away might be as useless as though in the Indian Territory.

"'Course the broncs aren't tied," he demurred. "I'm holding them. I don't reckon there would be any objection to that."

"I'm objecting. Me, Guy Reed, if you don't know who I am. Marshal in this man's town. An' no buckaroo off the trail can hurrah me, fellow. It ain't ever been done, an' it won't be."

"I got too much sense to try, Mr. Reed," Dave said meekly. "I reckon everybody knows you, by reputation, anyhow. Would it be all right, do you reckon, if I moved the broncs to the road and waited there? It won't be but a minute now."

The marshal moved a step nearer and glared at the horse wrangler. "Don't argue with me, lunkhead. Do like I say."

"Where will I take 'em?" Dave asked, having no intention of taking the animals anywhere.

"Take 'em to Texas. Take 'em to Little Rock, Ark. I don't give a billy-be-damn where you take 'em so's you get 'em away from here."

Looking over the shoulder of the marshal, Dave saw and heard something that withered his heart. A woman walked into the Burke City National, stopped, flung up her hands in alarm, and gave a wail of terror. She turned, scuttling out to the street like a frightened hen. Her shrill scream carried far and arrested the attention of fifty men in the offices upstairs, in the Last Chance Saloon, in the hardware and drygoods stores a little farther up the street. Into the echo of her cry cut a high, excited explanation. "They're robbing the bank!"

The news ran like an earthquake shock up and down Front and along Twelfth. It set the hearts of men throbbing with excitement. It moved their feet swiftly toward rifles and shotguns, their hands toward revolver butts. This was a big-game country. Everybody hunted and was familiar with weapons and their use. In a good many business offices rifles and shotguns were kept instead of at home.

Reed forgot Dave. He was like the proverbial old warhorse who scents the battle. Swiftly he moved down the street toward the Burke City National, dragging out two six-shooters as he went. His step had the lithe crouching stride suggestive of that other killer, the panther.

Dave shouted a warning to his brothers. He reached forward and pulled a Winchester from a case beside the nearest saddle.

The sun-warmed languor of the siesta hour had been torn to shreds by violent action. Hoarse voices called, one to another. Feet pounded up and down the stairs. Excited faces appeared at windows. From stores and restaurants men poured, as seeds are squirted from a squeezed orange.

The first shot was fired by the marshal. He stood in the doorway of the National and carried the battle to the three outlaws inside. Instantly the Tolts accepted the challenge. Luke and Steve sent bullets crashing at him. Cole did not stop for a moment the business that had brought him here. He continued to cover the teller and the cashier as they poured gold into the sack he had tossed them.

The bank officers showed extreme nervousness. The room was filling with smoke. One of Reed's bullets splintered a panel behind them. The cashier ducked. His face was ashen.

"Don't lose your heads," Cole advised sternly. "Get the sacks of gold in the safe and dump 'em in here." He spoke as evenly as he might have done if he had been cashing a check in the ordinary manner.

The marshal staggered back and slumped down on the sidewalk. Two bullets had torn through his vitals. He had scored one hit. Steve had been struck in the upper chest.

Four or five citizens, armed with shotguns and rifles, were at the windows of the bank firing at the robbers. Cole was hit in the left forearm.

"All ready," he called coolly to his brothers.

The three moved toward the front door, taking the bank officers with them as a protection. Cole passed the sack of gold to Luke and drew a second forty-five. He could shoot with both hands, even though his left arm could not support the weight of the heavy sack. As the outlaws reached the street, the cashier and teller broke and ran.

A dozen men were shooting at the bandits, from office windows, from open doors, from the street. The Tolts moved through a lane of fire, their guns smoking as they went. Cole recognized the freckle-faced cowboy with whom he had been playing poker an hour or two earlier. The young fellow was behind a water-barrel, set in the street for fire protection, and he was raising his head cautiously for a shot. The bullet from Cole's revolver struck him in the forehead, just above the eyes.

A red-headed man, hatless, came out of the hardware store carrying a rifle. He took a shot at Dave and hit one of the horses. Steve, wounded in three places, flung a bullet at him from a distance of fifty yards. The man with the flaming topknot slid down to the pavement, sat there coughing for a moment, then crawled back into the hardware store.

"Hell's broke loose, looks like," Steve cried savagely.

He had reached the horses at last, but he saw that Luke was down in the middle of the road, trying to raise himself on one arm to continue firing. Steve ran lurching forward to drag him to the horses. A sawed-off shotgun roared. Across the body of his brother Steve fell dead.

Standing among the horses, Dave wondered feverishly why his brothers did not come. What

147

was the matter with them? Did they not know what a hornets' nest they had stirred up? Already a dozen men were visibly in action. Every office window and saloon door seemed to frame a man with a gun. Half a dozen more citizens were running up the street. From Twelfth Street he could hear shots, though the brick buildings cut off his view of what was taking place there.

Dave dared not leave the horses. He dared not open fire upon the attackers, for that would be to call attention to the fact that this was the remuda of the outlaws. He could only wait, in an agony of dreadful apprehension.

The battle had spread now to include the Drovers' and Cattlemen's Bank. Burke City had discovered that two banks were being robbed.

Then Steve came out of the National followed by Luke and Cole. It was at this moment that the red-headed man in the hardware store realized that Dave was one of the robbers and fired at him. Steve, badly wounded as Dave could see, dropped the man a moment later with a long pistol shot. Cole was wounded too. Luke was down. As fast as he could Dave pumped shots from his Winchester.

Cole and Steve reached the cottonwoods. But a moment later, Steve was back in the street trying to rescue Luke.

The blaze and roar of the guns were incessant. Dave emptied one rifle and reached for another.

Back of the horses he and Cole had considerable protection. Two horses were down, a third was screaming with pain.

Why didn't Caldwell and Sam come? Had they been killed in the bank? As Dave shouted the questions at Cole he caught sight of the other two brothers coming down the lane beside the Drovers' and Cattlemen's bank. Caldwell was carrying a heavy sack. Both were firing as they came.

Dave felt a thud against his shoulder and knew he had been hit. He was surprised at the slightness of the pain.

A German wearing the apron of a butcher crowded in toward the Tolts coming down the alley. He had a sawed off shotgun. Sam caught sight of him and fired over his shoulder at the man. The butcher staggered against a wall, steadied himself, and succeeded in raising the short-barreled gun. He was at close range. A score of buckshot struck Sam in the back of the neck. Before the bandit's body thudded to the ground he was dead.

Caldwell looked at his brother's body once and realized the truth. He ran zigzagging across the street to the park. Twice he was hit before he reached the cottonwoods. So badly was he hurt that he could not pull himself to the saddle without help.

The outlaws swung to their mounts and made

for the alley back of the park. Dave carried the sack of gold across the saddle in front of him. They galloped out of the firing zone with bullets whizzing past them as they rode. Into open country they raced, mile after mile.

They had to travel fast, for they knew that soon a posse would be on their trail. Wounded though they were, there could be no rest for them now. The whole countryside would be aroused. Farmers and trail-drovers would be watching for them. They must keep going until they reached the relay horses, if they got that far without being brought to bay.

"You hurt bad, Cald?" Dave asked, his voice trembling. The tragedy that had befallen them, that had seemed to leap at them out of the warm and friendly sunshine had shaken him to the marrow. It had all been so sudden. One moment, his brothers full of lusty life; the next, three of them dead and the others wounded.

Caldwell set his teeth. "Pretty bad. How about you, boy?" He spoke with difficulty.

"In the shoulder. Not so bad, I reckon. And you, Cole?"

"Hit three times. In the left arm and in the left leg, and this one in the cheek. We'll be lucky if we make it to the relays."

"We'd better stop at this creek here and make repairs," Caldwell decided. "They won't take the trail for an hour or two and we're ten miles from town. Got to patch ourselves up or we'll bleed to death."

What they could do for one another they did. Wounds were washed and bound with strips of cotton from torn shirts. Caldwell was in worse case than the other two. Watching him anxiously, Dave doubted whether he would ever get home alive. One of his wounds was in his side, below the heart. It did not bleed much, but the youngest brother was oppressed by a dreadful fear that Caldwell was dying before his eyes. He did not complain. He would not do that, no matter how badly he was hurt. The stoic Indian blood in him would keep that immobile face from telling stories. But there was a drawn look, a pallor in the brown cheeks ghastly to see.

Once more they lifted Caldwell to the saddle. His eyes were glazed. He clung to the horn with both hands. The bay he rode had been wounded, struck in the flank by a rifle ball. Neither horse nor rider could go much farther.

They met a pair of ranchmen jogging to town. The eyes of the two men opened wide at sight of the wounded trio. One of them drew up to ask a question, but without a word he started his horse again when Cole turned on him a black threatening look and flung out an imperative gesture for him to be on his way.

Cole was watching Caldwell closely. Sheer will was keeping the oldest Tolt in the saddle, but the strength was ebbing from him fast. They came to another creek.

It was a shallow stream with a hard bottom. Cole turned up it, his horse splashing through the water.

"Can't go any farther," he said to Dave in a low voice. "Cald is through. We'll hole up in the brush somewheres."

The country was rough, with a good deal of shinnery and sage. Cole wanted to get as far from the road as possible. His black eyes scowled over the landscape looking for a good place to hide.

"Not far now," Dave said to Caldwell. "We'll get you off where you can rest."

The boy's heart was flooded with distress. They must do something for Caldwell . . . soon . . . or it would be too late.

Caldwell did not answer him. His thin lips were pressed tightly together. The boy rode close to him when he could, trying to steady the swaying body in the saddle.

In a small arroyo, nearly a mile from the road, Cole stopped and dismounted. The place was well filled with brush. It would do well enough.

He and Dave lifted their brother from the saddle carefully and put him on the ground. They made him as comfortable as they could, readjusting the bandages. Dave noticed how tenderly Cole's fingers touched the flesh of his brother adjoining the wounds.

When they had done all they could for Caldwell, which was little enough, Dave asked again about the condition of Cole. He knew he would get no information as to how serious the wounds were unless he probed with questions.

"I'll make the grade," Cole said curtly.

"That cheek wound. It has bled a lot."

"Before I tied it up. Bullet went through clean and out my mouth. Knocked out a front tooth here. Nothing to worry about, that."

"Your other wounds. How about the one in the leg?"

"It's there," Cole answered grimly. "I'm getting notice from it a-plenty. But the bullet missed the artery. It'll heal up nice. So will my arm." He added, impatiently: "Quit worrying about me, boy. There's hell enough ahead of us without that."

"Yes," agreed Dave unhappily. The bottom had dropped out of his world. A few hours ago, life, adventure, sunshine; now, death, grief, the gloom of complete disaster.

Cole stabbed a fierce inquiring look at him. "How about that shoulder of yours? Can you stick it out? You've got a man's job ahead of you."

A cruel pain was beating in the wounded shoulder. At first the shock had deadened it, but the jabbing thrust of red-hot activity was present now.

"I can stand the gaff," Dave said evenly.

"Good. I'm tied here with Cald. He can't possibly travel—not yet."

Caldwell opened his eyes. "You've got to leave me, boys. It's every man for himself now. Hit the trail and go on the dodge."

His voice was weak, but he spoke with decision.

"By jacks, that sounds to me, Cald," Cole flung back scornfully. "What do you take us for? We're all in this together. We'll stay in it."

"Steven didn't quit Luke. He went back and got shot," Dave said with a gulp.

"Sure," Cole cut in sharply. "We'll take our medicine . . . together."

"If you'd leave me by the road, they would find me and take me to a doctor," Caldwell said diplomatically.

"If they found you, like enough they'd fill you full of holes," Cole retorted savagely. "None of that for us! We'll make a getaway yet, all three of us, or else—"

He let the conclusion of his sentence be guessed.

"What am I to do?" Dave asked.

"We're going to lose this bay. You've got to ride back to the park where we picketed the last bunch of broncs. Bring the scarface claybank with you. He rides easiest. And food enough to carry us a couple of days. Better bring all the grub we cached. Turn loose the other horses. They'll work back home by and by."

154

Dave's troubled eyes rested on Caldwell. "I hate to leave him. There's no rush about getting a horse here. Food's different. We've got to have that, of course. What's the matter with me going back to Burke City and bringing supplies and a doctor?"

Cole looked at him in amazement. "Are you crazy with the heat, boy?"

"No. Why couldn't I do it? A doctor could fix us all up fine. It's a jim-dandy idea."

"How do you aim to explain that shoulder to the folks back there?" Cole demanded with sarcasm. "And is it yore notion to tell the doc he's going to have three wounded bank robbers as patients? Might as well tell the sheriff where we're at."

"The shoulder won't show. I'll keep it covered with a bandanna. Nobody will take two looks at me. It's the last place in the world anybody would expect one of the bank holdups to be. We were seen riding out of town. Why would one of us come back?"

"You might be recognized."

"No chance, not if I'm careful. The only fellow who got a good look at me after the boys went into the banks was Reed, the marshal. And he's dead."

"You haven't explained yet how you expect to get a doctor to come." In spite of himself, Cole found merit in the plan, if it could be worked. There was danger in it, but whichever way they turned there was peril. And one grim fact that stared him in the face was that without medical aid Caldwell probably would not live.

"I'd tell him a fellow got hurt by a threshing machine," Dave said. "A fellow up the valley here."

"And if he told you he was right busy in town fixing up a bunch of citizens who had been shot up by outlaws? If he said he hadn't time to come now?"

"I'd persuade him to change his mind," Dave said quietly.

"Could you do it—alone?"

"I robbed a train alone," the boy reminded him.

"By jacks, you did," Cole agreed. "But there's one thing you've forgotten. After the doc had fixed us up and gone back to Burke City, a passel of sheriffs would come hotfooting it out here *muy pronto*."

"Yes, if the doc went back to Burke City. But he wouldn't go back till we were ready to have him go. He'd stay with us till we turned him loose."

Cole looked closely at him, brows narrowing to a frown. What did the boy mean? How far was he prepared to go?

"We're not running a hotel—nor yet a jail," the older brother said harshly.

"We're down to the blanket," Dave insisted. "It ain't what we'd like to do, but what we've got to do."

"Let's get it straight, kid. Are you proposing to dry-gulch this doc when he's fixed us up?"

"No," Dave broke out quickly. "I wouldn't stand for that. If it came to a showdown, I'd rather let him go and then fight it out with the posses."

Cole nodded, only the black eyes in his swarthy, immobile face alive. "Good. Here too, I never fired a shot at a man who didn't have a gun in his hand. I never will. All right. Go bring yore doc. It's neck meat or nothing."

"The way I look at it too," Dave said in a low voice, with a glance at Caldwell, who was lying on the ground with his eyes closed. "He won't make it if we don't get help. No use fooling ourselves."

"I hate to let you go back there," Cole said. "If it wasn't for this game leg of mine—"

"You couldn't go," Dave interrupted. "Soon as you was out of the saddle and started limping some guy would spot you."

"Yes," the older brother agreed.

"But I'm only a fool kid cowboy. Nobody is going to bother about me."

Cole wished he could be sure of that. This raid had been tragic enough already. He dared not go back and tell his mother that he had sent her Benjamin back into the danger zone and lost him too. Yet he had to let Dave go. He had to do it to save Caldwell.

"For God's sake, be careful, boy," he urged.

They washed the sweat stains of rapid travel from the flanks of a sorrel Cole had been riding. Dave reloaded his revolver. He put it in the right saddlebag.

"Stay in the brush until you're close to town," Cole went on. "When you slip back to the road, be sure nobody sees you. Better have the doc fix up your shoulder soon as you get him out of town. You don't want to take a chance of keeling over. That would sure stop our clocks for us."

"I'll be right careful," Dave promised.

With a heavy heart Cole watched him go. Boy though he was, if there was any slip-up, if anyone should discover he was one of the outlaws, he would probably be rubbed out instantly.

The excitement in Burke City, the rage against the bank robbers, must be intense. Four or five citizens had been killed and as many wounded.

The town would be in no temper for anything but swift vengeance.

XI

A Narrow Squeak

Doctor Watson, just back from hours of strain, measured himself a small drink of whiskey. In Burke City there were only two physicians and both of them had had their hands full. They had attended to four wounded men and examined briefly seven dead ones. The frontier had been the home of Norman Watson for a great many years. Men wounded and killed by weapons were a familiar part of his experience, but he had never known such a holocaust as today.

A good law-abiding citizen, the wantonness of this crime filled him with anger. What kind of men were these who came bent on robbery and carried it through at such cost? He hoped they would be captured and dealt with severely by the law, those of them who had escaped.

He was not sure how many had got away. In the excitement men saw double. According to some stories five or six had ridden out of town. Others who had been in the battle made the number three. Already two or three posses were out after them. It was known that at least one of the bandits was wounded. There ought to be a good chance of a capture.

He drank a chaser of water after the whiskey, put down the glass, and turned. Somebody had come into the outer office. He hoped it was not a patient. Most of the night he would be up with the wounded men, and he did not want to take on any extra work.

Watson stepped to the door of the inner office and opened it. "Do you want to see me?" he asked.

A young cowboy moved forward. "You Doctor Watson?"

"Yes."

"A fellow has been hurt up the valley—got his foot caught and badly crushed while we were putting up hay. They sent me to get you."

"I can't go," the doctor snapped. "I've got four wounded men on my hands right here in town."

"This fellow is hurt bad, doctor. Someone has to look after him or he'll die. It ain't but five miles out. Couldn't you have some other doc look after your town patients till you get back?" The cowpuncher's wistful smile pleaded for consideration. He was a dark, good-looking lad. His eyes had the stricken look of one who has lived through something terribly shocking.

"Why couldn't he pick some other time to get hurt?" Watson demanded testily. "I'll have to go, I suppose, if it's no more than five miles. But I can't stay after I've dressed the foot. Understand that."

"We'll sure be much obliged, doc," the boy said gratefully.

The doctor began to put medicines and instruments in his case. "Meet me here in ten minutes. I've got to get my horse. While you're waiting, go to the office of Doctor Ridley and ask him to look after the wounded men alone until my return. Explain to him I'll be back before eight o'clock. Ridley's office is in the next block, above the National Bank."

"Yes, sir," Dave said. "Better take some whiskey along. Or shall I take that?"

"You get it. In ten minutes, young fellow. Right here in front of the D. & C. Bank. I won't wait."

Dave dropped into a saloon and bought a quart of whiskey. Two ranchmen were drinking in front of the bar. The boy looked at them, and his heart stood still. They were the men who had passed them on their flight from town. The ranchers were talking excitedly to the bartender.

"Yes, Jim, we passed 'em six or seven miles out. The very birds. One of 'em was badly wounded. So was his horse. Aleck here started to stop, but one of the guys waved him to keep agoing."

"I'd sure know that blackbird again," Aleck contributed. "Or any one of the three for that matter. Texas men, I'd say."

"Needn't wrap the bottle," Dave said, and wondered whether his voice was quite steady. "It's for immediate use, you might say."

One of the ranchers glanced at Dave. He was full of his story. It had not got him much atten-

161

tion so far. Too many men had been in the actual battle to listen to a tale not tied closely to the thrill of the fight. "A kid almost, the youngest one was. No older than this boy here. But you could see he was a tough *hombre* like the others."

"Y'betcha," the other man agreed. "All three of 'em. Give us another of the same, Jim."

Dave went quaking out of the place. If the man had taken a second look! If he had shouted, "This is one of the robbers."

Young Tolt climbed the stairs to the second story of the National Bank building and walked into the office that had upon it the name of Doctor Ridley.

The doctor was a young man, not long out of medical school. Dave delivered his message.

"Tell him not to worry," Ridley said. "I'll look after them until he gets back."

As Dave reached the street, he came face to face with one of the wranglers at the Alamo Corral.

"Hello, fellow!" the man cried. "Two of those Texas fellows we were talking to this morning were in the bank holdup gang. Soon as I saw their bodies I knew 'em. They're over at Jig Sullivan's place now. Come along over an' see if I ain't right."

He caught Dave by the wounded shoulder. The boy let out a yell of pain. The wrangler fell back and stared at him.

"What the heck, fellow!" he cried.

Tiny beads of perspiration stood on young Tolt's forehead. The clutch of that heavy hand had changed a throbbing pain to a knife-thrust of fiery agony. For a moment the boy leaned against the brick wall, white to the lips, fighting against a wave that seemed to lift him from his feet toward unconsciousness. He fixed it in his mind that he must not faint. He dared not. He had to think fast, to avert any chance of suspicion suggesting itself to the Alamo man's thought.

"Didn't you know?" he boasted faintly. "One of the gang hit me. In the shoulder here. I was right there when he came out of the bank, with my sixgun a-foggin'. Doc Ridley has just been dressing it. Hurts like billy-be-damn."

The mouth of the corral helper opened. "I'll bet it does. Lordy, I'm sorry I grabbed the place. Why don't you wear a bandage so folks can see it? Those devils certainly pumped lead into a mess of good citizens. Hanging's too good for the ones that made their getaway, if they are ever caught. Ain't I right?"

The pain was still shrieking through Dave, but the danger of fainting was past. He had satisfied this dumb wrangler. It was time to be gone.

"Y'betcha, Bill! Well, I got to push along back to camp."

"Stick around a while in town. I got the evening off."

Dave had heard the footsteps of someone

descending the stairway of the National Bank building. Doctor Ridley emerged from the entrance.

"'Lo, Doc!" the wrangler grinned. "I'll bet you're the busy white-haired lad tonight. I didn't know till right damn now that this buckaroo here—"

Boisterously Dave interrupted. "Fellow, Doc's too busy to listen to all you don't know, if he's got any patients. Come along, Bill, and have a drink."

Ridley came to Dave's aid, unintentionally. He was still young enough to be full of professional dignity. One thing he could not stand was to be called "Doc." He was not a veterinarian, but a full-fledged practitioner of medicine licensed by reason of a certificate from a good school. Moreover, he had a bride of four weeks' standing anxious to meet him after six hours of separation. If he hurried, there would be time for supper before he had to return to his patients. This had been the most dramatic day of his life. He anticipated the pleasure of sharing its thrills with her in eager talk.

"You'll have to excuse me," he said stiffly, and turning on his heel he walked swiftly down the street.

Bill looked after him. "That guy won't get anywheres in this man's town," he predicted with a sniff. "All right, Mr. Texas Cowboy, I heard you when you said drink."

Dave's brain was working by flashes. He had to get rid of this fellow. Quick, too. As soon as they got inside, the wrangler would begin to talk about his wound. Any excuse would serve, since the man was a lunkhead. As they walked toward the Last Chance he began framing his story.

"The boss gave me what-for on account of me getting plugged," Dave explained. "I was s'posed to be out with the herd an' I slipped away. He came awful near giving me my time. I'm to get right back to camp soon as I'm fixed up by the doc. That's what he told me. The old man is still sore at me."

"He must ride herd on you buckaroos mighty close. I been up the trail myself. When a fellow gets to town he's entitled to some fun."

They pushed through the swing doors of the Last Chance. Dave took one look at a group of strangers near the back of the room and whispered excitedly to the wrangler.

"The boss. I've got to *vamos*."

Dave turned and ran out. When he reached the street he kept going.

During that first five miles out of town, more than once Dave felt a wave of sickness sweep over him almost overpoweringly. He was tempted to stop and have Doctor Watson dress the wound. But he rejected the urge. As a patient he would be in the power of the physician. One glance at Watson's rugged square-cut face had told him the man was no fool. He would guess that Dave was one of the bandits taking him to the hide-out of the others, and a whiff or two of chloroform would put the boy out of business for the time.

The waves of nausea came and passed. Dave lost count of time and distance. Once he just missed sliding from the saddle in a faint by hanging desperately to the horn.

"How much farther is it?" the doctor asked. "You said five miles."

"Not so far now," Dave replied evasively.

"Whose place?"

"A nester called Johnson."

"Must be a new man. Don't think I know him."

"Came from the Cross Timbers country."

"Is he the man that's hurt?"

"A fellow working for him."

"How did you say he got hurt?"

"Got his foot jammed while we were putting up hay."

They covered another two miles. An unease, scarcely amounting as yet to suspicion, came to the doctor and stayed with him.

He pulled up. "Just where is Johnson's place?" he asked.

Dave waved a hand to the right. "Back this way."

"Where? How does it lie from Allen's ranch?"

The boy fumbled in one of the saddlebags. When his hand came out there was a revolver in it.

"Don't ask so many questions, doc," the owner of the weapon advised grimly.

"Who are you?"

"Another question. We're leaving the road here. Head into the brush. No fool business. I'm a dead shot."

"You're one of the bank robbers," Watson said quietly.

"That's your guess," Tolt replied, his voice cold and metallic. "Mine is that if you want to stay healthy, you'd better start moving *pronto* and do like I say."

The doctor guided by the rein into the brush, Dave followed, his pony's nose brushing the rump of the other horse. For miles they traveled without a word. No sound was heard except the creaking of the saddles, the swish of shrubbery, and the occasional sharp clip of a hoof against a stone.

Watson did not attempt to escape. He knew better. A wide observation of gunplays in the Southwest had taught him that it was folly to take liberties when covered by a weapon. More than once he had acted officially as coroner upon the cases of those who had failed to learn this in time to be of practical use to them.

Out of the chaparral the horses came to an abrupt slope. Down this they went stiff-legged to a small brook winding among the land waves.

"To the right," Dave said brusquely.

Watson followed the creek around a spur of rimrock and came to a sudden halt. A tall dark man, his face bound with a blood-stained bandanna, barred the way with a rifle.

"All right?" Dave asked. "How are you both?"

"He's out of his head. This the doctor?"

"Doctor Watson. I looked over both docs and picked this one." Dave made answer.

"Get down," Cole ordered the doctor. "We've got a patient here for you. Fact is, we've got three."

Watson made no comment. He began his examination of Caldwell's hurts.

"Bring me water," he presently ordered.

Half an hour later, he rose from his knees, flexed his muscles, and looked coldly at Cole.

"Next patient," he said quietly.

"You, boy," Cole said to Dave.

The youngest Tolt shook his head. "No. You're worse hurt than I am. Let me wait."

"Do like I say, boy," Cole frowned.

As the doctor examined and dressed the boy's wound, he was amazed at the stoicism of the lad. He had ridden for hours beside him and had not even guessed that the young fellow was carrying a bullet in his shoulder. Now he endured, almost without wincing, the fierce pain of the probe.

Watson felt the same unwilling admiration for the third patient. The brown man with the goatee was a superb physical specimen. The long muscles of legs and arms rippled under the smooth skin like those of a tiger. During the operation of cleaning and dressing his wounds, he must have endured exquisite pain, but not a twitch of the hard, set face betrayed it.

These men were miscreants, wolves outside of the law, a menace to the honest men who had come as pioneers to the frontier. It was his conviction that they ought to be stamped out like wild beasts. But he discovered in them qualities worthy of better types. One of them, a few hours since, had plunged back into the zone of fire, though already desperately wounded, to rescue a comrade unable to save himself. Two of these three—the two who were masters of their actions —showed a rare unselfishness toward each other.

It would have been difficult for one not used to the frontier to understand the characters of such men. Doctor Watson made a good guess at them because he knew his West. They were intensely loyal one to another, brave, generous, full of lusty energy. Their virtues had become exaggerated until they were destroying vices. The individualism, so necessary to the pioneer, had gone to seed in them and run wild. Brought up in constant danger, they had little regard for their own lives or for those of others. They had the stuff of heroes in them, yet because they could not rule themselves they had become murderous outlaws. Like thousands of others who had "gone bad," the fine qualities in them had been unable to save them from their own lack of discipline and self-control.

Watson observed that they did not address one another by name. He interpreted this as a hopeful sign for himself. If they had intended to kill him, they need not have been on their guard.

After the wounds had all been dressed, Cole drew the doctor to one side. "What about him?" he asked harshly, nodding toward Caldwell. "Will he make it?"

"I don't know," Watson said frankly. "I can't tell yet about the wound in the side. He has lost a lot of blood. It hasn't helped his chances to come so far in the saddle after he was shot. Fact is, I don't see how he managed it. . . . But I've learned one thing about you outdoors men. You take a lot of killing. This man is in fine fettle physically. He has lived a clean, hard life. I'd say he has a fair chance if he's kept quiet. But he can't be moved, not for some time."

"How long?"

"I don't know. The longer he is kept quiet, the better chance he ought to have. Not for ten days, anyhow. A long ride would finish him."

"You mean now?"

"Yes. He couldn't possibly stand it." Watson frowned thoughtfully. "I wish I had him in a hospital. He needs constant attention, medical supervision, I mean."

"He'll get it," Cole said bluntly.

"Where?"

"Here. You're staying with us, doctor."

"I have wounded patients in town that need me."

"There's another doctor there. They can send and get two or three by train inside of six or seven hours. We can't."

"You mean you'll hold me by force?"

"We'll hold you," Cole answered, not specifying how.

"How long?"

"Long as you're needed."

"And after that?"

Watson was no coward. He looked the outlaw straight in the eyes as he asked the question. Tolt met the steady regard of the physician with a gaze just as direct.

"We'll turn you loose. Don't worry, doctor. Play square by us and we'll do the same by you. What's more, we'll pay liberally for your services."

The physician believed him. The man's word was good. Bandit though he was, he would see that his unwilling guest came to no harm. As for remuneration, he might be paid with the money of the bank, but he would be paid.

"Don't you think it likely you may be discovered here?" Watson asked bluntly.

"About an even bet," Cole said coolly.

"And if you are?"

Cole laughed, savagely, without mirth. "Why then, doc, you'll have more patients," he said.

"Do you expect to keep me tied?"

"Not in the daytime, anyhow, if you'll act sensible. How about it, doctor? Seeing as you have to string along with us anyhow, will you give me your word to play fair? It will be a lot more comfortable all around."

"You mean, not try to escape if I get a chance."

"I mean, not try to escape if you *think* you get a chance. There won't be any chance, but you might right easy commit suicide by making a break."

Watson considered. "All right. I give you my word. Under the condition that as soon as you've turned me loose I'm free to set the law on you. And under one other condition: I'll take no fee for my services."

"You figure our money is blood-money, eh?" Cole told him roughly. "All right. Please yoreself about that."

The outlaw turned away. He might jeer cynically at Watson's stipulation as to accepting tainted money, but he gave the man his entire respect. The doctor was game, and he was honest. Not many would have had the nerve to stand so uncompromisingly, given a situation where frank-ness was so dangerous. Courage was a virtue Cole could understand.

Dave was taking from the saddle a gunnysack filled with groceries.

"Got grub enough to last a week?" Cole asked.

"Don't know. I brought all I could carry. Bought it before I went up to the doctor's office."

"Good. If we run out, you can go to the cache. You'll have to go, anyhow, to turn the horses loose. . . . Have any trouble in town?"

"No trouble. Everything worked slick. I got a couple of scares, though." Dave told of meeting the two ranchmen who had passed them on the road and of his adventure with the wrangler of the Alamo Corral.

"Lucky none of 'em jumped you," Cole said. "But I reckon you made your own luck, boy. Pick up any news?"

"The town is crazy with excitement."

"It would be." Tolt's next question came almost roughly. "Hear about . . . our boys? They're all . . . ?"

"Yes." Dave gulped. "Before we left. All three of them. So a fellow told me. They . . . died right away."

"Thought so. Better that way. How many of the other fellows?"

"Four dead, four wounded."

Cole looked away, at the fading western light back of the hills. "We played hell," he said at last bitterly.

XII

On the Dodge

The Tolts showed an amazing recuperative power. Even Doctor Watson, used though he was to the stamina of the men of the Southwest, was surprised at the progress his patients made. They built blood rapidly. After a few days the temperature of the two younger ones registered normal. Cole still limped a little when he walked, but it was plain that he would soon be as well as ever. More slowly, strength flowed back into the lax, stricken body of Caldwell. His wounds were serious. They might have put an end to an indoor office man. But the Tolts had a splendid physical inheritance. The sun and the wind, good food, hard work, and clean living had toned up Caldwell's vigorous vitality so that it offered a potent resistance to dissolution. Within forty-eight hours he had turned the corner. Inside of four days he was beginning to relish food.

Doctor Watson was nurse and cook as well as physician. He was of a philosophic turn. These men were his patients. It was his job to get them well. That they got nourishing food and rested sufficiently he made it his business to see. He did not doubt that the law would get them in the end, dead or alive. Very likely he would contribute to their capture by information given to the police, and later to their conviction—provided they were taken alive—by witnessing against them. That had nothing to do with his present duty.

He and the bank robbers maintained an attitude of inimical friendliness. All of them knew exactly where he stood. None of them held any resentment. It was almost as though they were playing a sporting game. If he could score off them by contriving their capture, that was one to him; if they could outmaneuver him, score a point for the Tolts.

Meanwhile, he made no attempt to escape. Watson did not feel entirely easy in mind. They were desperate men, these outlaws who had him in their power. He knew they were not bloodthirsty, that he would not be shot down out of wanton impulse or out of savage cruelty. The pinch would come only if his life endangered theirs. Given such an emergency, what would they do? Would they destroy him?

It was characteristic of his blunt courage that he put the question to them boldly as they lounged on the sun-warmed sand one pleasant afternoon.

Cole aimed tobacco juice at a flat stone ten feet away and made a center shot. He did not usually chew, but he was debarred from smoking these days. A thin drift of smoke might betray them if anyone chanced to be near.

"I wonder," Cole said amiably. "We'd hate to bump you off, doc. Fact is, we feel real friendly to you. To be sure, business is business. You get that. No hard feelings, in any case."

"I'd be just as dead if you shot me, regardless of what your feelings happened to be," Watson said dryly.

"That's so," Cole agreed. "If you look at it that way."

Caldwell drawled reassurance. "Don't you worry, doctor. Play a straight game with us and we'll do the same with you. We've got our tails in a crack all right, but it's not your fault we're in a tight. If it comes to a showdown, we won't throw down on you, if you don't on us first. You certainly grabbed me by the hair and hauled me out when I was going under. I ain't liable to forget that, or the other boys either."

"Hump!" grunted Cole. "No sense in telling all you know, fellow. I wouldn't put doc out of business any quicker than you would. You know that. But it wouldn't have done any harm to keep him on the anxious seat."

"Nor any good either," Caldwell returned. "Doctor Watson has told us just where we're at with him. He's entitled to know where he's at with us."

"Why not?" the physician asked, relieved in mind. "If a sheriff's posse was fifty yards away, I wouldn't make a sound even though it was safe. I wouldn't leave you if I had a chance to slip from camp. I've given my word on that. After you've turned me loose, that's another proposition."

None of the Tolts asked the useless question as to what kind of a proposition it would be then. They knew. Accurate descriptions of them would be mailed all over this Southwest country, even to the location of the moles and scars on their bodies. Their wounds would be enumerated, their approximate ages given, the peculiarities of their features stressed. Too bad, but that was the price they would have to pay for medical services. They would have to stay in the chaparral on the dodge until they could make arrangements to leave the country. The chances against them would be doubled, as soon as the doctor told the officers what he knew.

The alternative was to put an end to Watson, leave his body dry-gulched under the rocks. But that was one thing the Tolts could not do. There are degrees of villainy. This man had served them, given them of his best. He had nursed Caldwell night and day. They did not value their own lives so highly as to murder him in spite of all decency. In this they differed from the modern city gangsters, the pasty-faced gunmen who look out under thick lids from cold leaden eyes almost reptilian. They had their perverted code of honor, these cattlemen who had gone bad. From it they would not depart a jot.

As soon as Doctor Watson would permit it, Dave set out on a night ride to the little mountain park where the J T horses had been left for remounts.

"You're just a kid," Cole had explained as they were eating supper. "If anyone sees you, they won't figure you're one of us. If I went, this game leg would be liable to give me away. But at that, I hate to let you go alone."

Dave had not needed to be told that there was another reason why Cole did not go. Any hour the camp of the outlaws might be discovered. If this occurred, Cole wanted to be present with Caldwell. It was likely that he welcomed an excuse to get Dave out of the danger zone.

After Dave had swung to the saddle, Cole had a last word with him. "Bring back two broncs and the one you ride. We'll have to take Doc a ways with us before we turn him loose. I don't expect we'll be in this camp when you get back. Too near the road and that ranch over to the south. We'll be in that pocket four miles farther up the creek. That's what I'm figuring on now, anyhow. If our luck doesn't stand up and we should have to fight it out, or if we should be taken, you can't help that. Soon as the word gets to you, turn loose your string and light a shuck for home. Stay on the dodge till you get a chance to slip out West. Understand?"

"Yes."

"Good. Don't forget it. You've got to think of Mother. Luck, boy."

It was a rough country. Dave had been only once in that small park which nestled in the rockrim. But he went to it as directly as though guided by a compass.

One of the horses had pulled up its picket-pin and was grazing near the others. The rest of the animals were wild for water. Dave took them to the creek and let them drink moderately. After an hour or two he watered them again. Three of the animals he repicketed. The others he freed. In the course of time they would wander back to their home range.

Across country he cut to the meadow where the first bunch of mounts had been left. Day broke before he reached the spot. He rode into a mesquite thicket and unsaddled, hobbling the horse so that the animal could graze while he rested.

There was no hurry. The fugitives in camp had plenty of food, nothing to do, and good medical attention. Until Caldwell was able to travel, the fewer men and mounts in camp the less likelihood there would be of discovery. Cole had given him positive orders not to show up again inside of four days. Though Dave knew his brother's real reason, or at least the chief one, why he did not want him back too soon, he recognized that the one given was valid enough.

The boy's own urge was to get back to Caldwell and Cole, losing as little time as possible, but he realized that his feeling was based upon fear for them. If the officers found them, he wanted to be there and share the danger. That, however, was largely a sentiment. He had to do as his older brothers had directed.

Dave lit a fire and cooked food. He lay down and slept. The sun shifted so that the mesquite no longer shaded him. He awoke, checked up on his cowpony to make sure it was not straying too far, and again lay down. When his eyes opened the second time, dusk was falling. After eating supper he packed the saucepan and supplies, resaddled, and set out once more.

The moon was up when he reached the meadow where the J T relay mounts had been left. The animals were gone. It was sure that all of them had not pulled their picket-pins, especially since they had been left within reach of water and there was still uncropped grass within the circles where they had been tied. Somebody had found the animals and had either released or removed them. Judging from the amount of grass that had been cropped and the other signs left, Dave guessed this had taken place the day following the one when they had been left here.

Not so good, young Tolt reflected. Whoever had taken or released the animals knew they carried the J T brand. If rustlers had stolen the remuda, they would of course keep quiet to protect themselves, but if an honest man had stumbled on the tethered horses he would guess, as soon as he heard of the bank robberies at Burke City, that the ponies had been left as relay mounts by the bandits. This could not be proved, but it would work in with the chain of evidence forged against the Tolts bit by bit.

The fugitives were outside of the news currents, but it was probable that before the bodies of the dead outlaws had been buried, someone had identified them as black Tolts. In any case, photographs would have been taken and sent broadcast to the officers of every county within a radius of two hundred miles. Given the knowledge that the slain bandits were Tolts, it would follow inevitably that those who had escaped were of the same family. The only chance for them was to get out of the country. Even Oregon might be too near. Over their breakfast one morning, when Doctor Watson had been out of hearing, the wounded men had agreed that the chase would carry far and would not be dropped without a most determined effort to capture them. Too many lives had been snuffed out. The Argentine might be the best bet as an objective. It was a cattle country, and there the fugitives could drop into oblivion. The chance of reaching South America was, of course, very slight.

Dave returned to the rockrim park where he

had left the three horses picketed. All was still well here. The cached food had not been touched. There was no evidence that anybody had been in the park since he had left it.

Below the rockrim Dave camped for three days. He took pains to remove frequently all possible evidence of long occupancy. Somebody with an inquiring mind might drop in and pay him a visit.

On the afternoon of the third day this occurred. An old bearded fellow looking for strays drifted over a break in the rockrim. When he saw Dave, he rode up to him, and relaxed in the saddle, putting his weight on one stirrup.

He was unkempt and ragged. His boots were run-down-at-the-heel antiques, the uppers broken and gaping. The funnel-shaped hat had three or four holes in it. Incessantly, throughout his visit, he chewed tobacco and fired shots of juice with deadly accuracy at selected targets.

"A one-gallus hill billy," Dave summed up to himself, but reserved the right to revise the judgment upon further acquaintance.

The old man cocked a curious eye at the boy. "I ain't met up with you before, have I? Where from, young fellow?"

"From down Sanford way. These doggone horses won't range in our country. My dad bought 'em north of Burke City. This is the second time they done lit out for their old home."

"Sure. The critters always will. Say, you weren't at Burke when the rookus was, were you?"

"No. I wisht I had been. Looks to me like I always miss everything. Anything new about that?"

"I been roostin' up in the hills at my place for three days. How would I know anything new? Listen to me. They never will get those birds. Our officers ain't worth shucks."

"Why won't they get 'em? I'd think they would, with all the country out lookin' for 'em."

"That shows how much you know. You're only a fool kid. Listen. Only yesterday a posse come nosin' around my place. No sense a-tall. The birds that robbed those banks struck a high tail outa here sudden. They ain't foolin' around waitin' to be caught. No, sir. They've drug it for home, an' they didn't move like snails climbing a slick log. Not none. They went like the Watsons, hell for leather."

One of these wise guys, Dave decided. For the sake of appearances he put up an argument.

"That's what you'd expect 'em to do. But maybe these lead-pumpers holed-up somewheres an'—"

"Mebbe they're right in Burke now, an' mebbe they ain't," the old man shrilled derisively, excitement in his voice. "No, sir. This bunch is bad medicine. They're rattlesnakes. If a skunk bit one of 'em, it would die from p'ison. They ain't a gang of crazy kid cowpunchers. They know what for. They've done holed-up all right, but it ain't anywheres around here. They're in the Nation. That's where they're at. If these sheriffs that run around like a chicken without a head had a lick of sense, they'd know it too."

"I reckon you're right."

"You know damn well I'm right. They've done rattled their hocks outa this neck of the woods with thirty thousand dollars the bank will never see again. Now if I'd been in charge of this here man hunt, it would sure have been done different. I wouldn't have fooled around for a minute. I'd a-wired to the Nation an' then hit the grit for there with a posse before you could say 'Scat.' By now I'd a-had my men. Don't you know it?"

The old nester was so well satisfied with himself and his abilities that Dave wondered how he explained to his own satisfaction that after sixty-odd years he was and always had been a nobody, a cipher who had no weight with his neighbors. Perhaps he bolstered his self-esteem by these delusions of power within himself.

"Can't prove it by me," Dave said. "Sounds good, what you say. I hadn't figured it out myself, but I'll bet my boots you've got it worked out according to Hoyle. Come to think of it, there wouldn't be any sense in those fellows stickin' around. Do you reckon there's a big reward out for the ones that got away?"

"Sure. The authorities got to do something,

ain't they? I'll tell you something else, young fellow." The old man leaned down and lowered his voice, with a manner of wisdom infallible as a Supreme Court decision. "The guys that did this job are the same ones that pulled off the Painted Rock and the Melrose holdups. Find the train robbers an' you've got the scalawags that stuck up the banks at Burke."

Dave's big eyes reflected astonished admiration at such perspicacity. "By golly, I'll bet you're right," he admitted, scratching his head to help him think. "I wouldn't of thought of that. You're certainly right up on yore toes, mister. If you'd been sheriff, like you say—"

"Nothing to it. If I'd been sheriff they would have been in the calaboose by now. Mebbe I can't fly, but I can catch birds."

Young Tolt gave an imitation of a country boy much impressed by superior intelligence. "Lucky for the holdups you ain't," he said.

Before the old-timer left he remembered to ask Dave if he had seen anything of a dun cow with a six-weeks-old calf, the mother marked by a twisted left horn.

Dave had not.

"Well, I'll be moseyin' along," the nester decided. "Don't let any tinhorn sell you a glass eye, young fellow."

Dave watched him and his broomtail disappear over the break in the rimrock.

"He's certainly a big wind pudding," the boy drawled aloud.

His reason for playing up to the old fellow had been to keep his mind busy. By concentrating his attention on the robbery, Dave had kept him from reading the signs of occupancy written all around him. The man carried away with him an impression that this country bumpkin had just arrived in the park and was leaving at once.

Part of his deduction was correct.

Within the hour Dave packed up and departed, taking the spare horses with him.

Dave rounded a spur of rimrock and saw at a glance that the camp was gone. He had expected this. Cole had said they meant to move to the hill pocket four miles farther up the creek. No doubt, Dave thought, he would find his brothers and Doctor Watson there. His eyes, trained to cut sign, swept the locale. They picked up a detail that startled him. Four empty shells, ejected from a rifle, lay on the sand where they had fallen.

The stomach muscles seemed to give way and let his heart fall. There had been a fight. Perhaps his brothers had been killed or captured.

He swung from the saddle and quartered over the ground. From what he read there he could guess at part of the story. The outlaws had been attacked. They had fought back. Hurriedly they had departed, *and they had gone up the creek.* This meant that they had not been taken by the posse, at least not during the first brush. For the sheriff would have headed with his prisoners down the creek toward the road.

Dave followed the creek to the hill pocket where Cole had told him he expected to hole up. There was no sign of his brothers there. Two horses had passed through it, but they had kept going. Moreover, they had been traveling fast. In the brush, half a mile beyond this point, Dave lost the tracks and could not again pick them up.

It was possible the fugitives had taken to the water. Certainly they had covered their trail. Though he spent hours trying to find it, no success rewarded his vigilant search.

While still looking for hoofprints, the boy had made up his mind what to do in case of failure. He hobbled his extra horses, left them, and rode to the nearest ranch.

A lad about his own age was shoeing a roan gelding. He was the only person to be seen on the place. Dave lent him a hand at the job. When they had finished, Tolt put a question. "Seen anything of a claybank mare with the Sixty Three Quarter Circle brand on the left hip?"

"No, I don't reckon I have," the boy answered. He was a guileless youth, freckle-faced and red-headed.

The reply was not surprising, since Dave had that moment invented the description.

"It strayed. Dad bought it up thisaway, and we allowed it might have drifted back."

"Maybe so. I ain't run across it."

"Like looking for a needle in a haystack."

"Y'betcha. Where's the Sixty Three Quarter Circle?"

"Down south of Regent. Say, you been having lots of excitement up here lately. Were you in any of it?"

The boy with the sorrel top grinned. "Depends on what you mean by in. I saw the last scrap."

"Where?"

"From the hilltop right north of the house here."

"Dad gum! Tell me about it."

"I was fixing a fence right over there when I heard shots," the boy began, eager to tell his story. "I'd seen a party of four riders headin' up the creek, an' I'd kinda 'lowed it was another posse out after the bank holdups. So when I heard the firing I forked my bronc an' lit out for the hilltop. It's about a mile from where I was at, an' Two Bits covered that mile like he'd stirred up a hornets' nest. Before I reached the top, I could see the posse backing off. One of 'em was wounded. I could notice how he slumped down on the saddle. The whole caboodle of 'em was getting out real unanimous. They hadn't lost any bank robbers. Not one. I could see 'em get panicky right before my eyes."

"Did you see the other fellows?"

"Fellow, I *saw* 'em. From the top of the hill. They were going up a draw. Three of 'em. One of 'em afoot. He was trailing behind. The birds on the broncs waved to him to light out. He ducked into the brush and came straight up the hill toward me. Me, I didn't wait for him. I scooted for the ranch. Well, sir, half an hour later that fellow showed up at our place. He was Doctor Watson."

"Doctor Watson! Was he one—?"

"No, sir. But it seems all the gang had been wounded, an' one of 'em went to town an' brought Doctor Watson out to look after them. O' course the doctor didn't know where he was going till they had him covered. They made him stay with them 'most a week, right within two miles of this ranch here."

"Were either of the robbers hurt in the fight you saw?"

"No. The way of it was that Bob Slink's posse jumped 'em unexpected. In the shooting Jim Lane got hit. The posse backed right off like I done told you."

"And the outlaws—have they been seen since?"

"No. Doctor Watson says he figures they came from down Indian Territory way. They had been shot up right consid'rable, but they were a whole lot better an' were good for a long ride if they took it in spells. Watson he got right to town an' descriptions of these gazebos were sent out everywhere. Sheriff Opdyke got busy with a bunch of fellows, but he couldn't seem to hit the trail of the robbers. I dunno whether he wanted to so doggone much. These fellows are bad *hombres*."

"Looks like," Dave agreed. "Well, I reckon I'll slope. If you see anything of that claybank mare, drop a line to Bill Butler at the Sixty Three Quarter Circle and we'll be obliged."

"Sure will," the boy promised.

Dave took his leisurely way back into the hills where he had left the hobbled horses. He had found out what he wanted to know. His brothers had escaped, for the time at least, though posses were still combing the chaparral in search of them. There was nothing he could do now to help them. No doubt they were working back cautiously toward the home country.

He must look out for himself now. With his description flung far by the authorities, he might at any moment be arrested. Any youth traveling alone would be suspect now, since Doctor Watson had told that he was separated from the others. It would be better for him to lie low in the daytime and ride at night.

The hunt would be fast and furious. The holdup of the Burke City banks had been too bold, too tragic in its result, for any merely perfunctory pursuit. Very likely Bill Tilghman and Chris Madsen, the men who had done so much to rid Oklahoma of its criminals, would be put on the job of running down the bandits. Dave's instinct, like that of a fox flying before the pack, was to get home and hole up. After that, if he could keep out of the clutches of the officers, arrangements might be made for getting him out of the country. It was a slim chance. Too many would be after the big reward. But it was neck meat or nothing with him. He was down to the blanket.

Just as a cold-blooded proposition, Dave was not sure of the wisdom of his decision. It might be better to try to slip down to Texas and sift into the cattle country. One young puncher among the hundreds there would attract no attention. But Dave gave this no consideration. His fate was tied up with that of his brothers. He did not want it any other way. Moreover, he had to see Ellen. Of course he had ruined his chances with her, but he must find it out from her own lips. In spite of the fatal facts a queer unreasonable hope burned in his heart. She loved him. Maybe . . .

XIII

'You Kept Still to Save Him'

Ellen stared at the poster with eyes fascinated by the dreadful shock of it. She had felt sure of it, ever since the news had been sent out that the three dead bandits had been identified as Sam, Luke, and Steve Tolt. But it was one thing to dread privately, always with a faint hope she might be wrong; it was quite another to see her fear certified in black-faced type under a reward of four thousand dollars for his capture dead or alive.

There were descriptions of Caldwell and Cole, then one of Dave. The most intimate details were given. She wondered how anyone could possibly know his body so well.

> David Tolt, about nineteen years of age, weight one hundred and fifty-five. Wounded in left shoulder during the battle at Burke City. Dark-skinned, with straight black hair and black eyes. Large mole on right breast. Scar on left arm above wrist. Teeth very white and well-formed. Smile pleasant and attractive. Body smoothly muscled. Carries himself well. He is handsome, has a nice manner, and

would never be taken for an outlaw. Like his brothers, he is a desperate man and will probably fight before surrendering.

A quick step sounded on the wooden walk. Ellen looked up, to see Allan Macdonald approaching. Even in her misery she was glad to see him. Always, nowadays, the sight of Allan was like good news.

"Have you seen this?" she asked unhappily.

He read the poster. "No, I hadn't seen it," he said.

Her distressed gaze went to his. "I knew it. I knew it before I saw this, as soon as I heard about Steve and the others."

"Yes," he admitted with reluctance.

"Why did he do it—this dreadful thing?" she wailed. "And now they want him, dead or alive."

Allan could not explain Dave Tolt, not in words that would make clear the strain in him that brought to nothing all his good qualities. For that matter, Ellen understood the conflict in him just as Allan did, and yet was mystified at his actions. The common interpretation of the Tolts, that they were bad *hombres*, might be true of them. But why were they bad? Why was Dave bad—Dave who was so gay and in a way so loyal, so brave and friendly and kind?

"I don't know," Allan said. "There's something in Dave that drives him. Even when he was a little boy he did the wildest things. He would never take a dare. He had to climb higher than anyone else and ride the worst outlaw broncs. Then, of course, he's a black Tolt. He was always crazy about his brothers. He just went the way they went."

"Yes, I suppose so."

But that did not make his actions any clearer to Ellen. She could ask the same question about the other brothers, though in their case without the same poignant ache in her heart. She had danced with Steve often enough. Any girl would have liked him, with his fun and laughter and good looks, combined with so much reckless strength. Why had Steve gone bad? No, to say he was a black Tolt was just to beg the question.

"Where do you think Dave is now?" she asked.

"I don't know. On the dodge in the brush somewhere, I reckon."

"He's been wounded, it says. All of them have. How do they know?"

As to this Allan could give her information. He had just come from the sheriff's office and had read a copy of the Burke City *Herald*. In it was Doctor Watson's story of his week with the outlaws.

"So Dave went back and got Doctor Watson for his brothers—went back to that town where a hundred men were wild to kill him?" she echoed. "Isn't that like him?"

"Never were gamer men than the Tolts. Think of Steve, after he had reached the horses, already wounded, going back to help Luke because he was down. And Dave is just like him. I never heard of anything nervier than his return to Burke City, wounded the way he was."

The girl turned to Allan, biting her lower lip to keep back a sob welling in her throat. Presently she spoke, in a stress of emotion.

"Sometimes I don't see how I can stand it, Allan," she cried.

"I know. It's . . . tough."

"That's not all of it—what you think. It's part. There's no use pretending to you, Allan. I loved him. If he'd been different I would have married him. But that's just it. He wasn't different. He isn't the Dave Tolt I loved at all. He used to be, but he isn't any longer. I told him, the very night he left here to go on that dreadful raid with his brothers, how it was with me. I gave him his choice. If he expected to marry me, he must be good. I was awf'ly plain about it, because I had a queer feeling he was about to do something desperate. He said he'd be good as soon as he came back, and he wanted me to run away and marry him. You see? He doesn't think straight any more. Where is that boy I used to . . . love? Did I just dream him, Allan? Wasn't there ever a Dave Tolt like that?"

"Yes—and no." He smiled ruefully. "Men aren't

ever what their sweethearts think they are, do you reckon? Lucky for us, too. A fellow has to keep on his toes to keep from disappointing his girl too much. If I was in love with a girl, I wouldn't want her to know how mean I am. I'd want her to be fooled a little bit in me."

"A girl wouldn't have to fool herself about you, Allan. That's the difference between you and Dave." Ellen blushed, thinking perhaps she had said too much. Wherefore she rushed into explanations. "You shielded Dave in the train robbery. I didn't guess it at the time, but I'm sure of it now. But even then I knew you couldn't be guilty because you are you, Allan."

It was his turn to flush. He did it with an energy that increased his embarrassment.

"Sho! I don't expect—"

"Dave did rob the express car, didn't he, Allan?"

"How would I know?"

"I don't know how you knew, but you did. 'Fess up, Allan. I'm going to keep after you till you tell me."

"I can't tell you, since I don't know."

"You needn't try to shield Dave from me. I'm not going to marry him now—ever. I couldn't, not after what he's done." She broke down and cried a little. "It's horrid to say so now, when he's wounded—and being hunted—and folks talk as though he was a wild beast. But I can't help it.

I'd be so dreadfully unhappy married to him, knowing what he's done . . . and might do again."

After a moment of thought, he said quietly: "I'm glad to hear you say it. In spite of what he's done, I'm just as fond of Dave as I ever was. But I wouldn't want you to marry him. It would ruin your life."

"Yes," she agreed. Then, quickly, she added a rider to her statement. "I'm not ever going to marry. I'm going to stay at home with Father and Mother. So we don't have to say any more about that."

He did not say any more about it. They were walking along the sidewalk. His eyes shifted to the shining sage on the far horizon line.

"You haven't told me yet what I asked you," she went on. "About Dave robbing the express car."

"I don't know for sure."

"You do know," she charged. "You know perfectly well. And so do I know. You kept still to save him. It was because you were trying to keep him out of it you were arrested. That was why you had the trouble with Clem Howland. You found out what Dave had done—and you just took the blame."

"I didn't take any blame. I kept yelling out that I didn't do it."

"But you didn't tell what you knew, the thing that would have cleared you."

"Since you know so much about it already, no

use for me to say anything," he drawled, smiling at her.

"Why didn't Dave speak out and clear you?"

"You certainly take a lot for granted."

"It doesn't seem like him, to let you be blamed for what he did, and then to quarrel with you while you were shielding him," she went on, frowning in deep thought. "Why did he do that, unless—"

"I wasn't in any danger. They couldn't prove a thing on me," he protested.

"Unless," she continued, paying no attention to his comment, "he couldn't say a word without bringing his brothers into it."

"You've got it all settled, haven't you?"

"Yes. That must have been the way of it," she decided. "He told me once that you hadn't a thing to do with it, that he knew you hadn't. But when I pressed him to tell me why he was so sure, he changed the subject right off."

"That's all in the discard now," he said. "This new trouble he is in is so much worse that the express robbery doesn't matter. I wish I could help him. If he could get clear away, maybe he could make a new start. He's still only a boy."

"Yes," she agreed sadly, "only a boy, and such a dear boy, too, once."

She stopped. That lump had come into her throat again. She was thinking how utterly lost he was. An outlaw and a killer, a wounded wild animal hunted savagely because it was not safe to let him live. What hope was there for him now?

He had chosen his road. There could be no turning back for him at this late hour.

He must follow it to the end.

There is a cave in Terry County still known as Black Tolts' Hole. Into it, late one night, Dave crept warily. His horse, still saddled, was in the brush a hundred yards farther up the river. The boy moved noiselessly, a rifle in his two hands. For an hour he had watched the mouth of the cavern, to make sure that nobody came out or went in. For the place might be trapped by his hunters.

He stole forward, ready to blaze away if any warning sounded. None came. He shifted the Winchester to his left hand, felt for a match, and struck a light. This would make him a mark in case his enemies were lying in wait for him. But he had to take a chance. The end of his resources had been reached. Four times he had doubled back just in time to avoid a posse.

For two days he had not tasted food.

From the flickering flame of the match he lit a candle lying on a ledge. He raised the candle and surveyed the black interior of the cave.

Nobody was here but himself.

So far good. But that was only the first of his problems. Food had to be foraged somewhere. He dared not go home. It was certain that his mother's house would be watched. To show up in Melrose would be fatal.

As he moved the candle, to throw first one and then another part of the den into the light, a gunnysack caught and held his eye. Where had that sack come from? It had not been there last time he had been here. He shifted the candle to see better, then moved forward a step or two. A string, twisted around the neck of the sack, had been tied with a sailor's reef knot.

The heart of the boy gave a queer little turn. Allan had been here. He had brought the sack. What for? What was in it? Dave let his rifle rest against the wall. With fumbling fingers he unknotted the string. From the sack he drew out bacon, a cooked ham, coffee, a pan of cornbread, flour, meal, and salt.

There was no note, no message other than the reef knot. That was like Allan. Not a word wasted. No preaching, no reproaches. What was the use of talk, anyhow? Dave knew how he stood with Macdonald.

His former friend would follow a straight trail and have no alliance with outlaws, but the warmth of an old loyalty would still burn in him.

As Dave ate, his sight was blurred with tears. Nothing since that dreadful disaster at Burke City had so touched his emotion. Hunted like a wild beast, he had crept home with a cold lump frozen in his stomach. Every man's hand was raised against him. He was alone against a ruthless world, and into his utter loneliness had come this sign from the friend he had cast off.

For a time he could not swallow food. He had to set his teeth to keep from breaking down like a child. All the accumulated misery of the past days, dammed up by his stoic will, was ready to break through like a flood.

Presently he got control of himself again. No use acting like a baby, he told himself severely. He had dealt himself the hand, and he had to play it.

Voraciously he ate, with the sharp appetite of an outdoor man who has been denied food until his hunger had become acute.

Before he had finished, his eyes were nodding. So closely had he been pressed that he had not dared sleep, except for short snatches, during the homeward flight.

He reminded himself that he must go out and unsaddle, but he could hardly shake off slumber long enough to do this. He hobbled the horse and carried saddle and blanket into the cave. It was dangerous to leave a hobbled horse wandering through the brush, one branded with the J T, but if his hiding-place should be discovered, he would need a mount that could be reached. Whichever way he turned now there was peril.

He had to make a choice of evils.

It was, for instance, hazardous to sleep. He

might be found defenseless by his hunters. But sleep he must have. The instant he laid his head against the saddle his lids closed. When he awoke the tessellated sunlight was slanting into the brush-covered mouth of the cave.

He lay, luxuriously at ease. Then memory stabbed him with recollection of the late past. His brothers . . . his mother . . . the clutch of vengeance closing in on his future.

To ease the pressure on his cramped muscles, he turned—and leaped to his feet with one lithe movement, rifle in hand. A man was sitting, tailor fashion, not six feet from him. The man was Allan.

"I didn't know you were awake until you turned," Macdonald said.

"When did you come?" Dave asked.

"Half an hour ago. I thought you needed sleep, so I didn't wake you."

"Lucky for me it was you that came."

"Yes."

In silence each took stock of the other. So much had taken place since they had last met that neither knew quite how to begin.

"I'm much obliged for the grub," Dave said.

"'S all right. I figured you'd make for the cave if you got through."

"I haven't spoken to a soul except a Mexican sheepherder for five days. What's new?"

"They've got posters out describing you. How's your wound?"

"Healed up. Giving my name?"

"Yes. Cole and Caldwell's too."

"They haven't got Cole and Cald yet, then?"

"No. There are a lot of rumors. They've been seen in Texas and Kansas and the Nation, according to different reports. But when the officers run down the stories, the men they want ain't there."

"I reckon Doc Watson gave those descriptions of us. We knew that fellow wouldn't do us any good after we turned him loose. No complaints there, though. He's a square guy."

"The descriptions are very accurate, even to the scar on your arm you got when Maddern's bull hooked you."

"How did they get our names?"

"The bodies of your brothers were identified by a barber who had shaved two of them at Ridgeville."

"I expected someone would know them." Dave added after a moment: "Have you seen Mother?"

"Yes. She's worried 'most to death about you. She told me just where this cave is and got me to leave the sack of grub. Of course your ranch is being watched all the time. She couldn't have come herself without being followed."

Dave looked steadily at his friend. "You know what would happen to you if it's found out what you're doing?"

"I reckon," Allan answered quietly.

"You'd go to jail for about 'steen years as an accessory."

"No use going into that. Point is, what are you going to do? Have you got plans made?"

"No plans. I know what I'd like to do—slip out of the country to South America or even to Mexico; that is, after I know Cole and Cald are all right. But it'll be a miracle if I get the chance. I expect the chaparral is lousy with fellows looking for us."

"There's a reward of four thousand dollars for each of you, dead or alive. That will look like a lot of money to some fellows."

"Sure will." Dave drawled out a cynical suggestion. "Better collect me and that four thousand dollars, Allan. I'd as lief you had it as anybody, and someone is liable to get it."

Allan looked at him and said nothing. Dave had the grace to feel ashamed.

"Take it back, Allan," he said impulsively. "'Course I didn't mean it, but I hadn't ought to have said it. By jacks, you've been a better friend to me than I deserve. I won't ever forget it, long as I live, which may be all of a week if I'm lucky."

"You might make a getaway yet. I'd say to lie low for a while until the hunt has died down a bit, then ride south. How many people know of this cave?"

"Not many. Three-four besides the boys. Spence Kinney does, for one. So does Tim Hayes. I've got my horse Billy hobbled in the brush, in case I'm forced to light out sudden."

"Not so good, that. A J T horse wouldn't look so innocent if someone found it hobbled in the chaparral. I'll turn Billy loose and picket one of mine. If you need a bronc, you'll need him sudden. I've got another notion, too. What's the matter with me bringing my boat up the river and leaving it close to here? Then you'll have a choice. If you're cut off from your horse, you can drift down the river to our old island camp and lie doggo there."

"No, sir, I don't deserve a friend like you," Dave reiterated. "I always knew you'd do to ride the river with. But I'm so doggoned high-headed. When you called the turn on me after the express robbery, I had to get on the prod instead of listening to you."

"I wish to God you had listened, Dave," his friend burst out fervently.

Dave lifted his shoulders in a shrug. "I'm a black Tolt, Allan. Let it go at that. I go the way my family goes. I'm not kicking, only—I wish I could forget what I saw that five minutes at Burke when my brothers went down."

The fatalistic philosophy of the boy failed him before he finished the last sentence. It ended in what was almost a wall of despair.

Allan said nothing. There seemed to be nothing for him to say.

"I reckon it had to be," Dave went on. "It was that way with the James gang and the Dalton and the Doolins. We figured it would be different with us. We'd quit in time. This was to have been our last raid. Remember how that red-headed teacher, Miss Stratton, used to tell us about the pitcher that went to the well once too often? That was us Tolts. We went on one raid too many."

"You went on one too many when you went on the first," Allan said.

"I reckon. Anyhow, the Tolts are done for." Dave flung out an abrupt question. "Have you seen Ellen?"

"Yes."

"What does she say?"

The boy's burning black eyes had the haunted look which rarely left them now.

"She can't understand it, Dave. It has shocked her dreadfully. She wonders where that Dave Tolt is she used to like so much, the one who was so gay and happy and full of joshing."

"He's dead," young Tolt answered harshly. "She'll never see that Dave Tolt again, not in this world."

"You don't know that," Allan corrected in a matter-of-fact manner. "You've had a great blow, a terrible one. But you're young. You'll recover in time, if you're given a good break and give

206

yourself a good one. First thing is to get you away from here to some place where you can make a fresh start. If we're lucky, we're going to do just that."

There was resonant strength in Allan's quiet voice. Dave watched him, surprised at some new quality of leadership in his friend. He had always been first and Allan second. With a flash of intuition the knowledge came to him that they had made a mistake. Allan was the one who ought to have led. He was far and away the bigger man of the two, more loyal, more faithful, a better friend, a truer man. Dave had made fun of that quality of steadiness in him born of his sense of right and wrong. He had called him the deacon, old sober-sides, squaretoes, always with a feeling of superiority. Now he saw himself and Macdonald in the light of naked truth.

XIV

A Shot in the Dark

Dave did not venture out of the cave for three days, except for a few minutes between midnight and morning to draw fresh air into his lungs. Once, from the mouth of his retreat, he saw a posse on horseback riding the far bank of the river. Among them he recognized Jim Sutter, the new sheriff. The boy ducked back into the cavern. When he looked again the riders were out of sight.

Young Tolt had no resources of entertainment within himself. He depended upon action, excitement, the give-and-take of human fellowship for his pleasure. Allan could not visit him, for fear of drawing attention to his presence. After a few days Dave's loneliness overcame caution. He wanted to talk with someone, especially with his mother and with Ellen. He wanted news. It was out of the question for him to go to Mrs. Tolt or for her to come to him. But he persuaded himself he could go to Ellen with reasonable safety. It was now the dark of the moon. If he was very careful, probably nobody would see him but Ellen.

He rode the horse that Allan had left picketed for him in the brush. On the way to town he crossed a road several times, but he did not follow one a foot of the way until he was forced to do so by the barbed-wire fences close to Melrose.

Dave traveled at a road gait, his flapping wide hat set at such an angle that the brim dropped low over his face. Of late he had become a twogun man. A revolver rested on each hip. As the horse moved down the street the black eyes in the young man's brown face swept to right and left to pick up any suspicious object that might appear.

He heard voices. Two men were talking. Dave drew up and waited. Vaguely he could see their shadowy forms. Had they seen or heard him? Would it have been better to have ridden boldly past them? He could not tell. They would very likely have hailed him in friendly fashion. Or they might be officers, stationed there to keep a check on travelers.

He sat the saddle, muscles taut, ready for whatever might occur. Laughter drifted to him, and the scent of tobacco. They were taking their time, whoever they were. Presently he heard a casual "So long, Spence." One of the talkers moved down a walk, opened the door of a house, and went inside. The other came along the road toward Dave.

Tolt could have swung his horse around and galloped out of town. But that would have created an instant suspicion. Nobody knew he was in the neighborhood. Better do nothing to support the theory that he was.

His heel touched the pony's flank and put it to a lope. Dave flung up a hand in greeting as he cantered past the man in the road. A voice shouted, " 'Lo, Allan. What's yore hurry?" Tolt kept going. His mind was relieved. He had not been recognized.

The man was Spence Kinney, a mean little fellow with a reputation none too good. In passing, Dave had caught a glimpse of the beady, yellowish eyes in the pallid face. The man's countenance was one lit only by cunning and cupidity. Nobody trusted Spence. It worried Dave that he knew the whereabouts of the cave.

A couple of hundred yards farther down the road, Dave turned into the lane that led to the Owens house. In front of the yard there was a willow thicket. With a slip knot he fastened the bridle to a sapling.

There were lights in the kitchen and the sitting-room. Evidently the family had not gone to bed yet. Dave sat down to wait.

Watching that little house, which to him was nearer the ideal of a home than any other in the world, Dave Tolt's heart seemed to flow out of him on a cold river of despair. He had spent happy hours under that roof, gay and carefree ones in the innocent past. Mrs. Owens and her husband had filled the place with an atmosphere of love. They had welcomed the youths who had come to visit their children, though the mother had watched over the welfare of her young with a jealous eye. That was the kind of a home Dave had meant to have, with Ellen beside him as his wife. Then he had gone wrong, had tried to take a short cut to wealth. And all the air castles he had built had come crashing down about his head. He had lost Ellen. He had lost everything in the world worth having. His bullheaded perversity had made him that unhappy creature, a hunted outlaw with a price on his head.

Dave could not stay seated. He moved forward out of the darkness and found a saddled horse tied to the fence. He recognized the animal, a baldface sorrel belonging to Allan Macdonald.

So Allan was inside, calling on Ellen. The knowledge gave him a pang. That was as it should be, he admitted to himself. Her heart would turn to Allan. How could it help but do this? He was a fine upstanding man, strong and true. She would be happy with him. That was good. But in the passionate heart of the black Tolt there rose a fierce resentment against fate. It would have been he instead of Allan, if he had not let his life get so warped and twisted.

The sitting-room door opened and let out a fanshaped shaft of light in the center of which Ellen and Allan were framed. They stood there for a moment, smiling into each other's eyes.

"You won't forget," Dave heard the girl say.

"I won't forget," young Macdonald promised.

The door closed. Allan came down the walk to the gate. Dave moved forward from where he had been standing in the shadow of a lilac.

"You!" Allan cried. "What are you doing here?"

"I'm here for the same reason you are," Dave answered. "I'm here to see Ellen."

"Are you crazy?" Macdonald asked. "Don't you know that if you should be seen—?"

"I know," interrupted Dave. "You don't have to burn that in. It's been branded on me with a red-hot iron." The outlaw touched with a finger the shoulder that had been wounded.

"You can't see Ellen. If Mrs. Owens knew you were here—"

"She won't know. I told you I was going to see Ellen. I am."

"How? Are you going to open that door and walk in? Jinnie Harshaw is staying there tonight. Might as well put it in the paper that you're back here for a short visit."

"I've got to see her," Dave said stubbornly. "Once, anyhow, before I leave here."

"Maybe I can fix that for you. But not tonight— and not here. Are you sure nobody has seen you?"

"I met Mr. Spence Kinney a while ago. He hollered for me to stop and talk, but I hadn't time."

"That scalawag!" Allan said, aghast. "Did he know you?"

"He knew your horse, but he didn't know me.

He called me Allan. I was disguised as a respectable citizen," Dave answered bitterly.

"That's queer," Allan reflected aloud. "He saw me turn down this lane about an hour ago. I spoke to him. He asked me if I had any notion where you were. The little skunk was figuring on getting something out of me. I could 'most see his mind work. He'd like that four thousand dollars' reward. Tell me this. How did he think you were me when he had seen me on this baldface sorrel not ten minutes earlier? He'd know it wasn't the same horse."

"I reckon he didn't have time to think. He knew the bronc and let out a yell for me to stop."

"He's had plenty of time to think since. What d'you reckon he's been thinking? Boy, you better burn the road up back to the cave."

"I came to see Ellen," Dave reminded him.

"I told you I'd fix that. Tomorrow night, say. I'm going to the Dunns' with her to a taffy-pull. Be at the place where I picketed the horse the first night."

"You'll bring her?"

"I'll bring her if she'll come."

"Tell her I've got to see her. If she doesn't show up, I'll walk into the Dunns' and find her," Dave threatened doggedly.

"Don't argue that here. Fork Cricket and light out."

"That's good medicine too," Dave drawled.

"Not that I give a billy-be-damn. Best thing that could happen to me would be a bullet right spang through my heart."

"That's no way to talk," Allan reproved sharply.

"No?" Dave looked at his friend hardily, desolation in his eyes. "You used to claim I wouldn't look at facts. Well, I look at 'em now. You're sitting on the top of the world. That's all right. I don't blame you. That's where you deserve to be. Only, don't think I'm a fool. You're going to marry my girl. Good enough. I flung my chance away. I'm nothing but a hunted wolf. One of these days I'll step into the trap and be rubbed out. I'm not kicking. All I've got to say is I want to see Ellen first . . . once."

"You'll see her. She wants to see you too. What's the sense of talking about my marrying her? She never cared for anyone but you. She doesn't now. If she can't marry you, it isn't because she is to blame."

"I know who's to blame," Tolt said bitterly. "All right. Tomorrow night. On your way to the Dunns'. I'll be waiting for you."

Dave turned and walked toward the willows. Allan untied the bridle of his horse, dropped it over the animal's neck, and swung to the saddle.

A shot rang out. He saw Dave plunging through the willows, whirled the sorrel, and drove it straight into the thicket after his friend. Something scuttled past in the brush. Allan made a half-turn and followed. The young willows whipped his face as he plowed among them. He could hear his quarry just ahead. It cut off at an angle to avoid his rush. The sorrel turned as on a dollar, just as it was used to do after a steer hightailing to escape.

Allan loosened his feet in the stirrups and leaned far out from the saddle. At exactly the right moment he leaped. His weight crashed heavily upon the dodging figure and brought it to the ground. The bulldogger's fingers fastened upon the wrists of his captive. He did not want any more bullets flung in his direction.

The man struggled feebly, but in Allan's hands he could make no more resistance than a child. He began to whimper weak apologies.

"I didn't go for to shoot. It went off, accidental."

Somebody else pushed through the willows.

Dave spoke. "He shot at me. Who is it?"

Roughly Macdonald swung the man over on his back. He put his face close enough to see.

"Spence Kinney," he said.

The door of the Owens house had been flung open. The voice of Ellen's father called.

"Anything wrong, Allan?"

"No. My gun went off by accident. I'll join you in a minute," Allan shouted. He lowered his voice. "Hold Kinney here, Dave, till I come back. I've got to satisfy Mr. Owens."

"Don't worry. I'll hold him." Dave said it grimly.

Allan borrowed Kinney's gun. He did not

have one of his own. Presently, after crashing through the willows, he appeared at the garden gate. Owens and his sons Jim and Bob were gathered there. Hovering in the background were the women of the family and Virginia Harshaw.

"I'm just dumb," Allan apologized, showing the gun. "Don't know how I came to do it. Reckon I must have brushed against a willow and let the darned thing go off."

"Why do you carry a gun?" Owens asked severely. "No sense in it nowadays. And if you must carry one, don't you know better than to have a cartridge in the chamber your hammer's resting on?"

"I was plumb careless," Macdonald admitted humbly.

"Don't you ever wear a hogleg in my house again."

"No," Allan promised. "I never will. Fact is, I didn't this time. Left it in my saddlebag while I was in the house."

"And then you had to go get it out. Why? Kid stuff. Wanted to tote a gun and be a man. I'm surprised at you, Allan. Thought you had more sense."

"You'd think I would have," Allan agreed.

"I suppose he didn't know it was loaded," Mrs. Owens suggested sarcastically. She had always been afraid of weapons and she did not like the idea of an admirer of Ellen carrying one.

"Lucky you didn't hit yourself," Bob said.

"Or someone else," his mother added. "I hope this will be a lesson to you, Allan."

"It will," the offender told her. "I see now how dangerous it is. If a fellow doesn't carry a sixgun, it can't go off accidentally, can it?"

The feminine contingent had moved down the walk to the gate.

"Where's your horse, Allan?" asked Ellen.

"Bucked me off and bolted when the shot came. Baldy will stop up the lane a ways."

Ellen looked at him, almost skeptically. It was not like Allan to have an accident of this kind. Moreover, she happened to know that since the affair with Clem Howland he had not carried a weapon. There was something back of this that had not been explained, but she knew better than to expect Allan's wooden face to tell anything he did not want known.

"All's well that ends well," Virginia Harshaw reminded them gayly. "I vote we let Allan off this time."

"If he leaves his old gun at home after this," Mrs. Owens added.

"Which he will," Allan assured her. "Well, I'll sashay along and pick up Baldy. Good-night, again."

He tiptoed up the lane in his high-heeled boots. As soon as he was sure the Owens family were back in the house, he cut through the willows to the spot where he had left Dave on guard.

"I got away with my story," he explained to his friend. "Everybody happy here?"

"You done broke my collar-bone when you lit on me thataway," Kinney complained fretfully.

"Too bad it wasn't your head," Allan said cheerfully.

"I told you my gun went off accidental."

"We heard you," Dave said coldly. "What do you aim to do with this buzzard, Allan?"

The alarmed beads in the pallid face shifted from one to another rapidly. "You dassent do a thing to me, boys. Not a thing. I'm a citizen of this community, an' I got my rights. I explained how this thing happened."

The assurance of his personal safety did not seem quite to convince Kinney himself. Damp perspiration stood out on his forehead. His lips were colorless. He realized that the only way for Dave Tolt to ensure silence was to put him where he could not talk. His captors could not hold him a prisoner. The alternative was . . .

Kinney swallowed his Adam's apple. Before him there jumped a picture of seven dead men lying in a row at Burke City, another of three desperadoes flying into the hills for safety. He knew how hard and callous the black Tolts could be. He did not know that there were gulfs of infamy that separated this young outlaw from him. To make sure of his own life, Spence Kinney would have killed without hesitation. It did not occur to him that Dave Tolt would hesitate now.

"We've listened, Spence, and we don't believe you," Allan said. "Now lie some more. Tell us how you came to be here."

Kinney found some difficulty in making that clear. He insisted he was telling the truth, so help him God. He wouldn't lie to them, not about this. He had come, so at last they understood him to say, to make a deal with Owens, about—about a milk cow. As to what cow it was he was vague, but neither of the young men pressed the matter. It was no pleasure for them to listen to his lies.

"Where do we go from right damn now?" Dave inquired of Allan harshly. "We know what this bird would do if we turned him loose. I reckon you'd better grab Baldy and light out, Allan. You're not in this. I don't want you responsible for what happens to this guy whose gun goes off accidental."

"My God, no, Allan!" the little spy begged. "Don't do that? Don't leave me! Listen. Here's a proposition. I won't tell a soul—not a soul. I'll padlock my lips. S'help me, Dave. I swear it."

Allan's steady eyes searched the man. "You're such a liar, Spence, that we can't trust you any farther than I could throw a two-year-old by the tail. How do we know you won't run right to the sheriff and start him on a hot trail?"

"I'll swear not to, boys. Honest, I will. I never did get along with Sutter, anyhow. No, sirree. I'm a clam. Bet your boots. Not a word out of me. I'll keep what I know under my hat."

"Too bad you don't shoot straighter when your gun goes off accidental," Dave jeered bitterly. "You'd be four thousand dollars richer. Think of that. Now you'd have to share with Sutter—if I let you go."

"Honest, I'll do like I say," the man whined. "I always liked you, Dave. I always claimed the black Tolts—"

"Fellow, if you make me sick enough I'll certainly bump you off," Dave interrupted roughly. "Keep your mouth shut and let me and Allan fix this up. Get this to start with; Allan didn't know I was here any more than you. Like I said before, he's not in this. But I don't reckon I can pump lead into you without his say-so. Not now. If he hadn't butted in, I would have got you when you had a gun in your hand. But it's too late for that now. Once more, what'll I do with him, Allan?"

"I don't know. I'll promise you this, Dave. If he swears secrecy and we let him go, and after that betrays you, I'll wear him to a frazzle with a horsewhip every time I meet him. That will be something for him to think about."

In the end they let him go. There was nothing else to do. But neither of the young men was at all sure that the oaths he had sworn or the fear of personal vengeance Allan had poured into him would keep him from going straight to the officers. He would hope to tie Allan up as an accomplice—and even a share of four thousand dollars was a lot of money.

"I'll try to break through to Mexico, soon as I've talked with Ellen," Dave decided. "I wanted to stay and make sure about Cald and Cole, but I don't reckon I can now."

Allan agreed that he could not.

As soon as the buggy had left the lights of Melrose behind, Ellen plumped at Allan the question that had been in her mind all day.

"Now you can tell me who really did fire the gun last night."

"You're smart as a new whip," he said, smiling at her. "My story is—"

"Yes, I know what your story is. You needn't go into that again. I don't want a story, but the truth." Her interruption had been peremptory, but she gave him back his smile.

Promptly he capitulated and told her what had taken place. She listened, almost breathlessly, without comment until he had finished.

"That mean little Spence Kinney!" she exclaimed. "He'll not keep still, will he?"

" 'Fraid not. He's money mad. I told him I'd beat up on him if he talks. That may do some good."

"What it will do will be to make him go after you too," she cried. "Don't you see, Allan?

221

You've made yourself an accessory, or whatever they call it. You'll be arrested too."

"Maybe," he admitted. "But I don't see how I could help it."

She flashed a queer little look at him. "I don't see how you could—not you. Some men could."

"I reckon you mean something by that, but I don't know what," he grinned. "Now I'm going to tell you something interesting. Guess where we're going."

The girl's heart fluttered. "To a taffy-pull at the Dunns'," she said, and knew that was not the answer.

"We're going to stop somewhere on the way," he contributed.

"Where, Allan?" she whispered.

"Do you mean where? Or do you mean who?" he asked.

"I think I mean who. Is it—Dave?"

"Rang the bell first shot, ma'am."

"I'm so glad. I want to see him. I want to tell him he must get away from here. If he stays—"

She let her last sentence die out unfinished.

"I reckon he wants you to tell him more than that," Allan contributed.

"What can I tell him that will do any good? What is there left to tell him?"

"I don't know. But when you see him, you'll know what to say. He's been living in hell and he still is. If you can bring the poor boy some comfort—"

She looked at him, wide-eyed. "Do you mean—tell him—that—"

"I don't know what I mean. I'm just warning you that he's desperate. I'd like awfully to help him."

In a low voice, she spoke her thought. "I could help him, if I'd promise—"

"No!" he cut in imperatively. "Not that. You're not to sacrifice yourself. I won't have him saved at that cost."

"Maybe it wouldn't be such a sacrifice," she murmured.

"I won't take you there, if you're going to do anything wild and foolish."

"I'm not. I was just thinking that he's still our Dave. It doesn't matter what he's done, does it?"

"Yes. It matters a lot. He's finished with his life here. Maybe he's finished with it everywhere. That's the only reason I'm taking you to him, because he's got to get out of this country in twenty-four hours. You're saying good-bye to him."

"Yes, Allan. That's sensible, of course. And we've got to be sensible, haven't we?" There was bitterness in the little sob of laughter that welled out of her throat.

"You won't make me sorry that I'm bringing you?" he asked.

"No. I'll be good, I reckon."

"You told me you could never marry him now —after what he's done."

"Then I'd think you'd be satisfied, if that's what you want."

Allan was disturbed. He was young in the ways of women. He did not know that they think one thing now and the opposite tomorrow. He wished he had not promised Dave. And yet, what else could he have done? Anyhow, it was too late to turn back now, though he had a feeling that Ellen was in a mood dangerous to her happiness.

They left the main road and followed a wagon trail through the brush. It wound in and out, around clumps of mesquite, deep gullies, and hills, but always bore in the same general direction except for short detours.

"Isn't that the river?" Ellen asked after a long silence.

"Yes. We're nearly there."

Presently he stopped the team and gave the hoot of an owl. An answering hoot reached them.

Allan handed her the reins. "I'll be back here in fifteen minutes," he told her as he stepped down from the buggy.

He vanished into the black night, but before the sound of his movements in the brush had died down, someone else came out of the darkness toward her.

Ellen wound the reins around the whip and sat there trembling. A man stood beside the buggy.

She cried, "Dave," and a weakness ran through all her limbs. Somehow she found herself out of the buggy and in his arms, the heart of her melting from her body into his.

He could not speak. He could only hold her close to him in a passion of despairing joy. She was his. In spite of all he had done, of the barrier he had built between them as unscalable as the ice wall of a great glacier, she was the woman who loved him. That no happiness could be possible for her with him he knew. But he pushed from him the realization. This hour, of all those that would flow by in swift procession until his death, belonged to him.

It was strange, if either of them had thought of it, that the magnitude of his crimes, producing so dire peril had wiped out the differences between them. He was again the boy of whom she had been so fond, yet a more appealing one. For he was humble, repentant, and unhappy, and the mother instinct in her enveloped him with a sympathy very sweet and healing. For the first time she found in him a strain of unselfishness. He made no claims. He was so grateful for what she gave, that she forgave him for the sin he had done their love.

In her bosom there was an ache for the hunger in his sunken eyes, for the gaunt, wolfish look in his bony face. They talked, when words came at all, not of the wrong he had done, but of what he had suffered and of his plans for the future.

There were times she glimpsed another change in him, but just now she drew back from recognition of it. It was both moral and physical. There was a movement in the brush. His lips became instantly a steel trap. Into his eyes leaped the pouncing menace of a cornered wild beast. He listened, something almost tigerish in his poised crouch. It came to Ellen, when she thought of it later, that one cannot escape the consequences of his actions. They are branded on the soul with a red-hot iron.

The hoot of an owl sounded. Back from the brush strolled Allan.

"So soon!" Ellen cried.

"My watch says it's been three quarters of an hour," Macdonald said dryly.

Ellen was not ready to go. Dave was very reluctant to have her leave. But a more dominant will than theirs was in charge. With quiet insistence Allan hurried their farewells. Before the girl knew it she was in the buggy, her lover a vanishing shadow. She cried, softly, into her handkerchief.

Allan had not driven more than a hundred yards when he dragged the horses to a halt. A shot had sounded, not far from them. He handed the reins to Ellen. "Keep going till you reach the bridge. Wait for me in the brush near the road. If I don't come—"

The uncompleted sentence drifted back to her

over his shoulder. He was running back to the spot where they had left Dave.

The flash of a sixshooter, scarcely a dozen steps from him, stopped Allan in his tracks. He heard someone crashing through the brush. Dave, he guessed, and cut across to meet him, forgetful of the fact that in the darkness friend and foe would look alike to the hunted man.

The other runner turned, threw down on Allan, and fired, at a distance so close that only the black night saved the target. Allan could neither stop nor turn. He dare not wait to explain. Crouching low, he dived at the man's waist, striking him hard in the stomach with his shoulder. Even as they went down together, Allan knew he had made a mistake. The paunch into which he had flung one hundred and sixty pounds of bone and muscle was that of a man far past his youth.

The assaulted man let out a gasp as the breath was driven from his body. His stocky figure crashed heavily to the ground and momentarily relaxed. Allan's hard brown fist drove into a jutting chin. The fingers of the young man's other hand reached for a thick hairy wrist and twisted it savagely. From a slack grip a revolver slipped. Swiftly the youngster scooped it up and scrambled to his feet. In another moment he was lost in the shadowy chaparral. The man he had left on the baked earth, all the energy for the present jarred out of him, was the sheriff, Jim Sutter.

There was, of course, a posse. Allan could do nothing here. He ran, in the direction of the tethered horse.

Voices, low and guarded, brought him up short. The horse had been found. He swung away, at a right angle, to put distance between him and the hunters. Dodging in and out among the mesquite, he circled back toward the buggy.

A voice, low, hard, stopped him in his stride. "Stick 'em up!"

"Dave," he called, not loudly.

The point of the revolver fell toward the ground. "Allan—that you?"

"Yes. Let's keep going."

They ducked through the brush, not losing sight of each other. After they had gone a distance far enough, Dave stopped.

"I'd better work back and get the horse," he said.

"Too late. They've found it."

"Too bad. Leaves me afoot."

"We're close to the river. Why don't you try for the boat and pull up to our island? I'll draw 'em off and give you a chance."

"How?"

"Fix it so they'll follow me."

"And get you, maybe."

"No chance. Not in this brush. Slip over to the right. When you hear a shot, edge down to the boat. They'll all head this way."

"Where did you get that gun? You didn't have it a while ago."

"Jim Sutter lent it to me."

"Who?"

"The sheriff. I bumped into him and borrowed it."

"Was that when I heard a shot?"

"Yes. Thought he was you. He took a crack at me and I landed in his fat paunch. Before he could ask any questions, I helped myself to his Colts. Didn't want him to plug me in the back as I was leaving."

"Did he know you?"

"Don't think so. We're losing time, Dave. They'll be spreading out after you."

"That's right. That little devil Spence Kinney must have brought Sutter to the cave. If I reach the island, how about grub?"

"I'll get you some. *Vamos.*"

Dave disappeared. Allan gave him several minutes, then fired into the air. Results followed swiftly. Voices called, one to another. Over to the left a horse crashed through the brush. Once more Allan flung a bullet skyward. He wanted to be sure that Dave would have a clear field.

But it was time to be gone himself. He ran, fast as his high-heeled boots would let him, diving into the brush like a rabbit. It seemed to him that the chaparral was alive with men. He dropped into a gully and waited to listen. Someone was thrashing around, not far to his right. Another man appeared out of nowhere and stood close to the ravine, just above the bush that sheltered Allan. He was joined by a third member of the posse.

"That you, sheriff?" the newcomer asked.

Sutter swore, with annoyed gusto. "I got one crack at him and missed. He rammed me amidships and knocked me galleywest. The young devil got away with my gun."

"You ain't hunting him without a gun, are you?"

"Buck lent me one. He must be near here somewhere. Don't take any chances. If you're sure it's him, blaze away. He'll pack just as well dead as alive."

They moved along the edge of the gully and disappeared.

Allan waited a minute or two before he scrambled up from his hiding-place. The dragnet of the pursuit had swept past him. Better be gone before its return. The sooner he rejoined Ellen the better. By this time Dave was probably on the dark river heading for the island. He had been saved by an eyelash. If it had not been for his appointment to meet Ellen, the posse Spence had brought would have caught him in the cave.

Macdonald moved warily but swiftly across the plain. His mind was busy with the adventures of the night. He told himself he should be elated, but instead he was depressed. For he felt sure, as far as Ellen was concerned, he had done harm and not good. How could he forget the moment when he had returned to her and Dave and been stabbed by the rapt look in her eye? By the sight of her slim virginal figure in the young outlaw's arms, the lifted expression of dedication, as though she were a modern Joan of Arc? Apparently she had forgotten his sins, that he was a robber and a killer beyond the pale. She had remembered only that he was her lover being hunted for his life.

In Allan's regret there was sharp jealousy. She had turned to him in these last months. He had been the one friend upon whom she could depend. He had known, by the same sure instinct as his rival, that with Dave out of the way, her love might some day pour toward him. Now he had brought them together again, and when Dave had held out his bloodstained hands she had run to him with a cry of joy.

Well, what else could he have done? Loyalty was one of the deepest traits in his character. No matter how badly Dave had gone wrong, he had to stand by him now. Tolt had been determined to see Ellen. He had needed her so badly, even though it could be for so short a time. But what about Ellen? It had not been in Allan's thought to sacrifice her for the sake of Dave. That would be absurd. Worse than that, it would be criminal. She was, in young Macdonald's eyes, a fine, clean, brave, young soul to be protected from all things soiled and sordid. Dave had put himself out of the running.

But what if she did not think so? What if she had

some romantic idea of dedicating herself to his reformation? She was generous and impulsive. She was capable of throwing away her happiness for love. To be sure, she had told him she would never marry Dave. But when the boy looked at her, when his voice shook, when the hunger for her stared out of his haggard eyes, the heart of the girl had turned over and she had forgotten everything but his need and her love.

Allan was working steadily back toward the river. For some time he had heard nothing of the posse, though he watched alertly for any sign of them. They might possibly sweep around and come back over new territory, in which case they would be very likely to pick him up.

Something moved just ahead of him. He stopped. It might be a coyote or a jackrabbit. It might be a longhorn grazing in the brush. But he was not taking any unnecessary chances.

Whatever it was had turned and was heading in his direction. Not a wild habitant of the desert then, for the wind was from him to it and already the keen scent of a coyote or a rabbit would have sniffed danger. He cut off at a right angle, moving lightly and swiftly. His eyes searched the gloom behind him as he went.

When his gaze swung back to see where he was going, it was a fraction of a second too late. His reaching foot found no ground upon which to rest. His body plunged downward into space.

XV

Caldwell Lays Down the Law

Ellen waited near the bridge for Allan as he had directed. Dread flooded her whole being. That Spence Kinney had betrayed to the sheriff the hiding-place of Dave she did not doubt. Had they captured or killed her lover? And what of Allan who had rushed back unarmed into the battle zone?

She had heard more shots after the first, three of them, fired at long intervals. The sound of them stabbed her with fear. In her imagination she saw her two friends lying on the rough plain, face downward, life stricken out of them.

Her impulse was to fly to them. But Allan had told her to wait at the bridge. He and Dave might come back, one of them wounded, expecting her to be in the brush with the buggy. She must not fail them.

So she waited, hope dying out of her from the long delay.

And at last she heard voices, the sounds of jingling bits, of creaking saddle leather, of a shod hoof striking a stone. The murmur of speech took on the coherency of occasional words and phrases.

"—son of a gun slammed into me and—"

"—been daylight, why—"

"All of 'em there—all three."

And then one complete remark. "What became of Spence? D'you reckon the li'l' cuss figured we'd be waylaid? Did he take us there to be bushwhacked?"

She recognized the cool, almost scornful, drawl of the answering voice. It was that of Pete Evans, the former sheriff.

"Hell, no! What would be the sense in that? The Tolts ain't looking for us. We're looking for them. And you can bet all the *dinero* in your pants that all three of the Tolts weren't among those present tonight. If they had been, we'd have had casualties a-plenty. Me, personal, all I met up with was one bronc tied out in the brush."

"One of Macdonald's string," Sutter said significantly.

"And you're asking, sheriff, howcome that bronc there," Evans said by way of interpretation. "And you're answering by saying the Allan kid left it there for young Dave Tolt. Right. Go to the head of the class, Jim."

The horses clattered across the wooden bridge and the sound of the voices was blotted out. But Ellen had heard enough. There had been no ring of victory in the sullen words of the sheriff. Dave had slipped away from them and apparently Allan had not been seen at all.

The girl waited a little while and then drove out

from the brush. She did not cross the bridge, but turned back along the road she had traveled with Allan a little more than an hour since. Presently she took the wagon trail into the brush. In the darkness she lost it. There was a good deal of rough growth. She twisted this way and that in the shinnery, trying to get back to the trail. Once or twice she had to back the buggy out of mesquite through which she had been attempting to force a passage. With a sigh that was half a groan she dropped the reins on her lap and for the moment gave up. She was lost.

Ellen decided not to be alarmed. She must think quietly. The road must be on her right, unless she had made a complete circuit of a half-circle. Surely she had not been off the trail long enough for that. If she made a right angle turn now and then held to a straight line . . .

Something was moving. Her heart jumped. Two shadowy forms crossed a small open space. Men on horseback. In a moment they would be gone.

"Dave," she called at them, just as they were disappearing into the bushes.

There was an instant pregnant silence. Ellen did not need to be told what was taking place. The riders had stopped and were listening. Who were they—friend or foe? She could not tell. But even if they were stray members of the sheriff's posse, it would do no harm to Dave to ask help from them.

"I'm lost!" she cried, in a weak little voice.

Came out of the darkness a harsh demand, "Who are you?"

"I'm Ellen Owens."

"Alone?"

"Yes. If you'd please put me on the road again."

There were slight sounds of someone moving cautiously toward her. A shiver like the cold feet of mice ran up and down her spine.

Then, close to her, from the back of a mesquite, a threat lifted to the girl. "If you're lying—"

"I'm not. Please."

"What you doing here?" was asked roughly.

"I . . . lost my way."

A figure emerged. "Why were you calling Dave? Dave who?"

She gave a little sob of relief. "Cald Tolt!" she cried.

Caldwell stood beside the buggy. "Girl, what in tarnation are you doing here alone?"

"I came with Allan to see Dave."

"Dave! He got through, then. Where is he?"

"I don't know. He was in your cave, but that Spence Kinney led the sheriff there. Dave wasn't in the cave, not when they were looking for him. He'd been talking with me. I think he got away from what I heard Mr. Sutter say as the posse passed me."

"Passed you—where?"

"By the bridge. The posse was going back to

town. I was waiting for Allan, hidden in the brush."

Cole had joined his brother. "Where was Allan?" he asked.

"He went back to help Dave when the firing began," Ellen explained. "I was dreadfully afraid, for both of them. Allan didn't have a gun. There was a good deal of firing."

"What makes you so sure Dave got away?" Caldwell carried on.

"I'm sure they didn't have him with them. And Mr. Sutter acted kinda sullen, like he'd been disappointed. Some of the others did too. One of 'em said all three of you were there. Mr. Evans didn't believe that."

"Evans was with them, then?"

"Yes. I think they gave up the hunt because they were afraid of being ambushed in the darkness. One of the men said so."

"How is Dave? Has he had food?"

"He's all right, only . . . he's not happy. But he's had food enough. Allan had some waiting in the cave. Your mother told him where the cave is. She couldn't take food there herself. Her house is watched. So Allan took some. He thought you might hide there if you got back."

"He thought right," Cole answered. "But that little cuss Kinney has ruined that plan. I'd like to wring his neck. We can't go to the cave now, not after Sutter has raided it. There wouldn't be any grub there now, anyhow. But we could certainly do with some chuck."

Even in the darkness Ellen could see how gaunt and famished they looked.

"We took some food in the buggy to Dave tonight," she said. "Allan bought it today in town. Dave wouldn't have had time to take it to the cave before they discovered him. Maybe it's where we left him—if they didn't find it."

"Maybe so—and maybe they're waiting there to bushwhack us," Cole said roughly.

"I don't think so. That Spence Kinney wasn't with the posse on the way home. One of 'em said they'd lost him. But the others were all there, I think. 'Course I'm not sure."

"We've got to eat," Caldwell said definitively. "Can you lead us to the place where the grub was, Ellen?"

"If you'll take me to the wagon trail," she said.

"Good. We'll see you don't get into the ambush, in case Sutter has one set for us. We'll put you back on the road. Then you skedaddle for home. You don't want to get mixed up in this, girl. I don't see what Allan was thinking of bringing you here." Caldwell frowned his disapproval.

"I had to come. Dave was at our house last night—outside in the darkness. Allan had to promise him I would see him once before he left . . . It was while he was there Spence Kinney shot at him."

"Spence shot at him, did he?" Cole commented, a rasp in his voice.

"Yes. Allan rode him down and bulldogged him, Dave says. He promised—Spence did—not to tell he'd seen Dave."

"Didn't they know that yellow coyote would run straight to the sheriff?" Caldwell asked, with asperity.

"Yes. But there was nothing else they could do."

"Except bump him off," Cole said brutally.

"They couldn't do that," Caldwell commented quietly. He asked Ellen a question. "Of course you've got no notion where we can find Dave?"

"Allan had his boat tied up near the cave. He had a saddled horse there too. I don't know what Dave did. If he took the boat he was to go to the old hide-out of the boys on the island."

They did not follow the wagon trail, but kept to the brush.

Caldwell drove. It gave Ellen a queer feeling to be sitting beside this man wanted so badly by the law. He was the leader of a band of outlaws. He had come red-handed from the crimes of robbery and murder. Yet she felt entirely safe with him. It was part of his code, not only not to harm her, but to protect her as long as he could stand and fight. She was not afraid, much less so than when she had been lost in the brush. But her heart beat fast. She had the sense of having been snatched into the center of thrilling drama.

Cole led the way, threading in and out of the brush skillfully. His brother followed. Once Cole stopped to question Ellen as to just where she had met Dave.

Presently Caldwell pulled up and stepped down from the buggy.

"The road is only a few yards to the right. Wait here for us, unless you hear firing. If there's trouble, hit the road for home as fast as you can. Understand?" he asked.

"Yes," she told him.

She waited, every nerve in her slender body strung taut. To her it seemed they were gone for hours, but it was only a matter of minutes, not more than ten at the most, before they rejoined her. With them they carried a sack of food.

"We found it, right where Dave must have left it when he lit out," Caldwell said. "Now we'll take you as far as the bridge."

"You'd better eat first," she advised.

"We'll eat as we go," Cole replied. "Anyhow, we'll take the edge off our hunger. Did you ever pass two days and a half without a bite, Ellen?"

"No. You must be starved."

"I could eat a pair of leather boots," the outlaw told her with a hard laugh.

He cut a hunk of bread from a loaf, which he handed to his brother, then found a piece of salt pork to go with it.

After they had chosen what food they wanted

240

for their immediate needs, Cole tied the sack to the thongs back of his saddle-tree. Ellen noticed that another sack was tied to the saddle of the other horse.

A fugitive guess flitted through her mind that this held the thirty thousand dollars taken from the Drovers' and Cattlemen's Bank at Burke City.

Caldwell rejoined her in the buggy. The Tolts still stuck to the brush, Cole leading the way with a rifle across the saddle in front of him.

After a long silence, Ellen spoke in a small, timid voice. "I hope you can get across the line into Mexico."

"We expect to make it now we've found grub," the driver answered.

"Will you try to find Dave first?"

"You don't think we'd go without him, do you?" He turned, peering at her curiously through the darkness. "Looky here, girl. Get Dave out of your head. I don't know what that boy's been telling you tonight. But he's through, far as you're concerned. Get me? He's in this business up to his hocks. No way for him to get out and come clean. Too bad. I'd give my right arm to have him out of it. But it can't be done. He's gone the way of all the black Tolts. Forget him. He's got no right to be making any claims on a nice girl like you. After tonight you'll never see him again. Better you shouldn't too. You're far too good for him after what he's done."

He spoke roughly, to hide his feeling, she guessed. Following a moment of hesitation, she asked in a low, shy voice: "He's still the Dave Tolt I . . . used to like, isn't he?"

"Not far as you're concerned. He's got to lie in the bed we've made for him," Caldwell said bitterly. "Maybe it's not his fault. That doesn't matter. He's through with girls like you. Don't ever think anything different."

This was what Allan had told her, but much more gently. It was what Dave himself had said, when he could long enough forget the joy of holding her dear slim body in his arms.

Her own good sense had told her so, when she had faced the facts in sober solitude. Now Caldwell was repeating it with brusque, cruel kindness. The only dissenting voice was the cry of her rebellious heart. She could not give him up, not when he needed her so, not when all the world was hunting him down like a wolf.

Again, timidly, she gave words to a remonstrance. "Can't anyone reform? I've read in my Bible that the mercy of God is from everlasting to everlasting."

There was a strange tenderness in the dark look with which he scanned her. "Mercy is one thing, and love is another," he said.

"It would be a funny kind of mercy if I forgave him and wouldn't ever speak to him," she murmured.

His harshness was a mask for emotion. "Girl, he's going out of your life. If he gets away, by luck, he's got to hide like a fox, slip away from the country, change his name, make a new start. What kind of a man would he be to let you take up with him now? Dave wouldn't do it any more'n I would, not after he's thought it over. You're through with him, from right now."

She made no answer. There was nothing more to say. The warmth went out of her bosom. She felt cold and dead. The chill tears were still dripping from her heart, so she felt, when the Tolts left her at the bridge.

Neither Cole nor Caldwell had asked Ellen not to tell that she had seen them. She was a friend of Dave. It was not likely that she would mention to anybody but Allan their meeting in the brush. There was much of self-containment, they guessed, in her quiet shyness. She was not the kind of girl to babble all she knew. In any case, the Tolts had a scorn of whiners. They had brought trouble on themselves and they were not asking mercy of anybody. Whatever punishment fell upon them would have to be endured. They could set their strong teeth and bear it.

Just now Caldwell was troubled about Ellen rather than about their own plight.

"That li'l' girl has no right to be in this," he told his brother. "What's Dave thinking about?

Don't he know better than to drag her into our trouble?"

"I reckon Dave would pay high right now for a nice girl's kisses—if she happened to be Ellen Owens," Cole said dryly. "He's only a kid, Cald. Can't blame him much, can you?"

Caldwell had a wife and two children of his own. He did not blame Dave at all. His heart grew heavy whenever he thought of having let the boy be dragged into such a hopeless situation. But he could not let his young brother tie Ellen up to his life as though he had a straight open road ahead of him.

"She's one of the nicest kids in the country," he concluded. "We got to keep her out of this. I reckon I've got to have a powwow with Dave about it."

"Y'betcha!" Cole agreed. "Right now that boy's got to keep his mind off women. Too many unhappy women in the Tolt outfit already. Any more would be surplusage. Give the boy hell."

They rode back to the cave. There was a slit in a rock fault where they had been accustomed to leave one another messages. Dave might have slipped a note in there for them.

Cautiously they approached the place, leaving their horses in the brush a hundred yards away. Every bush they scanned, to make sure an enemy was not lurking behind it. Like cats, they had eyes that could see in the dark.

At the entrance to the cave, Caldwell laid a hand on the arm of his brother in warning. A faint gleam of light could be seen. Evidently it came from back of a bend in the cavern.

Perhaps Sutter had left a candle burning. Perhaps someone was inside.

The Tolts listened. A sound of scraping came to them.

Caldwell whispered in the ear of Cole. "I'm finding out about this. Stay here and watch nobody comes."

Noiselessly the older brother soft-footed forward. After what seemed like a long time, Cole heard his harsh, imperative voice.

"Stick 'em up, Spence!"

A yelp of startled dismay answered the summons. Cole followed his brother as far as the bend. Spence Kinney, tripe-visaged, stared at them in horrified fascination. In his hand was a pocket-knife. With it he had been digging the floor.

"Looking for a gold mine, maybe, Spence," suggested Caldwell in a derision behind which lurked a threat.

"I—I—I—why, boys, I—"

"Stuck around looking for the loot, eh?" Cole jeered. "If you want *dinero*, why don't you stick up a bank your own self?"

"Glad to—to see you, boys," the little man gasped. His face was colorless. The fear in his eyes, active as that in those of a squealing, trapped rabbit, darted first at one and then at the other.

"I'll bet you are," Cole said, with a grin not reassuring. "Just sitting around on your heels waiting to welcome us."

"I—figured maybe I could—kinda help you if you got back."

"So you brought Evans and Sutter and some more of the boys along as a welcome committee. Good of you, Spence. We got to make that up to you somehow, haven't we?"

"No, Cole. I wouldn't throw down on you thataway," Kinney whined, almost in a whisper. "You know I wouldn't, after I been such good friends with you-all."

"I hear you've been a good friend to Dave since he got back—took a shot at him last night, and after he turned you loose brought Sutter here to trap him." Cole's mouth was a thin, cruel line. In his eyes cold lights gleamed fiercely.

Tiny beads of fear stood out on Kinney's forehead. His fingers twitched. The pasty face was bloodless.

"It wasn't thataway, boys," he pleaded. "My gun went off accidental, like I told Dave. I didn't bring the sheriff. Soon as I heard he was comin', I straddled a horse an' split the wind to let Dave know, but I didn't get here in time."

"Liar!" Cole spat out explosively. "Fellow, draw your cutter and let's decide this here and now. Just you and me. Cald will stay out. We'll give you an even break."

Dark, grim, and handsome, Cole in his lithe stillness offered the threat of swift and violent death. Kinney shuddered at it. His knees sagged. He was ready to sink down and beg for mercy. Throat and mouth were parched. Words came from him in a whisper.

"No—no. Listen. I—I ain't a fighitng man. Cripes' sakes, Cole, don't—don't—"

"Why don't I cut down on him?" Cole demanded in disgust. "Do I have to let him live after so many game men died at Burke?"

"Hold your horses, Cole," his brother interposed. "I know a better way than that."

"Why won't he fight? Why don't he make a break to get away, with a gun in his hand?" Cole cried furiously.

"Claims he's not a fighting man," Caldwell said, with cold contempt. "All right. He doesn't have to fight. We'll put him where he'll have plenty of time to think over how good a friend he is of ours."

"What d'you mean?" Kinney asked.

Caldwell did not look at him. He spoke to Cole. "We'll fling him down Ranse Dunkley's Folly."

A decade before this, an old prospector had drifted across from Arizona. He was half-cracked from a sunstroke suffered years ago. He had decided there was gold on the plains. For two years he had labored on one hole, selected for heaven-knows-what reason, and at last had packed up and vanished from the place. Perhaps he had gone back to Tombstone. Perhaps he had drifted to a new field of operations. Behind him he had left only an empty prospect hole as a memento of his lost hopes.

"You can't do that, boys!" Kinney objected, moistening his lips with his tongue. "Why, nobody ever goes near there. I'd starve to death."

"Unless you are lucky," Caldwell said coolly. "Someone might drop around looking for strays. Anyhow, starving ain't so bad after the first couple of days. We've been trying it. Your insides kinda fold up and quit yelling for food when they find out it's no use."

The beady eyes in the yellow, wrinkled face darted from Caldwell to Cole and back again in wild and terror-filled appeal.

"You wouldn't let a dog starve to death!" he whimpered.

"Not a dog," Caldwell agreed. "Not even a wolf. Listen, fellow. You've eaten our bread and drawn our pay. You've gone up the trail with our outfit. When you got in the jam with that tinhorn at Dodge, who took the difficulty off your hands and made the fellow back down? Cole here. When you got sick, who nursed you till the fever went down? Dave Tolt. When you came squealing to us after Evans 'most caught you branding a

Cross-in-a-Box flitter-ear, who talked the sheriff out of it on account of your wife and three kids? Steve and Sam Tolt. Then, when we got our tails in a crack, you threw us down for the reward. You tried to kill Dave. You sold him out to Sutter. If we turned you loose, you'd run to him again. By jacks, you'll not get a chance. We'll throw you into Dunkley's prospect hole. You been looking for gold in the ground. Maybe you'll do better than he did and find some there."

"It would be murder," Kinney urged, swallowing a lump in his throat.

"How about shooting Dave, the kid who nursed you day and night? What do you call that?" Cole demanded savagely.

"Think of my family."

"Why should we think of them?" Caldwell asked contemptuously. "You never think of them. Your wife had to take the kids and go back to her folks because you wouldn't provide for them. It's up to you. If you don't like Dunkley's Folly, you can take up Cole's proposition. You're so handy with a gun, maybe you'd like to take a crack at some other Tolt than Dave. There's a reward on us, too. You can have your pick—either Cole or me. Only one of us. If you win you can run back to Sutter and claim the reward. The one that's left of us won't interfere. How about that?"

"No," the victim of their vengeance wailed. "I don't want to fight ary one of you boys. I never claimed I was a killer. I always been a peaceable citizen. And I'm your friend. Why, would it be reasonable, after all you did for me—"

"Don't call yourself our friend," Cole interrupted harshly. "We're particular who uses that word to us. Take your choice. Is it to be a gunplay? Or Dunkley's Folly? If you've got any sand in your craw, hop to your cutter and come a-fanning."

Kinney's fingers moved jerkily toward his thigh. Cole, still as a statue, watched him closely. There was no movement of Tolt's muscles, not a hairline shift of hand or body. He was giving his foe every chance for a better than even break.

His hands hung loosely beside him. Only the cold, hard light in the eyes and a certain catlike poise of the strong figure showed alertness.

The fingers of Kinney did not reach the butt of his pistol. The will of the man could not drive them to that desperate choice, even though Cole's weapon was still in its holster. The perspiration beads stood out on his clammy forehead. The muscles of the face twitched. The courage in him wilted, flowed out of his arteries and left him in a trembling chill.

He was physically incapable of carrying through.

"Thought it would be thataway," Cole sneered. "All right. We'll hit the trail for Dunkley's prospect hole."

They took Kinney's weapons from him and put him on his horse.

Through the chaparral the three men rode for about fifteen minutes.

They dismounted. The prisoner's knees buckled under him, so that he had to be supported as they moved forward in the darkness.

His teeth chattered. He tried to beg for mercy and could scarcely whisper words from his parched throat.

The open well loomed darkly before them. The Tolts propelled Kinney forward. He went down through the rotten casing, which had fallen across the shaft and jammed, with a crash of rending wood.

From the bottom there came a shout echoing up.

As they rode away, Cole made comment. "Funny. That didn't sound like Spence. 'Course it was. Must have been. Anyhow, he couldn't have been hurt bad in the fall."

The night swallowed the two Tolts.

XVI

Company for Each Other

Allan crashed down through brush and timbers into a pit of darkness. Jarred and bruised, the breath driven from his body, he lay for a time motionless. The orientation of his mind was gradual. First he made sure by careful groping of his hands that he was at the bottom of the precipice over which he had plunged and that there was no danger of a second fall.

The flare of a match showed him that he was in a well. From above there came a faint glimmer of light. The night was dark, but not as dark as the prison in which he found himself. He knew where he was. By some malignant chance he had flung himself into Ranse Dunkley's Folly.

No bones had been broken. He felt pretty sure of that, though he was sore and would later be a great deal sorer. His bruises were comparatively unimportant. What mattered was that he had been hurled into a prison from which escape might prove very difficult. More than once he had looked down into the prospect hole when he had passed this way hunting strays. The walls were sheer. Near the top they had been cased with timber. Below the casing was a stratum of rock.

Now, as far up as he could reach, he found the surface of the sides to be of clay. There had been a ladder once, but this had succumbed to rot. A bit of it still clung to the vertical shaft, but the rounds crumbled away in his fingers when he put any pressure upon them.

It might be days before anybody passed near the prospect hole, and, even if a rider chanced to be within hail, he might go on his way without suspecting that Dunkley's Folly had become a prison. Allan felt that his best hope lay in Ellen. When he did not meet her at the bridge, she would worry. Perhaps, after waiting a day or two, she might go to his mother for news. Search parties would be sent out to find him.

He wondered if Dave had reached the river and got away. If so, young Tolt would go to the island and wait for him. He would be unable to understand why Allan did not bring food to him. He would probably worry for fear his friend had been shot.

Mrs. Macdonald would be anxious, too, when he did not show up at home, though for a day or two she would persuade herself that he had driven out to the camp where a drover named Mulligan was assembling a herd for the trail. Allan was sorry he had mentioned going to the camp. The sooner she began to get alarmed, the better it would be for him.

Allan found he had four matches left. No use

wasting them now. He might need them a lot more later. The best thing to do would be to wait until day and then take a survey of his prison.

He rolled a cigarette and smoked it. There was no use getting excited about his situation. If a fellow couldn't get crumbs, he would have to eat crust. And since the matter of eating was up— well, that didn't do to think about.

Into the silence there came a crash of rotten timbers and falling débris. Allan's first thought was that the walls of the pit were caving in on him. He gave a cry of alarm and crouched close to one of the sides to avoid the avalanche. A queer fear jumped to his throat. For his foot was weighted down by something soft, something that let out a strange sound between a squeal and a groan.

An animal had fallen into the pit. That was his secondary reaction and he braced himself for possible attack. Then he became aware that the huddled mass was human. It had uttered a whining curse.

"Who is it?" Allan asked.

The object gave a scream of terror.

"It's all right," Allan reassured. "I fell in a while ago. Don't worry about that. Are you hurt?"

"Every bone in my body's broke," the new prisoner groaned. "Who are you, fellow?"

"Allan Macdonald. And you?"

There was no answer. Allan did not understand

why. He felt in his pocket for a match. The light of it flared up. He held it close to the face of . . . Spence Kinney.

"How did you come here?" Allan asked.

"They threw me in," whimpered Kinney. "I reckon they've killed me."

He did not sound to Allan like a dead man or even a seriously injured one. His voice resembled that of a weakling schoolboy complaining to the teacher that someone had abused him.

"Who threw you in?" Allan demanded, astonished.

"Cald and Cole Tolt. That's who. I'll get even with 'em too. You see if I don't."

"What for?"

"Wouldn't you, fellow, if they dragged you here and—"

"I mean, why did they throw you in?" Macdonald interrupted.

"Account of me shooting at Dave accidental. They claimed, too, I brought Sutter to their cave. Ouch! My leg an' shoulder hurt like sixty. Wouldn't wonder if I'd busted both of 'em."

Allan had not much sympathy for him. He was a traitorous cur. It was the business of Sheriff Sutter to capture the Tolts. Every decent citizen summoned by him to serve on a posse was justified in going out after the outlaws. They deserved to be caught and punished. But young Macdonald's gorge rose at the thought of this little spy leading the officers to the hiding-place of the men who had befriended him. The fellow was selling his friends for blood-money. On the frontier nobody but the scum of the earth betrayed those who had stood by in trouble even though they were wanted badly by the law. One had to be loyal under such circumstances. A miscreant could claim no sanctuary.

Not very graciously Allan offered aid. "Show me where you're hurt."

"I'm hurt all over."

"Where you think your bones are broken, then."

Allan felt the leg and shoulder, after the clothing had been removed from them. He was as gentle as possible, but Kinney yelped at his touch.

"I don't believe they're broken, either your leg or your shoulder," the young man said. "They don't feel that way to me. You're only bruised, I reckon."

"Not their fault if I'm not killed," Kinney growled. "Think of it: throwing a man down this hell-hole to get killed or to die of starvation. That's the Injun blood in the black Tolts coming out. That mother of theirs—"

"Leave Mrs. Tolt out of it," Allan cut in sharply. "She didn't throw you down here."

"Tha's all right. I was just aimin' to say—"

"You needn't say it."

"You're a friend of theirs, eh? Everybody knows

that. You an' Dave were runnin' round together before he'd been back here a day. Mighty funny, I'd call it."

"But my business and not yours," Allan suggested. "Don't forget I promised you a whipping every time we met if you threw down on Dave. I'd work you over right now if you weren't already black and blue. My advice would be for you to sing sort of small while we're here together. I might forget you're some stove-up."

"Don't you dass touch me, Allan Macdonald," Kinney warned. "I got something on you. I can send you to the pen for life just like that." He snapped his fingers triumphantly.

"If you ever get out of here," Allan corrected.

"What you mean by that? If you're threatening me—"

"Did you leave your address with friends before you headed for Dunkley's Folly?" asked Allan.

"They'll find me. Don't worry about that, fellow."

"I'm not. I wouldn't care if they never found you," the younger man returned callously. "But I'm some curious to know who you think will find you. Far as I know, there isn't a soul in the world will figure he's lost you. About a week from now someone in the Jerry Dunn Saloon will say, 'What's become of that no-'count Spence Kinney?' And someone else, hoisting one, will stop to say, 'Maybe we're lucky and a rattlesnake bit him.' That's about how it will be."

"Shows how much you know. Jim Sutter an' the other boys will miss me. They've done missed me already, point of fact. When I don't show up in town tomorrow, Jim will know something's wrong an' will start looking for me."

"Will he? Why would he do that? Say he kills or captures the Tolts. He'd have to divvy on the reward with you on account of you having sold your friends. I'll bet my boots he wouldn't walk across the street from his office to look you up. Good riddance is how he'll figure it when you don't show up."

They settled down to a long night of waiting, as far apart as the limits of their prison would permit. Allan took from his fellow prisoner the knife he found in his pocket.

"Just to make sure you don't get any notions while I'm asleep," young Macdonald told him. "I don't reckon you would be durn fool enough to knife me, but it's a whole lot better to be safe than never to get a chance to be sorry."

"You got no sense a-tall," Kinney snapped. "What for would I want to kill you?"

"Don't know. Can't read the mind of a rat like you. You've got a lot of first-class whalings coming to you from me. Maybe you'd like to fix my clock so the black-snakings wouldn't ever happen. You'd probably claim I was in cahoots with the Tolts and get away with it."

Allan slept, intermittently, very lightly. With the first gray light of pre-dawn he could hear a pair of coyotes yip-yip-yipping on a hillside.

Kinney woke up and began to complain. His aches hurt like blazes. He had not had a wink of sleep all night. And why didn't someone come and get them out of this hell-hole? He was hungry, and he wanted a drink of red-eye. Like as not, nobody ever would come and they would die like a pair of trapped weasels.

"Weasels is good, for one of us," Allan assented. "Listen, Spence. I've got to stay here with you whether I want to or not. But I don't have to hear you crying all day long. And I won't. Get that."

"You ain't my boss," Kinney protested. "I'll do like I darn please."

"Suit yourself. We'll both do as we please. If you annoy me by your yapping, I'll give you something to yelp for. There's room enough here to swing this belt of mine. A fellow needs exercise, anyhow, when he can't move around."

"That's a nice way to talk to a man about half your size and fifteen years older, already stove-up from falling in here. I'd think you'd be ashamed."

"I am," Allan admitted. "I hate being here with you. It would make me sick to touch you. Fellow, I've got as much use for you as I have for a skunk. Just the same, if you drive me to it, I'll wear you out. We'll get along better if we don't talk."

Kinney looked venomously at him, but conversation ceased.

It was the morning of the second day after Ellen had talked with Dave near the cave. She had heard the expedition of Sheriff Sutter to the cave discussed at table by her father and her brothers Bob and Jim. They had talked with two members of the posse. Both of them reported no casualties. Ellen could not understand why Allan had not been to see her with the story of the affray.

Perhaps he had joined Dave in his flight to the island. But he did not have to hole-up there. Why had he not come to put her mind at rest? It was very strange, since Allan was always kind and thoughtful. There was something wrong. She was sure of it. Dave had been hurt—or Allan.

Ellen could not think of anything else. At last she decided to find out what was the matter. She made an excuse to ride out to the Macdonald place, just as Allan had thought she might do.

The eyes in Mrs. Macdonald's brown, wrinkled face brightened at sight of her visitor. She and Ellen liked and understood each other.

"What's wrong wi' you, lass?" she asked, after one long look at Ellen.

Tears welled up in the big blue eyes of the girl. "It's about Allan—and Dave," she confessed. "I'm worried."

"What about them?" Mrs. Macdonald asked quickly.

Ellen told what she knew.

"So Allan's helping Dave," the mother commented. "I might have guessed that. The boy will be in a peck of trouble yet for that worthless Dave."

"He isn't worthless, Mrs. Macdonald."

The Scotchwoman looked keenly at her. "Is he no'? You can choose your own word for it, my lass. Allan went to jail for him, and he hadna the common decency to speak up and say he robbed the train himsel'."

"But Dave couldn't, not without bringing his brothers into it."

"And so he let the innocent suffer instead of the guilty," Allan's mother returned dryly. "He's a fine friend, that lad."

"He would do anything for Allan."

"I'm sure he would, if it was no trouble or cost to him." Mrs. Macdonald made up her mind to speak the plain truth as she saw it. "You're trying to fight against plain facts, Ellen, because you're fond of Dave. He's gone bad, with the rest of the black Tolts. They're a' a gang of murdering robbers. You've no business to be thinking about him or seeing him. He's made his choice, and he's done with a decent, upstanding girl like Ellen Owens. So there's no sense in your being romantic about him."

"Is Allan romantic about him, too?" Ellen asked, a tide of color beating into her cheeks.

She knew that what her friend said was true. She did not have to be told that in this whole affair he cut a sorry figure beside Allan. There were times when her heart repudiated the young outlaw, when she knew the love she had given him had gone out to one unworthy of it; and of late sometimes she had wondered if what was left of her feeling for him had not its basis in pity for his desperate plight. But she could not surrender it without a fight to justify it.

"Allan is a loyal young fool," the older woman answered composedly.

"Then I'm proud of him for being one," Ellen cried hotly.

"I'll no' say that I'm not. But that's neither here nor there. The point is, what's become of him? I haven't seen him for two days. I thought he had gone to Mulligan's camp. Can he be hiding with Dave? What would be the sense in that?"

"I don't know. I'm dreadfully worried. Mrs Macdonald, will you keep a secret if I tell it to you?"

"I'll keep it if it's one that ought to be kept."

"No. That won't do. There's life and death in it."

Ellen had an inspiration. "Will you keep it if it's one Allan would want you to keep?"

The mother thought swiftly. "Yes."

"And not tell anyone?"

"No." Mrs. Macdonald made a mental reservation. She would tell her husband if she thought best. That would not be betraying it to anybody outside.

"I think Dave may be on the island over there. Allan had his boat waiting under some brush near the cave so he could escape in it."

"Losh!" the Scotchwoman exclaimed.

"If he's there, he might be able to tell us about Allan."

"And that's true, too."

James Macdonald rode up to the house and swung down from the saddle. Through the window the women saw him.

"We must tell him," his wife said.

"Oh, no—no. You promised."

"He's a Hielandman, like Allan. He'll stand by his boy and his boy's friend. You can trust him."

Jean Macdonald did not wait for Ellen's consent. As soon as her husband came into the room, she began to tell the story. He listened, asked a few questions, and looked down at the floor in frowning thought.

"I'll pull over to the island and see if the lads are there," he announced.

"Take me with you," Ellen said quickly.

"What would I do that for?" Macdonald asked.

"If I were with you, Dave would know you didn't come to make him trouble," the girl explained.

"You mean he wouldn't shoot me down without asking questions," the ranchman said bluntly.

"He would know you weren't someone like that Spence Kinney snooping around to betray him."

"That's good sense, too," Macdonald agreed after a moment's reflection. "We'll go together."

In an old flat-bottomed boat they crossed to the island. Macdonald made the boat fast. The two walked up the slope to the dugout Allan and Dave had built when they were boys. Not a sign of habitation met their eyes. No smoke came from the chimney. No horses were in sight. Not till they had reached the dugout was this impression of solitude lifted.

Macdonald lifted the latch and opened the door. From the comparative darkness within, a voice drawled an invitation that might be interpreted as a command.

"Come right in and make yourselves at home."

There were three men in the cabin. One of them cried, "Ellen!" excitedly. Macdonald looked around, his eyes gradually getting accustomed to the subdued light. He saw the three Tolts for whom rewards were out.

"Looking for something in particular or just

making a friendly call?" Cole asked with derisive but steely irony.

"I'm looking for my son Allan," the ranchman said.

"He's not here," Caldwell said harshly. "What's the idea, Macdonald? Did you come to look for us? That's about as safe as walking into a grizzly's den without a Winchester."

The eyes of the Scotchman met those of the outlaw steadily. "I didn't know you were here. I thought Dave might be—and my boy. Where is he? Where is Allan?"

"Are we Allan's keepers?" Cole demanded. "We don't know where he is. If you thought Dave was here, why didn't you call 'Hello the house!' before you started in?"

"What do you mean about Allan, Mr. Macdonald?" Dave broke in.

"I mean that he hasn't been seen since the night he helped you escape at the cave. That is, if he did help you get away."

"Yes. Allan drew the posse away and I reached the boat. Do you think maybe—?"

Dave broke off. He didn't want to put his fear into words.

"I don't know. The men with Sutter claim nobody was shot on either side. That's another queer thing. They wouldn't find Spence Kinney. He hasn't showed up yet—or he hadn't when I left town two hours ago."

Cole and Caldwell looked at each other. Neither of them volunteered any information. Dave spoke, in a low voice, to his brothers.

"Let me tell Mr. Macdonald."

Caldwell lifted his broad shoulders in a shrug. "Go ahead, young un," he said indifferently. "It doesn't matter now. We'll have to get on the dodge again, anyhow."

"He tried to kill me," Dave told Macdonald. "He brought Sutter to the cave, after all we had done for him. The boys dropped him down Ranse Dunkley's prospect hole."

"Alive?" Macdonald asked.

"Squealing like a stuck shote," Cole said, with disgust. "The yellow coyote wouldn't fight. Sure he's plenty alive."

"What does it matter about him?" Ellen cried. "It's Allan we're worried about. Where is he? What's become of him? Don't you truly know, Dave?"

"I don't, Ellen—honest. Why would I lie, after all he's done for me? Could he have been hit and be lying out in the brush—wounded?"

"Or dead?" Macdonald put into words the devastating fear in his heart.

"Oh, no!" Ellen protested unhappily. "Not that."

"There was a lot of shooting. He might have been hit without any of the posse knowing it," the boy's father said. "I'll have to start a hunt for him."

He spoke quietly, with no apparent emotion. Inside, he was a mountain torrent of woe.

"Yes," Dave assented eagerly. "If he's hurt, he wouldn't be more than a mile or two from the cave. We can search with you."

"No," Macdonald refused brusquely. "You've done the boy enough harm already. I'll get my honest neighbors to help me."

"That would be better," Cole agreed, in a voice even and critical. "And what about us, Mr. Macdonald?"

"I care nothing about you."

"Maybe not. But we do. Do you aim to put Sutter on our trail? Because if that's your notion—"

"You'd put Ellen and me down Dunkley's Folly, too, I reckon." Macdonald stood straight and four-square, his rugged face like granite.

"What's the use of talking that way?" Dave interrupted impatiently. "You know better."

"We'd like intentions declared, Macdonald," Cole insisted coldly in almost a murmur.

"Very well." The blue eyes of Macdonald fastened upon him. "I'll have no truck with outlaws. The country would be well rid of the whole pack of you. But I'm Allan's father. He's got himself into trouble helping you—if he's still alive. I'm with him to the finish. Get along with you out of here and scurry into the brush. I'll say nothing of having seen you, not unless I'm asked."

"Sounds reasonable," Caldwell agreed. "We don't want Allan dragged into this, just because he helped Dave. It would be better for him if we can get out of the country."

"I hope you find Allan all right," Dave cried impulsively. "I wish I could help look for him."

Macdonald looked grimly at him. "You've made your bed, my lad, and you'll have to sleep in it. If my boy is lying dead in the brush, I'd rather have him there than where you are this day."

"And you'd be right, too, Mr. Macdonald," Dave answered, choking on a lump in his throat.

He was thinking of Allan, not of himself. Had he brought to death by his criminal folly the one friend who had stood by him in spite of everything? Not that. Surely not that. The thought of it was too terrible to face.

Ellen and Allan's father walked back to the boat and crossed the river to the ranch. The handkerchief of the girl was wadded to a tight wet ball clutched fast in her hand. Her heart was crying, "Allan—Allan—Allan!"

Jean Macdonald came running down to the river to meet them. "Any news, James?" she called to her husband.

His arm went around her shoulders in a quick, strong pressure of comfort. "None, lass. They haven't seen Allan since he and Dave separated the night before last. I'm starting the search for him."

"But where? Where will you look? Do you think it just possible he went out to Mulligan's camp?"

"Not likely, but I'll send a man out there. We'll search first near where he was last seen. You'd better pack what food you've got cooked. We may need it."

"What's the use of searching the place where he was last seen?" Jean asked. "He wouldn't stay there, would he?"

James Macdonald did not look at her as he answered. "I don't know. Maybe we can pick up his trail there."

Macdonald roped and saddled a fresh horse. As he did so, Ellen described to him as closely as she could the location of the spot where she had last seen Allan.

"You'd better get to town and let Sutter know Kinney is in the Dunkley prospect hole," he told the girl. "You needn't mention the Tolts put him there. The sheriff will find it out soon enough from him, anyhow. By that time the Tolts will be on the dodge somewhere in the brush."

As Macdonald rode swiftly across the country to summon his neighbors, Ellen turned her horse's head down the river toward town. Anxious and fearful thoughts flashed through her mind while she traveled. They had to do with Allan, not Dave, at least primarily. She knew now, with a certainty not to be shaken, whom she loved.

XVII

Dave Sends a Message

Out of the brush beside the river Dave stepped. He was barefoot. His only clothes were trousers and a hickory shirt. Water dripped from his lank black hair.

Ellen pulled up her horse and stared at him. "You swam the river!" she said.

"Yes. I had to see you. Just once more."

"You oughtn't to have come. Someone may have seen you in the river or might see you here."

"It doesn't matter." He brushed that aside as of no importance. "I had to tell you. I've fought against it, but—no use. Allan's father is right. I've made my bed and I've got to lie in it. I reckon I've always been selfish as the devil. When you told me where I was heading and asked me to quit, I was too bullheaded to listen. Well, it's too late now . . . I got to give you up, Ellen."

"Yes," she agreed in a low voice.

"I was crazy to think anything else, after what has happened. You were crazy not to tell me so."

And again she said "Yes." All her pity welled out to him. He was still a boy, and he had become enmeshed in such a net of hopeless circumstance.

But she could not tell him less than the truth now that she was sure.

"You're the sweetest girl I ever knew. There's nobody like you. Howcome I got to be such a bad *hombre*? I wasn't like this a year ago. Or even six months. I always wanted you. Why couldn't I act right?"

She had no answer for that. It would do no good to tell him that he had wanted to follow his own willful way more.

"I got started kind of in fun," he continued. "To get a joke on my brothers. Now I've gone bad. Three of us black Tolts are dead and I reckon the rest of us soon will be. It's . . . tough on Mother. That's what I came to see you about, Ellen. She's not to blame, but folks will stay away from her. Like she had the plague. Will you be good to her? She always liked you, Ellen. I got no right to ask it, but—"

"I'll do my very best, Dave," she promised, and big blobs of tears rolled down from her eyes to the soft cheeks. "Right away I'll go see her. Tomorrow."

"That's good. I knew you would. We're going to see her tonight, before we make our break to get away. But if anything happens, if we don't get through to her, will you tell her that I—I—"

He could not finish. She said it for him, very gently. "I'll tell her, what she knows already, that you always loved her no matter what you did."

"Yes," he gulped. "That's it."

"It's queer, isn't it, Dave?" she went on, her soft voice tremulous. "I mean . . . what life does to us. Just a little while ago—less than a year, as you say—we were so happy and so gay, you and I. I've thought about it, a lot. I wonder if there isn't something outside ourselves . . . something terrible . . . that takes and twists our lives."

"I couldn't seem to help it," the boy pleaded. "I knew it was wrong. What I really wanted was to go straight . . . and to look after you. But I couldn't seem to do it. Something drove me on. I reckon it was the devil in me."

"Yes. What I mean, Dave, is that maybe you couldn't help it. Maybe we're not free to do what we want to do. I don't know how to say it. Parson Brownlow might call it original sin, whatever that is. The Bible says we're punished to the third and fourth generation. I've been thinking maybe you're being punished for what your great-grandfather did in England 'way back a hundred years ago. Only, it's not only one ancestor. Maybe all our forebears help to make us what we are. It's all mixed up in my mind. But—even though it's all been so wrong—I don't blame you so much, Dave."

"I'll remember that in all the hell I've got to go through," he said gratefully. "Will you remember one thing too, Ellen? You've been the best thing in my life." After a moment, he added, with a rueful, bitter laugh: "I always put myself first. If I'd thought about it, I would likely have felt it was nice for Allan I picked him as my friend. I've had my eyes opened. He was the strong one in our friendship. He's got me beat every way from the ace. I'm weak and shifting as water. He's like a rock. Never was anyone more faithful and true than Allan. And me—I haven't got sense enough to know what to be true to. If he's been killed through me—"

They looked at each other in a mutual unhappiness.

"I don't believe he has," the girl said at last.

"Nor I, somehow. But—where is he? Allan wouldn't ride away and let you and his mother suffer. He's not like me."

"No," she agreed. Then, gently, "You'd better go now, Dave, before anyone comes," she said.

His eyes devoured hungrily her blonde loveliness. He did not so much as touch her hand. He did not say good-bye. Without a word he plunged into the thicket. A moment later she heard him wading into the river.

Ellen rode into town, her mind a welter of emotions. Snatches of her thought touched various people—the outlaws on the island, James and Jean Macdonald, Jessie Tolt, Dave, and most of all Allan. She could not believe that he was dead. That could not be, not without her ever once having uncovered to him the secret of

273

her heart. Fate could not be so unkind as that.

She wondered if she ought to despise herself. Was she fickle? Did a nice girl shift her love with the breeze? Did she let one man kiss her passionately, to find out two days later that she was in love with another? Not according to the code by which Ellen had been trained. A good girl waited till a man told her that he loved her, then gave her affection to him reluctantly and coyly. She did not invite him to storm the citadel of her heart and then discover afterward that he was the wrong man. Was there something . . . wanton . . . about her? She had been thinking of herself as well as Dave when she had suggested that we are not free to be what we want. By choice, if she could have had her way, she would have stilled the wild insurgent impulses that swept so stormily through her. Her desire was to be good and tepid and proper. She flogged herself because she had such an eager zest for life.

Jim Sutter was in his office with his predecessor, Pete Evans. He was in his shirt-sleeves, tilted back in a chair, dusty boots on the desk. When Ellen entered the room, he brought his feet down to the floor and got into his coat. Sutter was not a ladies' man, but this was a country where everybody showed respect to women.

Without any introduction the girl plumped out her news about Spence Kinney.

"In Ranse Dunkley's prospect hole!" the sheriff repeated. "How do you know?"

"It doesn't matter how, does it? I know. He's been there two days, without food or water."

"Two days! Then he fell in the night he took us to the Tolts' cave. That's why he didn't show up to come home with us."

"Yes," Ellen confirmed.

Evans spoke for the first time. "How long have you known this, Miss Ellen?"

"I just found it out. I came straight here."

"Where did you find it out?" Sutter asked.

"Please don't waste time about that now," Ellen urged. "Won't you send someone out to get him, with some food and a canteen of water?"

"I'm not saying I will, and I'm not saying I won't. What's the idea of this secrecy, Miss Ellen? I'm entitled to all the information you've got. I don't allow to go out to Dunkley's Folly and find you've been joshing me."

"I'm not! I'm not!" she assured the sheriff earnestly. "It's true. He's there. I've positive information."

"I'll be the judge of how positive it is when you tell me where you got it."

Ellen turned to Evans. "Won't you believe me, Mr. Evans? He's down in that hole starving to death."

The ex-sheriff studied her, with watchful,

puzzled eyes. He was convinced she was telling the truth. Why was she holding back the source of her knowledge?

Before he answered, Ellen broke out hurriedly. "If you're not going to help him, I'll get my father and my brothers."

"We're going," Evans said quietly. "But I reckon Jim will want a talk with you afterward, young lady."

Sutter stepped to the door to call a deputy to make arrangements for the trip. This did not look good to him. Already he had decided to take an armed posse.

While he was away, Ellen asked a question that was very much on her mind. "Are you sure, Mr. Evans, that nobody was hurt the night you went to the Tolts' cave?"

Evans's narrowed eyes did not lift from her flushed face. "Hurt! Well, Jim 'most had a couple of ribs caved in when that young hellion Dave Tolt plowed into him."

"Yes, I know, but I mean—really hurt."

"Well, you seem to have later information than we have, Miss Ellen. Spence may be stove-up considerable for all I know. I wouldn't guarantee to fall down Dunkley's Folly without busting a leg or maybe two."

"I wasn't thinking of Mr. Kinney. What I meant was— Did anybody get shot by the posse?"

"Who might you be meaning by anybody, Miss

Ellen?" he drawled, his gaze steadily on the anxious eyes beseeching him.

"I mean—anybody."

"Dave Tolt, for instance?"

"If you like. But you'll tell me, won't you?"

"If he was hit, we none of us know it," the former sheriff said slowly. "Maybe you have information on that, too?"

"No. Could someone have been shot without anybody else knowing it?"

"I reckon so. It was dark. There was considerable shooting. What's on your mind, Miss Ellen? Come clean. It will be better for you if you do."

"Nothing. I've got nothing to tell. I just wondered. I've got to go now."

Ellen turned and walked quickly out of the office.

Evans watched her go. He stood, without moving, trying to piece together what she had told and what she had not told. She knew a good deal she had not divulged, and she was afraid of something else she did not know but guessed. Evans wondered what it was she knew and what she feared.

Allan wondered how long it took to starve to death when one had plenty of water. There was enough seepage through the walls of the shaft to eliminate thirst as a problem. Just now he was ravenously hungry. Somewhere he had read that after a few days of starvation the acute desire for food passes away. He wished he had read that newspaper article more carefully. Anyhow, before he got through with this—if the luck broke his way and he got out—he was likely to know a lot more about fasting than the fellow who had written about it.

"Fellow, ain't you going to do anything about this? Are you 'lowing to let us starve to death?" Kinney wanted to know for the fiftieth time.

Macdonald did not answer. What was the use? Kinney understood the situation as well as he did. The man had seen him dig arm and foot holds in the clay and had watched him try a dozen times to climb by means of these the precipitous wall. They had shouted at intervals. They had fired shots to attract attention until not a bullet remained. Now there was nothing to do but wait for release by rescue or death.

"Why don't you keep a-hollerin'?" Kinney complained. "Someone might pass right by an' never know we were here. My voice has done played out. We got to get outa here or . . ."

The little man broke down and wept. It was not the first time.

"I can't holler all day long," Allan protested. "What's the use of crying? We got to stand the gaff. Betcha some fellow comes along and finds us. Buck up and grin for a change."

From far above came a shout. " 'Lo! You down there, Spence?"

Kinney gave a little gasp of joy. He tried to call back an answer, but his voice had become almost a whisper.

"We're down here—two of us," Allan replied. "Spence Kinney and Allan Macdonald."

"Hurt—either of you?"

"No. That you, sheriff?"

"Yes. We'll lower a rope."

Watching the rope descend, Allan did not notice that Kinney slipped between his shirt and trousers the revolver taken from Sutter. Spence could not have explained why he did it, except that he knew the weapon belonged to the sheriff. He had recognized the ornamentation on the butt. There was something here he did not understand. So he followed his instinct of sly secrecy.

Kinney grabbed at the rope loop greedily. "Me first," he demanded.

"Sure," Allan agreed. Already he had decided on that.

The loop was fastened around the waist of Kinney. It began to move jerkily toward the surface. After a time the man disappeared and presently the rope came down a second time.

Allan slipped the loop under his armpits and called "Ready." Two or three minutes later, Allan was pulled out of the mouth of the pit by several reaching hands.

Food was waiting for him. He ate, not exactly sparingly, but with a certain discretion. He knew that a starving man cannot eat all he wants without incurring penalties.

After the first two or three remarks, Sutter pounced on Allan with a question. "What you doing with my gun?"

Allan looked at him with cool, hard eyes. "I haven't got your gun, Sutter."

"You had it. Spence brought it up with him. Did Dave Tolt give it to you?"

"Dave Tolt? Why, no. Is Tolt around this neck of the woods?"

"You know he is, Macdonald. You were with him and helped him to get away the night Spence tried to arrest him. Where did you get my gun?"

"I thought I mentioned that I haven't got your gun. If Spence has it, like you claim, why don't you ask him about it? What's in your craw, anyhow, sheriff? Did someone steal your gun?"

Evans spoke, apparently discarding the subject of the gun. "How did you get in this prospect hole, Allan?" he said casually.

"I fell in."

"When?"

Allan knew the ex-sheriff was pinning him down to the exact time. There was no chance to dodge the hour. He had been seen in Melrose that same evening. He was there when Kinney had been flung in by the Tolts. They knew already within half an hour the moment of his plunge into it. Allan mentioned eight o'clock, Tuesday evening.

"Howcome you to be here?" Evans asked, still speaking in the manner of one who was seeking information of only passing interest.

"You'd be surprised, Mr. Evans," Allan said coolly, helping himself to a ham sandwich. "I lost my way."

"Why, no, that doesn't surprise me," Evans returned easily. "You were probably in a hurry and weren't watching where you were going."

"Dumb of me," Allan admitted.

"I don' know," Evans excused. "If a fellow was on the dodge, ducking this way and that, he might easily lose his way for the time being, and if his luck was bad fall in here."

"I don't reckon I quite get your drift," Allan countered, looking puzzled. "But it doesn't matter, anyhow. Point is, I fell in and now I'm out again."

"That's not quite the point," Evans corrected. "The point is, Sutter, that Macdonald here took your gun from you and not Dave Tolt, if I'm a good guesser."

"What!" snapped the sheriff.

"He was out here with Dave when we jumped the kid. Maybe I'll have to revise my opinion about Cald and Cole. Looks like they were here, too, by Spence's story. It was Allan knocked you over and grabbed your gun. He still had it when he went down into this hole."

"Cald and Cole hadn't met up with Dave yet

when they threw me in here," Spence volunteered. "Anyways, they claimed they hadn't, but they knew all about me trying to arrest Dave the night before and me bringing the posse to catch Dave. How did they know that?" he whispered in excite-ment. "If they hadn't seen Dave, another member of the gang must of told 'em. Who? Why, Allan Macdonald. That's who."

"Sounds reasonable," Sutter agreed.

"I haven't seen either Cald or Cole since the bank holdups," Allan said.

"You'll get a chance to prove that, young fellow," the sheriff snorted. "At your trial."

"I'm going to be tried, am I? What for?"

"For aiding and abetting outlaws. For being in with the Tolts on the bank robberies—and maybe the holdup of the Flyer, too."

"You'd better come clean with what you know, Allan," the ex-sheriff advised. "You're not in this as deep as the Tolts, but you're in deep enough. If you tell everything, you may get off. We'll try to fix it so you do."

"That's right, Allan. You maybe weren't in the actual robberies at Burke City. I expect we can use you as a witness and get you off," Sutter added.

"Got it all fixed, haven't you?" Allan said hardily. "Fine. Well, listen. I'm not in with the Tolts. I had nothing to do with this last robbery or any other. I've got nothing to confess. You can save quite some time by taking that as it stands."

"We're your friends, Allan—"

"That's good, sheriff. Looks like I'm going to need friends by your way of it. I'll mention that my friends know I'm not an outlaw—and anybody who doesn't know it is not my friend."

"Don't pull your picket-pin, boy," Evans advised. "Talk with your father and see what he advises."

"Good medicine. I'll do that, and I'll bet my best spurs he won't tell me to confess something I didn't do."

Sutter pounded a closed fist down in an open hand. "Don't get biggity, boy. You're in one hell of a hole and don't you go to forgetting it for a minute. I'm going to send you to Burke City to see if anyone there can identify you as one of the bandits. Evans says you ain't as deep in this as the Tolts. Well, you're gonna have a chance to prove it. Nobody can tell me you're covering up just for them. You're playin' your cards close to your belly because you're in this too."

Allan was startled. He had not expected to be charged with direct complicity in the crime.

"I can prove I was here twenty hours before the bank holdup," he said.

"Who by?"

"By my father. I was out at our Three Willows dugout riding the line."

"You dad don't go as a witness with me. Who else?"

283

"Nobody else that day. The day before, in the morning, I bumped into Jack Sampson."

"No good. You could have made it to Burke City by hard riding. Anybody see you the day after the robbery—or the day after that?"

"Yes. On the second day after the Burke City business, I was riding close to the Tolt place and dropped in there for dinner."

"Two days after the holdup is no alibi. But who did you see at the Tolts?"

"Only Mrs. Tolt."

"She don't count either," Sutter said promptly.

"You seem to be unlucky in your witnesses, Allan," Evans said dryly. "Kinda interested parties, both of 'em."

"I always did claim he was one of the stick-up birds at Burke City," Spence Kinney said maliciously. "If he could have got away with it, he would have bumped me off down in that hole. 'Count of what I know. He threatened me plenty."

Scornfully Allan looked at the man who had been a prisoner with him. "You're a liar, and the truth isn't in you," he charged.

Sutter asserted himself. "Suit yourself, fellow. I reckon you got a mighty good reason for padlocking your tongue. If you feel thataway, you can take a trip with me to Burke City. Quite a lot of citizens there claim they would know the birds in the holdups."

"Fellow, you're going to hang," Kinney's hoarse voice whispered vindictively.

Evans did not contradict this opinion. He did not for a moment believe that Allan was actually in the bank holdups, but he was sure he knew more than he was telling. If the fear of God was flung into him, he might be frightened into talking. Of that the ex-sheriff had his doubts. The Maconalds were both game and dour.

His opinion was that they were going to get precious little information out of this lad.

"If you've had enough to eat, we'll be moving," Sutter announced.

On the way back to Melrose, Allan rode between the sheriff and Evans.

The latter put an abrupt question to him that disturbed Macdonald.

"What do you boys—Dave Tolt and you—mean by dragging a young lady's name into this business?"

"I don't get you," Allan parried.

"You do, too. Dave and you were at her house when Kinney pulled off his fool gunplay. Next night you started with her to the Dunns' for a taffy-pull. You never got there. Instead, you drove to the Tolts' cave."

"You can't prove that."

"I can prove you were there and that a buggy traveled over the wagon trail from the bridge to within three hundred yards of the cave. I found

285

the tracks next day. I can prove that Miss Ellen knew Kinney was down Dunkley's Folly. She's the one that told us. How did she know? Nobody else knew he was here but the Tolts."

Allan said nothing. What could he say? Of course she must have got in touch with Dave again and learned what had been done with Kinney. There was no other way she could have known.

"I'd say mighty little about that if I was you," Allan spoke up at last. "Everybody knows she's one of the nicest girls in town. Better not bring her into this, Mr. Evans."

"I'm not bringing her in. It's you fool boys who have brought her in. But we aim to go to the bottom of this. You'd better tell us what you know, Allan, if you want to keep her clear."

Allan gave this consideration and decided not to talk. What he could say would only drag her in deeper. . . .

Sutter chose two men to go with him as a guard for Allan Macdonald on the trip to Burke City. One of them was Evans, the other Spence Kinney. He chose Kinney only because of the bitter animosity the man was displaying toward the prisoner.

He was too full of hate to give the young fellow any chance to escape.

The news had reached Burke that one of the

suspected bandits was being brought to town and the place seethed with unrest.

Even before the arrival of the party, excitement had reached a high pitch.

Sutter rode into the town ahead of the rest of his party and met the sheriff of Faber County, a politician named Homer Opdyke.

The latter hurriedly called together four deputies and went out with Sutter to meet the prisoner.

"Folks seem kinda het up," Sutter mentioned to Evans. "We better slip him in a back way if we can, don't you reckon?"

"I'm sheriff in this town," Opdyke announced. "There won't be any trouble. I'll guarantee that. Anyhow, the jail is on the main street, so we've got to go that way."

The rumor fled before them that the posse was near. It filled Main Street with men and boys eager to see the suspect. Every minute the jam grew thicker.

"Here they come!" someone shouted.

Eight armed men rode down the center of the street. In the midst of them was one handcuffed youth.

"That's him!" a dozen voices cried. "The one next Opdyke."

Allan heard someone call to another, "The tough-looking guy in the middle." Twenty times in the next minute he learned what a villainous face he had, how much he looked the part of a killer. That it would be like this he had had no idea. The mob hatred beat upon him in waves. He had to set his teeth to keep back the panic fear that rose in him. For the crowd pressed close and impeded the little cavalcade. Its voice rose in a roar of blind rage.

"Keep back!" Opdyke ordered. "Give way and let's get through."

Instead, men began to sift in among the horses. Evans took one long look at Odpyke and knew he was a broken reed. He spurred his horse into the crowd and drove it back, then gave curt orders to the deputies.

"Keep close, boys. Don't leave room for any-one to get through. Get your sixshooters out. I'll see 'em in hell before I give 'em this boy."

Slowly the horses pressed forward through a dense pack. Voices screamed curses at Allan. Lifted fists were shaken at him. Furious, distorted faces focused on him their passionate lust to destroy. There was in the implacable mass emotion a cruelty more deadly than any individual alone could have projected.

Allan crushed down the panic wave that had risen to his throat. The clenched jaws gave the boyish face a grimness accentuated by the cold, steely eyes. He looked down at the twisted, upturned countenances, scores of them, all swept by one common surge of feeling, with a curious detachment that was later to surprise him in retrospect. He was no longer afraid. There was in the very violence of this raw passion a confession of weakness. Pete Evans, riding the storm quietly, his hard gaze sweeping the press with no more excitement than if he had been herding cattle, brought courage back to the prisoner's heart in a rush.

Not for a moment did Evans let the posse stop moving. He spoke evenly, but in a harsh, dominant voice, now to one or another of the posse, now to the crowd.

"Closer, Sutter . . . Keep your head, Kinney. We'll make it . . . Outa my way, fellow. This kid isn't one of the robbers. He's only a witness . . . Shove up, Opdyke. We're 'most through. . . . Clear the road, you damn fools!"

They were through. The mob had given way before the determined front of the officers. Five minutes later, Allan was in the office of the sheriff.

Within the hour more than thirty men had passed through the office and paused in front of him. They were there to identify if possible the prisoner as one of the bank robbers. Among these were bank officers, wranglers and loafers at the Alamo Corral, men who had been engaged or claimed to have been engaged in the street battle. A good many said positively they had not seen Allan among the bandits. Others could not be sure. Four witnesses claimed he was the one who had held the horses while the banks were being robbed.

Once Kinney lifted his voice in shrill approval. "Sure! Betcher life he's the fellow. I done said so all the time."

Evans looked at the little deputy. "That'll be enough from you, Spence," he said quietly. "We're not going to railroad an innocent man."

"D'you claim he's innocent, Pete?"

"We're here to find that out. If you're asking my opinion, I don't think he had anything more to do with this crime than I did. Anyhow, he's going to get a square deal."

"What kind of a square deal did the Tolts give the men they shot down in the street out there?"

"Allan isn't a Tolt. Keep your trap shut, Spence. You hear me?"

Evans had with him a photograph of Dave Tolt taken by an itinerant picture-maker who had set up his tent for a while at Melrose. Each man who passed through the office looked at it. A dozen witnesses immediately recognized the print as a likeness of the youngest of the outlaws.

The two ranchmen who had passed the escaping robbers on the road did not believe Allan was one of them. The most convincing witness in his behalf was Doctor Watson.

"Not one of them," the doctor said as soon as he looked at Allan.

"Not one of those you saw," Opdyke interpreted.

"I saw all three of them—lived with them for a week," Watson replied.

"But there may have been more than three got away."

"No. There were six of them altogether. They didn't make any bones about that. I heard them say so repeatedly."

"Four men have identified him, doctor, as the fellow holding the horses."

"Then they've made a mistake. The young fellow that came to town to get me held the horses. He said so. The others said so too."

"This his picture?" Evans asked, handing the photograph to the doctor.

"That's the man."

"You've never seen this young fellow here until today?"

"Never, as far as I know. He's not one of the robbers."

"Seems conclusive to me," Evans said.

"Not to me," Opdyke differed. "The vote's four to one against this fellow."

Allan spoke quietly. "Everyone who has seen the bandits closely is for me. The boys at the corral all agree I wasn't one of them. The two ranchmen say so. Doctor Watson is sure I'm not. The only ones against me are those who saw the robbers at a distance during the fight. I wouldn't say their testimony is of much weight."

"I'll bet you wouldn't," Kinney sniggered maliciously.

"Keep your mouth shut, Spence," ordered Sutter.

The marshaling of the evidence had convinced the sheriff that Allan had not been with the robbers of the banks. He had never really believed Macdonald was a principal. Now he was sorry he had brought the boy here.

Later in the day his regrets increased. A good deal of drinking was going on in the town. He consulted with Evans.

"They're working themselves up to a lynching, looks like," he said. "That li'l' devil Spence Kinney is going around claiming we've got it fixed to turn loose Macdonald after he's been identified as one of the outlaws. What's your idea, Pete?"

"My idea is we'd better get this boy out of town right off. Let's go see Opdyke."

The hours had changed materially the point of view of Opdyke. He was a politician, and he sought popularity as a lizard follows the sun. But he did not want the backfire of a lynching against his record when he ran for a renomination. That would be fatal. The applause of a mob was fickle. If it was proved later that this young fellow Macdonald had not been one of the robbers—and Opdyke was privately convinced he was not one of those who had been in the battle—the crowd would turn on him and rend him for not defending his prisoner. It was an awkward position to face. He certainly was not going to kill anybody if the jail was attacked.

Yet he would be in a poor light if he tamely surrendered this boy to a mob to be hanged. Already he was beginning to sweat fear.

"Better take the prisoner back to Melrose," he agreed. "There's going to be trouble in town tonight if you don't. It may be too late already. The jail is being watched. I doubt if we could get through the crowd again without a fight."

Evans had a suggestion to make. The others agreed to it, not without reluctance on the part of Sutter.

XVIII

'Good-Bye, My Lover, Good-Bye'

Through the barred windows of his cell Allan had watched the rising tide of indignation against him as it expressed itself in Main Street. Men came and went, gathered in knots, talked, and looked up at the window through which he saw them. Someone had picked him out early, and, as group succeeded group, always at least one of the preceding idlers remained to point out his cell to the others.

At times men shook their fists at him. At times they shouted curses and threats. As the day grew on, he noticed that the number of those in the street became larger and more excited.

The jailer, bringing him dinner, was a frank pessimist.

"Fellow, you're in a sure-enough jam," he confided gloomily. "Those guys out there mean trouble. They sure do."

Allan felt a queer, cold sinking of his stomach muscles. "What kind of trouble?" he asked.

"What kind would you think? They want you."

"And your sheriff—what will he do?"

"How do I know what he'll do? What can he do, with hundreds of 'em milling around?"

Macdonald's appetite vanished. He found he could not swallow food. They had brought him here as a victim and would surrender him to a mob clamorous for vengeance. He paced the cell, stopped a moment at the window, took up his short beat again. All the swift, eager youth in him protested wildly against such a fate. It could not be true. There must be some way—somehow . . . Never again would he look on his mother or his father. He would never see Ellen Owens. He could never tell her now how he had loved her for years. Oh, Ellen, Ellen! Not for him the gifts flashed by her fluttering, winged eyes. Not for him her warm, brave friendship.

Through the window he could see the shadows of the buildings on the other side of the street grow longer and longer. The day was beginning to wane. Soon that strip of sunshine on the road, narrowing every minute, would be snuffed out. He would never again ride in the warm sunlight, the wind blowing across the plain. He was done with life. They would take him out and throttle . . .

No, he mustn't think of that. He had to buck up and play the man. He had to game it out, go through without whining, without begging for a mercy that would be denied him.

If he could see his father and talk with him! No chance of that. Sutter had slipped him out of town without letting anyone know where they were going.

But at least he could write—to his father and mother, and to Ellen. He called the jailer and asked for paper.

The man hesitated. "I dunno about that. Well, all right. You'll have to write with a pencil."

He wrote brief messages, put them in stamped envelopes, and gave them to the jailer.

The strip of sunshine in the street had vanished now. A dozen men stood in the road. When he stepped to the window, they gave a cry of rage.

The door of his cell opened. Evans was there, and the two sheriffs. Also there was a young man of about his own age, not unlike him in appearance.

Evans spoke, rapidly, evenly. "We've got to get you out of here, boy. If we don't, there will be trouble and plenty of it. Are you game to take a big chance? We're down to the blanket, son."

Courage flowed in upon Allan like a tide. They were going to give him an opportunity to fight for his life, to use his nerve and his brains.

"I'm ready," Allan answered, level-eyed.

"We're going to turn you loose, to ride out of town alone. We can't go with you, any of us. You'd be spotted right away. Maybe you will be, anyhow, but if you are, we'll try a rescue. This boy is going to stay in the cell, near the window, so as to attract the attention of those outside. Four or five men have walked out of here in the last half-hour. I'm figuring they'll think you too a witness or a visitor. Act natural. Don't hurry. There's a horse tied in front of the Silver Palace, about fifty yards up the street, a roan with white stockings. Fork that bronc and ride out of town. Don't hurry unless they get after you."

"Do I get a gun?" Allan asked.

"No gun," Opdyke said promptly. "There's been enough killing in this town."

"You're to ride to Melrose and give yourself up to the jailer there—if you get through. Will you promise?"

"Yes."

Evans tossed upon the bed some wearing apparel. There were a pair of shiny leather chaps, a red bandanna handkerchief, a wide flopping sombrero, and a blue checked shirt.

"Get into these, Allan," he said. "And don't forget to roll out of here like you hadn't a care in the world. If you get scared and start to run, you're a gone goose."

"I'll not forget," Allan said. "There's a gun in the pocket of these chaps. What about that?"

"Not loaded," Evans explained. "Just a part of the bluff that you're a fool cowboy."

Allan dressed. He cocked the flapping sombrero jauntily a trifle to one side and he knotted the bandanna carelessly in the current fashion of the range.

"If you throw down on me and don't show up at Melrose—" Sutter threatened.

"I'll be waiting at the gate for you, Sheriff—if I make the riffle," Allan assured him.

At the front door of the prison, Evans had one parting word for Allan. "Make your luck stand up, boy."

The eyes of the ex-sheriff and young Macdonald met. Evans was reassured. He knew that the prisoner knew there could be no rescue. If he was discovered, fifty men would swarm on him before he could move a dozen steps. That fifty would become hundreds in the space of a minute. It was up to him alone. Not in words, but in that long cool look Allan told the older man that he understood this. His were the steely eyes that would not accept defeat until the game had been played out to a finish.

Evans was reckoned a hard man as well as a game one, but as the door closed behind Allan, his feeling went out in warm sympathy to the intrepid youth. If he could have done it without spoiling Macdonald's chance, he would have liked to take that long short walk with him.

The men behind the door waited, scarcely daring to breathe, fearing the sudden yell that would denote betrayal. There drifted back to them a sound of whistling. Allan was offering the world a solo, "Good-bye, my lover, good-bye."

Sutter slapped a hand on his thigh. "By jinks, did you ever hear anything like that?" he whispered. "He's sure got sand in his craw."

The sound of that cheerful solo was drowned in a yell of triumphant execration.

As the door of the jail closed behind Allan, the blood in his arteries streamed fast. He felt a curious lift of the spirit, an odd gayety born of excitement. From this moment he was on his own, a hundred enemies within a stone's throw. An unconscious quickening of the step, a gesture of alarm, might destroy him. His life was staked on the turn of a card, but at least he was playing the hand.

At sight of him one of the groups across the street broke off its talk. It was then that Allan's cheerful whistle sounded in the chorus of "Good-bye, my lover, good-bye." He moved with the careless, bandy-legged roll of a cowboy without a care in the world.

"Say fellow, what's new?" someone called.

Allan shook his head, not interrupting the solo. He cocked an eye toward the window of the cell above. This had two advantages. It turned his face from those nearest him and their attention to the figure that had moved forward to the bars. At the sight of the lad in the window, dressed in Macdonald's hat and coat, a cry of anger swept across the road and beat against the wall of the jail.

The sound of that roar chilled Allan. It was meant for him, might in another instant fling itself at him. There was something inhuman about it.

Individually these men were like a hundred others that he knew, good neighbors, kindly, full of friendliness; but thrown together in a mob with the bloodlust they became by some strange chemistry members of the wolf pack.

He sauntered on his way, brushing shoulders with men who did not even look at him. Their gazes were lifted to the window of the cell. Again the figure behind the bars showed itself and brought out another yell. Allan joined in the bitter cry, though he blessed the boy for playing his part so well.

Just ahead, not thirty yards away, Allan saw a sign, "The Silver Palace." In front of it was a hitchrack. Tied to the rack were three ponies. One of them was a roan with white stockings.

It was all he could do to keep from hurrying. These men he passed had seen him brought down this street a prisoner only a few hours since. If one of them recognized him . . .

The roan was tied by a slip knot. In a few seconds now he would be in the saddle. Funny, how crazy a fellow's thoughts ran. " 'They'll have fleet steeds that follow,' quoth young Lochinvar." The piece was in his McGuffey's Reader. He had had to learn it once. . . . Out of the saloon poured a little jet of men. The liquor in them was noisy. One of them waved a big weather-beaten hat. "All set for the neck-tie party!" he shouted. "Soon now."

Another held a fat black cigar in his fingers. "Gimme a match, fellow," he said to Allan.

Macdonald's hand moved to the pocket of his shirt where 'the makings' would be kept. As he felt for a match, his heart died within him. Spence Kinney was pushing through the swing doors to join the party. In another moment he would turn and see Allan.

"No can do. Nary a match," Allan said with a forced grin.

He circled around the group toward the hitchrack. Doing this, he had to come face to face with Kinney. There was no alternative. His one faint hope was that the little man might turn away to speak with someone.

Kinney started to do this, and for some reason changed his mind. His shifty glance fell on Allan. He let out a yelp of amazement and with it the fighting epithet of the West.

Allan's left fist lashed out savagely for the man's chin. Kinney went down like an ox hit with a pole-axe.

"Can't any man alive call me that," Allan blustered. "This li'l' scalawag beat me out of forty dollars for a saddle."

"Say, cowboy, do you always knock 'em cold?" a fat man demanded, half in challenge, half in admiration.

Their eyes were all fastened upon Allan. Without shifting his gaze he could see others running toward the saloon. It was time for him to be going—if he was to get away at all.

The luck broke against him. One of the men in the knot already gathered recognized Allan. He had been among those invited to the jail earlier in the day to identify him.

"By Gad, it's Tolt!" he cried. "He's broke out of jail."

Allan beat them to the draw. They were caught by surprise, and he was not. He backed off, revolver moving in a quarter-circle that threatened each in turn. He crouched slightly, snarling defiance. Through narrowed eyelids gleamed deadly points of light. The fingers of his left hand groped for the bridle rein behind him.

"Don't you monkey with me!" he growled, voice low and harsh. "An' don't crowd. If you do . . ."

His fingers had found the rein and tugged it. The horse was free. With one lithe swing of the body he vaulted to the saddle.

But in doing so he had been forced to turn his back on them all. Instantly three or four had plunged forward. The second horse barred escape that way. He dragged the roan abruptly against them. One man stumbled and went down. Another caught at the bridle. His hat had been knocked off. Allan swung the heavy barrel of the revolver up and down. It struck the fellow on the head.

With a groan he staggered back, clutching at his red hair.

Allan gave the roan the spur. The bronco went into the air, came down on all four feet, and shot forward like an arrow from a bow. Reaching hands clutched at the rider, but failed to drag him from the saddle. He was out of the press, in the middle of the road, racing for his life, body bent low above the horn.

He could hear the roar of guns and knew they were firing at him. Excited voices came to him, shouts, curses, explanations. Faces flashed before him for a moment and vanished in his wake. The false fronts of stores and gambling-houses gave way to residences. These became more scattered. He was out of town in open country. To the right he could see the camp of a trail herd. Another long line of dust showed him where another bunch of longhorns were in motion. He deflected his course to avoid these.

Already he knew that Evans had picked him a good horse. The roan was fast and probably had stamina. Both speed and endurance would be needed, for already Allan could see the dust of his pursuers. They were riding together, well bunched. At that distance he could not tell how many of them there were. He guessed that he had a start of nearly a mile.

It was none too much. No doubt they were armed with Winchesters. If they could get near enough, they would pick him off with no risk to themselves, or they would shoot his horse and capture him alive.

Allan knew nothing of the country through which he was traveling. It was new terrain to him. His eyes searched for heavy brush, but found none either to the right or left. There were no hills, no timber, no pockets into which he might duck to escape observation. He had to keep going, straight and fast.

The sun had set. That was one thing in his favor. Within an hour or two darkness would fall and cover him . . . if it did not come too late.

The posse was stringing out. One or two riders were falling back, one was coming fast, far ahead. That he was gaining on him Allan knew, and lessening the distance between them very rapidly. He must be on a race-horse, the fugitive thought. Already he could make out that the man wore a yellow bandanna.

The leader must be almost within firing distance. Any minute now a bullet might kick up a spurt of dirt within a dozen yards of Allan. But no sound of a shot came to the young man. Perhaps the man on the racer did not have a rifle.

Allan did not give up hope. It would be horrible to be dragged back to a rope now, after he had come so near escaping. But he did not let himself think of that. They had not got him yet. A race-horse is good for a certain distance. At any moment now the iron-gray pounding along in his wake, gaining stride by stride, might falter and lose ground.

The roan was blown. Its lungs were going like a bellows. It galloped heavily. Allan knew there was not much distance left in the animal. He had kept it to a pace too cruelly fast.

It jumped to Allan's mind that the iron-gray was no longer outrunning the roan. At first he was not sure, but presently he knew there could be no doubt. The man in the yellow bandanna pulled his laboring horse to a walk.

He was the only pursuer to be seen. The others, far in the rear, had dropped into a dip in the plain. A voice, faint and indistinct, came to Allan on the wind.

Macdonald spoke grimly, to himself. "Nothing doing, Mr. Yellow Flag, I've got hurry-up business anywhere but with you."

Presently, out of rifle range, he, too, pulled to a walk. It was possible he had already mined the roan. In any case he had to give the pony a breathing spell or he would find himself afoot on the desert. Even now he was not safe. The iron-gray plodded along, neither lessening nor letting increase the distance between them.

Once more Allan heard the faint far shout. He wondered why the fellow wasted his breath calling to him. Was it likely he would stop to exchange the time of day with a man inviting him to be hanged?

If night would only come. Anxiously Allan looked at the sky, at the horizon light fading away. It could not be long now. In the darkness he could slip away.

The man wearing the yellow bandanna was persistent. He became a vague shadow in the gloom of deepening night . . . He was entirely blotted out. But Allan knew he was still jogging along back there.

Better let him pass, Allan decided, then cut off at a right angle from the course he was now following. There was a jog in the prairie, and to the left a dark outline which looked like a small hill. Allan swung into the draw, rounded a curve, and waited.

The roan betrayed him by nickering a greeting to the iron-gray. Out of the night a voice called.

"That you, Allan? This is Evans."

Macdonald drew a deep breath of relief. Yet he held the revolver for its effect in case the pursuer was lying.

A shadow showed around the bend.

"Near enough," Allan said. "Till I know who you are. I'm covering you with a gun."

"Which isn't loaded," the other said casually. "Boy, didn't you hear me calling?"

Allan recognized the voice now. He thrust the revolver back into its pocket. "You certainly scared me to death," he said. "How did I know who you were?"

"I didn't reckon you could know, but we certainly didn't either one of us do our horses any good."

"What about the other fellows with you?"

"We better lose 'em, don't you think? Might as well keep moving this way as any other. We'll mosey along kinda easy."

Allan followed his lead.

XIX

Ellen Breaks a Plate

Pete Evans, back from Burke City, was eating dinner at the house of Owens. He was a friend of the family and sat at the table frequently. There was a home feeling in the atmosphere that he liked.

Just now they hung on his words, for he was telling a thrilling story. Even the boys, their fascinated eyes fixed on him, forgot to eat. At the door leading to the kitchen Ellen stood, an empty plate in her hand. She had started to the stove for hot biscuits and had become absorbed in his tale to the exclusion of everything else. Her face was an index of the girl's emotions. The color came and went with the ebb and flow of the ex-sheriff's drawling narrative. She was like a charmed bird, all the quick life in her eager being suspended. Scarcely did she dare to breathe, lest she break the spell of the words that so enthralled her.

After all, it was a simple enough story, with no dramatic art in the telling to enhance the stimulation of high adventure, this account of a man caught in a current of stark tragedy from which he had escaped by virtue of the gay recklessness rising out of the stores of courage within himself.

"It was a fool business taking him to Burke," Evans admitted. "We didn't know it till we got there. He didn't have a chance—not from the first. I knew it. I reckon he did, soon as we started down the main street and the crowd pressed in on us. Owens, I could feel waves of hate beating up to that boy. I'll sure never forget it. We had 'most to fight our way through to get him to the jail. Allan never batted an eye. He was that cool, that easy, though he knew if they broke through and dragged him from his horse he was gone."

"The poor boy," Mrs. Owens murmured.

"You can bet that Sutter and I cussed ourselves proper for bringing him there," Evans went on. "We could feel what was in the air. They were talking it in every saloon, and they were doing a lot of drinking to work themselves up to it. The sheriff at Burke is a politician. We could see he wouldn't put up any real fight to save Allan and wouldn't let us do it either. But he didn't want a lynching. That wouldn't be so good for his chance of reëlection. So I fixed up a plan. It was a mighty long shot at that, to have Allan change his clothes and walk right out into the crowd that was aiming to kill him come night."

"Lordy!" Bob Owens cried softly.

"I put it up to him," the ex-sheriff said. "He wasn't fooled, not a little bit. He knew if he was recognized—and hundreds of people had seen him, some in the street and some real close when they came to the jail to identify him as the kid bank robber—he wouldn't last any longer than a snowball in Yuma. It never fazed him. He grabbed at the chance like it was a Fourth-of-July picnic we were offering him. Talk about your Tolts. This boy has got 'em all beat both ways from the ice. You never saw anyone cooler than he was. I was scared to death myself. If there had been another chance on earth, I wouldn't have sent him out into those howling wolves . . . Another thing, first to last he never said a single word blaming me or Sutter. I reckon he knew how we felt."

"Bully for Allan!" cried Jim Owens, waving a spoon in excitement.

"I wasted time telling Allan not to act excited when he got outside," Evans explained, a sardonic grin on his hard, leathery face. "Excited! Do you know what he did? Sauntered out whistling 'Good-bye, my lover, good-bye.' He could have fooled me like he did those outside. I would have said he was a kid cowboy without sense enough to say 'Sic' 'em.'"

The starry eyes of Ellen never lifted from the man telling the story. She could have added one small detail to it over which she had wept in a stress of passionate emotion. Above her heart, close to the immature bosom that rose and fell so fast, lay a letter written her by a boy who had thought himself about to die.

"And he made the grade—reached the horse unnoticed and rode out of town," Owens said. "He was lucky, Pete."

"It wasn't quite thataway," Evans corrected him. "Just as he got to the horse I had waiting, that little devil Spence Kinney rolled out of a saloon with a crowd of scalawags. Allan knocked him galley-west, bluffed the others with an unloaded gun, forked the bronc, slammed through the fellows trying to stop him, and lit a blue streak down the street. It was the slickest getaway I ever saw."

From Ellen's fingers the biscuit plate slipped to the floor and broke into fifty pieces. Her mother looked at her, started to speak, and changed her mind. She was startled at the rapt look of the glamorous-eyed girl. This was no time to fasten all their attention upon her.

"I was right out there with the first bunch that hightailed it after him," the officer continued. "At that I fooled around and held 'em back long as I could. I was kinda particular to get the best mount in the lot. My idea was that if I got to Allan first, the two of us might stand off these hurry-up lads. It worked out better than that. Night came. I was a long way ahead of the other fellows when I bumped into the boy by chance. That was all there was to it. We drifted along home and Allan is here in the jail now."

"I don't see why you put him there," Ellen broke

out indignantly. "He had no more to do with the bank robbery than I did."

Evans looked at her. "Maybe not. Did you ever hear of anyone being accessory after the fact?" he asked dryly.

"Would you want him to desert his closest friend because he'd got into trouble?" she demanded hotly.

"I'm not running the law of this Territory, Miss Ellen. If you're asking me what I think, I'd say Allan Macdonald is a man to ride the river with. You've told the story. He stuck by his friend after Dave went bad. I don't blame him any, but the United States Government doesn't take that view. Sensible folks quit their friends when they get themselves into trouble."

"The way you quit Allan at Burke City," the girl flung back at him.

"I figured I'd got him into a jam and it was up to me to get him out. Besides, I always figured young Macdonald was a pretty decent citizen."

"Even if he is a what-d'you-call-him after the fact. Mr. Evans, you're a fraud. If it had been Dave there instead of Allan, you would have stuck by him just the same."

"Is it your idea to put me in jail, too, Miss Ellen?" he asked with a grin.

"It's my idea to get Allan out. I never heard of anything so ridiculous as the way you sheriffs hound him for no reason at all."

Spots of hot color flamed on her cheeks. As on the night when she and Allan had gone to the cave to meet Dave, Ellen looked like a slim young Joan or Arc ready to give inspired battle to the enemy.

Her mother spoke gently. "Don't you think, Ellen, you'd better let older folks decide what is the best way to help Allan?"

The ardor died out of the girl. She bit her lip to hold back the tears. By her unmaidenliness she had laid herself open to rebuke. Why did she have to be so impulsive and so—so brazen? Other girls didn't always say what they thought. They did not give themselves away as she did.

Swiftly she turned and ran out of the room.

Bob took up the cudgel for Allan. "Honest, Mother, I'd think they'd let Allan out. Maybe he did meet Dave after he got back from robbing the bank. Golly, I might have bumped into him myself. No jury in this country will send Allan to the pen for that."

"It's some worse than that, Bob," Evans told him. "Sutter figures Allan gave the Tolts active aid when they got back here. Somebody fed them and acted as a lookout. It is known he bought food here in town that he didn't take home. Some of us think that the Tolts are still on the dodge in this country and that Allan knows where they are. I think Sutter is doing right to hold him."

"I wish the Tolts would hurry up and get across

he line before they make any more trouble," Mrs. Owens said. "Either that or get caught. They deserve punishment if anybody ever did."

"They'll make their break to get through soon as they think it's safe. I reckon," the ex-sheriff said. "My advice to them would be to make it soon. They've got to depend on their friends in he brush for food. One of these days, if they don't look out, some bird will drop into Sutter's office the way Kinney did looking for a reward."

Evans rose from the table, filled his pipe, and walked out with Owens to the porch.

The sun had gone down in a splash of splendor, one of those vivid pictures done in flaming color by the master painter Nature. It had, indeed, been a score of pictures and not one, for almost each moment had seen it touched to new values, to softer, more harmonious tints, until dusk had fallen over the plain and filled the crotch of the far hills with a lake of velvet not quite blue, not quite black.

Now dusk had given way to night. This suited the three riders moving through the chaparral toward Melrose. What they had to do could be done only in opaque darkness. They traveled in silence, except for the swish of brush dragging against their legs or the occasional ring of a hoof striking a stone. There was something almost sinister in their silence, as though they were savage denizens of the desert slipping furtively through the jungle to stalk their kill.

Their physical conformation supported this fancy. They were lean and gaunt of body; tigerishly lithe. The bony structure of their faces was marked. The eyes were fierce and sunken, their lips were like steel traps. A hunted man takes on the visible characteristics of a wild beast, and these three had been harried by a vengeful pursuit for weeks.

It was necessary to their purpose that they be not seen. They rode through pastures instead of following a road, nipping barbed wire to let them in and out. So they came to Frater's ten-acre alfalfa field unobserved. The lights of Melrose gleamed below them. To some young cottonwoods they tied their mounts. With them they had a led horse, saddled and bridled.

The men stalked through the green alfalfa, slipped between two strands of wire, and came to a dry wash upon the edge of which a square building had been erected. Close to the wall, in single file, they stole to the front and knocked on the door.

A man opened to the knock, and gasped in astonishment.

"The Tolts!" he murmured.

"Right first guess, Hank," answered Caldwell gently. "I hear voices. Who's with you?"

The jailer stared into the barrel of a forty-four that looked to him as big as a cannon.

"The sheriff and Spence Kinney," replied Hank.

"Good enough. Step into the room ahead of us and don't say a word. We'll do the talking."

The officer nodded. He would have preferred to be anywhere but here. His guess was that the hunted had turned hunters.

At sight of the Tolts, the two men seated by the table playing seven-up were struck dumb. Sutter tried to grin, in rather a sickly way. They had come here, he supposed, to pay him off for the persistence of his hunt for them. Kinney almost collapsed. He slumped down in his chair, the color washing from his tripe face.

Caldwell glanced around the room. The blinds were down. Dave had locked the front door after entering. Probably they would not be interrupted.

"A nice quiet little party," the chief of the outlaws said. Sutter took the lead offered, not very confidently. "You kinda—took us by surprise, Cald."

"Did we? You've been advertising for us." Caldwell glanced at a placard on the wall, showing photographs of himself and his brothers. "Quite a reward you're offering. Thought we'd come and collect it. Have you got it here?"

"Not right here, Cald. We don't leave that much money lying around loose," the sheriff explained. "You wouldn't hardly expect that, would you?"

"Why not?" Cole put in hardily. "We've been

letting a good deal more than that lie around loose in a gunny-sack for several weeks."

He did not add that this was at the presen moment tied to a saddle on the back of a horse ir Frater's alfalfa field.

"So you weren't looking for us, Jim," Caldwel said. "Not even though you claim you were righ anxious to see us."

"I'm sheriff of this county, Cald," Sutter responded uneasily. "Would you expect me to lie down and not hunt for you? I'd say if you think that way you're unreasonable. I'm paid to rur down men who break the laws."

Cole laughed harshly, with no pleasant mirth "Well, here we are, Jim. All run down for you. Wha do you aim to do with us now you've got us?"

"I'm like that Irishman that got the bear anc hollered for help to turn it loose, don't yot reckon, Cole?"

"Except that you don't figure on calling for any help," Caldwell added.

"That would hardly be wise," Sutter admitted "Well, boys, it's your say-so. What do you want?"

He managed to put the question quietly, withou obvious fear, though his eyes betrayed an inner dread.

"No harm to you, Jim, if you keep your heac and act sensible. We've got no grudge against you for doing what you've been elected to do.' Caldwell turned his gaze on Kinney. When he spoke to him, his voice was still low and disturbingly gentle. "What's the matter, Spence? Why don't you join in this friendly little powwow? Don't tell us you're not pleased to see us now you've met up with us again."

Kinney swallowed a lump in his throat. "Boys, I never did ary one of you any harm. You got the wrong idea about me."

"Why didn't you have the sense to stay buried when we flung you down Dunkley's Folly?" demanded Cole harshly.

"I ain't ever got over that," Kinney whined. "You stove me up terrible, an' I got rheumatism from being down in that hole."

"I'd better put him out of his misery, don't you reckon, Cald?" asked Cole, with a laugh of savage irony. "No use letting him suffer thataway."

"Spence ain't worth your powder, boys," the sheriff said. "You didn't come here to get him. You claim you don't want me. What can I do for you?"

"Always the little business man, Jim," Caldwell derided. "Don't hurry us. We'll let you know what we're here for without you pushing on the reins. Like you say, Spence ain't worth a barrel of shucks, but once in a while we burn up shucks to get them out of the way. How about it, Spence? Shall we burn up this trash here?"

Kinney begged for his life, beady eyes stabbing fear at the outlaws from a chalk face.

It made Dave ashamed to listen to his groveling.

"Hell's bells, boys! Let's do what we come to do," he said impatiently.

Caldwell turned on the sheriff. "We want Allan Macdonald."

"What you want with him?"

"We want to get him out of here. I know you Jim. You're holding the boy to make political capital for yourself. Because you couldn't get us you aim to unload trouble on him, claiming he was one of us. Well, he wasn't. He hasn't had a thing to do with any of our raids. What I can hear you came damn near getting him lynched at Burke. Looks like you'll finally cook up something against him if you get rope enough. A jury wouldn't be any too particular if it figured he was a friend of the Tolts. So we'll collect him and take him along with us."

"This is a jail break, then."

"That's whatever," Cole agreed. "Get the keys Hank. I'll go with you and get Allan while the other boys stay here and keep your friends company."

Hank took the keys from a nail in the wall. He and Cole left the room.

Kinney began again his hypocritical protestations.

Presently Caldwell interrupted. "Your friend will talk himself into his grave yet, Jim," the bandit said brusquely.

"Don't call him *my* friend, Cald," the sheriff implored.

"Not your friend? Thought you'd had him on our posses. Thought he was here having a ociable game of seven-up tonight with you."

"Does that make him my friend? If you're ever heriff, Cald, you'll know a fellow has to use vhat stuff comes to hand."

Dave spoke abruptly the thought in his mind. 'Did Allan have as narrow a squeak at Burke as olks say he did?"

"I made a bad mistake there, Dave," admitted utter. "Didn't realize the town was so crazy wild r I'd never have taken Allen to Burke. Yes, sir, he boy was sure enough in a tight. They aimed to ynch him come night. No doubt about that. We id the one thing possible in letting him walk ut. If we'd tried to take him out of town, they vould have torn him to pieces."

"And he's no more guilty than you are," Dave old the officer bitterly.

"He's got sand in his craw, that boy. Walked out nto the howling mob like David into the lions' len."

"If you'd gone to Sunday School and read your 3ible when you were young, Jim, you'd have grown up into a respectable citizen like me," Caldwell said, with a sardonic laugh. "I reckon ou mean Daniel, not David."

Cole and the jailer returned with Allan.

"Says he reckons he'll stay here if we don't nind," Cole reported to his brothers. "One on us, after we've taken quite some trouble to get him out of his jam. Seems he enjoys being in the calaboose."

Allan glanced at Cole, then at the other brothers. All three of the Tolts bristled with weapons.

"What good would it do me to run away?" he asked. "I'd have to come back and give myself up. My intention is to live my life in this neighborhood."

"Jim here has another idea, Allan," Caldwell mentioned. "He has a notion you'll live several years of it in the pen."

"I can't help that," Allan said evenly. "I'm not going to run away."

"Didn't I tell you?" Dave demanded bluntly of Caldwell. "Didn't I say he wouldn't go with us?"

"He figures he can't touch pitch and not be defiled," Cole snapped, with caustic acrimony. "Well, he can have another guess this time. He's going with us, anyhow."

"If I do I'll go under protest," Allan replied quietly.

Dave waited with Allan in the jailer's room while his brothers took the two officers and Spence Kinney upstairs. The three men were handcuffed, gagged, and locked in cells.

"I allowed you wouldn't want to go with us, Allan," young Tolt explained to his friend. "Reckon you're right, though it looks like they're fixing to put you in the pen for helping me. Bu you've got horse-sense enough to know that if you go you lose Ellen, and maybe you can make it without having to go to the pen."

Allan felt the blood mounting in his cheeks beneath the tan. "Sometimes you talk crazy, Dave. You know Ellen doesn't care for me. She never did. You of all men ought to know that."

"I've got some brains in my noodle too, Allan," answered Dave, with cynical recklessness. "When I went bad I lost out with Ellen. One of these days she'll marry you, if you don't get sent up to the pen, and when she does she'll marry the right man. You can name your first kid Dave, so she'll always have a reminder of the bad luck she missed."

"That's no way to talk," Allan said sternly. "It's not Ellen's fault you followed a crooked trail."

"Did I say it was?" Dave flared up. "I'm not saying anything against Ellen. I never have. I never will. Trouble with you is you're always right. You'll make a hell of a husband."

"I'll not make any kind. If you want to know, Ellen told me she meant never to marry. She's going to live at home with her folks."

Dave snorted discourteously. "And you're the guy who once told me you knew women."

"I never told you that. I don't know a thing about them."

"Bet your boots you don't, not if you think a girl knows today what she means to do tomor-

row, or tells you if she knows. Listen, fellow
There's so darn much you don't know I'll give
you one good steer. Camp on a girl's trail and by
and by she'll marry you to get rid of you."

The other two Tolts returned.

"Got 'em all put to bed nice," Cole said
"Tucked 'em up right comfy. I hated to leave
Spence without kissing him good-night with a
wipe of my hogleg barrel. But my worse feelings
got the better of me and I didn't."

"We've got to take you with us for a couple o
hours, Allan," Caldwell explained. "Can't have
you rousing the town and getting a posse out on
a hot trail after us. Maybe you'll change your
mind and travel on with us to mañana land
Anyhow, you'll have some time to think it over."

"I've done all the thinking that's necessary,"
Allan replied.

"You're the doctor," Cole agreed. "Well, we'd
better get going. I reckon, Allan, you're not foo
enough to try to break away or call for help."

"No. I'll go with you quietly."

They slipped out of the jail and around the
corner of the building, keeping close to the wall.

"This way," Dave said, and Allan answered
"All right."

None of the four men saw two figures passing
under the heavy shade of a cottonwood on the
other side of the street. One of the two had the
slender, willowy grace of a girl.

XX

A What-D'You-Call-It After the Fact

'Where you going, Ellen?" Mrs. Owens asked.

"Bob's taking me to Jinnie Harshaw's," Ellen answered, turning her slender neck to see how her hair looked in the glass.

Her mother gazed at her with a troubled frown. She had Ellen very much on her mind these days. The girl was not herself. Sometimes Ellen showed her old gayety. A snatch of joyous song would ripple from her throat. Again she would be depressed or absent-minded, lost in some inner vision she did not share with those near. Mrs. Owens guessed she was in love. If so, with whom?

The girl's mother had been fearfully afraid it was Dave Tolt. Nothing but tragic unhappiness could come of that unless it was nipped in time. But today, at dinner, another idea had come to her. Was it possible that Allan and not Dave was in her mind, that thoughts of him had quickened her sweet prettiness to such rapt loveliness?

There are times when love must be blunt, even harsh. Mrs. Owens felt that this was one of them. She had to know what this withdrawn young thing, to whom she had given life, was thinking in her secret soul.

"Sit down, Ellen. I want to talk with you," she said.

The blue eyes of the girl fluttered a swift winged question at her mother. She sat down.

"Is it Dave or Allan?" Mrs. Owens asked quietly, watching her daughter steadily.

Ellen felt hot flags of color in her cheeks. "What do you mean, Mother?"

"You know what I mean. I'm asking you whether it is Dave or Allan that you love."

"I don't have to . . . love . . . either of them, do I?" Ellen parried, panicky at this bold assault upon her secret.

"I'm waiting for an answer, child."

The girl was driven by an imperative impulse to hide her blushes. She flung her arms around her mother's neck and buried two burning cheeks in an ample bosom.

"Oh, Mother, Mother, I'm such a fool!" she cried.

"There—there, child. You're not the only one," Mrs. Owens comforted. "I've been one myself several times, at your age and since. Tell Mother dearie."

Ellen faltered out her story to a relieved parent. At least it was better than it might have been. Allan was an honest boy, even though a foolish and obstinate one. Mrs. Owens did not scold.

It was on the tip of her tongue to say dryly, "Are you sure you have made up your mind now?" But she knew that caustic comment might dry up her child's confidences instantly. Instead, she told her not to worry, and to be a good girl, and perhaps everything would come out the way she hoped.

A few minutes later, Ellen, shining-eyed and glowing with happiness, set out with Bob for the house of Virginia Harshaw. That young man reproved her for frivolity. Gusts of soft laughter welled out of her for no apparent reason. She skipped instead of walking decorously. Naturally he criticized her behavior, as brothers do.

To please him she achieved outward sobriety. He did not even know that, when she took him past the jail instead of by the short cut, he had been slyly maneuvered into thinking the choice of ways was his.

Under the cottonwood, just opposite the jail, she caught him by the arm. "S-sh!"

Four men came out of the front door. The lantern in the hall shone on the face of each in turn for a moment. The first two were Caldwell and Cole Tolt, the next Allan Macdonald, the last Dave Tolt.

"Gee!" Bob whispered, awed at this silent procession of outlaws. The sight of them, filing into the darkness toward the dry wash in the rear of the jail, give him the thrill of his young life. Just as the James brothers, the Youngers, the Daltons were heroes as well as villains to the boys of their generation living in the Southwest, so the Tolts were becoming mythical figures as their notoriety spread. For years young Owens would boast of this glimpse of the night raiders on their last dash for liberty. "Gee, Ellen! Did you see them?"

The heart of the girl was beating wildly against her ribs. What did this mean? Where were they going? What had they been doing? Why was Allan with them? She had heard Dave's whispered "This way" and Allan's answer. Did it mean that Allan was, after all, one of them, a silent partner in their lawless enterprises? That was what some people said. He was a spy, they claimed, who gave them information, did errands for them, and shared in their gains.

Ellen pushed this treasonable thought from her. It wasn't true. Allan had stood by Dave because of friendship. For that alone he had risked reputation, liberty, and life. She knew that. All the Tolts had admitted as much to her. James and Jean Macdonald had both understood that without the need of further explanation. It was written in the character of Allan.

But why was he with them now? How had he got out of jail? Had the Tolts freed him? If so, had they shot the jailer first? Questions flung themselves at her tumultuously. She was dreadfully worried. This was the last place in the world, except perhaps Burke City, for the Tolts to be. If they were seen there would be swift and tragic trouble.

"Golly! Where d'you reckon they're going, Ellen?" whispered Bob.

"I don't know."

"What we better do?"

"Nothing. It's not our business."

Her heart denied that. It was very much her business. But whatever they had done or were about to do, she must stand aside.

That night she slept little. At the breakfast table Bob, who had already been uptown on an errand, was bursting with news. The Tolts had come to Melrose, overpowered Sutter and the jailer, locked them in cells, and taken Allan Macdonald with them. Some time in the small hours Allan had come back, roused several citizens, and freed the officers. The boy's own story tumbled out on top of what he had been told.

Later in the day, other details reached Ellen. Allan had gone with the Tolts under protest and had returned as soon as he was released. The outlaws were riding for the border to get across to safety. They had cut all the telegraph wires out of Melrose. A posse was in pursuit. If the officers caught up with them there would be a battle.

As to Allan public opinion was divided. If he had no connection with the bandits, why should they risk so much to free him? Ellen met this question several times during the day. The excitement in her bosom mounted. Her mother would forbid her to get mixed in the affair for fear of starting talk. A girl's reputation was so easily smirched, and to have had dealings with the Tolts now would be enough to condemn her with the gossips. They would say . . .

Ellen burned with hot shame, not for what she had done, but for how it would be interpreted. Her thoughts shrank from crossing that borderline of scandal. They went as far as one epithet, a bad girl, and then drew back in panic.

But she had to think of Allan, not of herself. If she didn't speak, they would send Allan to the penitentiary on suspicion. There was enough against him to convict.

She went to Pete Evans. He was a friend of her father. He had been sheriff and would know best how to work effectively for her. To him she told everything. Her intention was to give only the facts, not her emotions, but she was too inexperienced to conceal her feelings. As soon as she had finished, she flung out an almost defiant comment.

"I know what you think, but it isn't true."

To see the hot cheeks of the girl, the proud lift of the white throat, the shamed eyes forced to meet his steadily, was to know that the gesture of defiance was purely defensive. She was afraid, but she had made up her mind to carry through. He set himself to restore her wounded self-respect. At bottom she was a shy, fluttering young thing easily put in the wrong.

"I reckon it's true," he drawled, with his slow, easy smile. "I think you're a mighty sweet young lady to take so much trouble for these triflin' no-'count boys just because they're friends of your folks. Allan's father has been to Sutter and told him what the Tolts said, that Allan wasn't in with them. 'Course what James Macdonald says won't go so far with the law, since he's the boy's dad. But it is different with you. I think it's right important that all three of the Tolt boys said to you Allan wasn't in cahoots with them. We'll send for Sutter. Since that Burke City business I can see he's been swinging round to Allan's side. All he needs now is an excuse to turn him loose."

Sutter came and listened to Ellen's story. The point in it which stood out like a sore thumb was one she stressed quietly herself after she had covered all the facts.

"You can't send him to the penitentiary unless you send me too. I helped him take food to Dave. I knew they were on the island and visited them there to find out what had become of Allan. I'm in just as deep as he is."

"I don't reckon a young lady like you would want to get mixed up in this. If Allan is any kind of a man, he wouldn't want you to do anything but keep still. All you say proves he helped Dave escape. Your story won't do him any good and it will do you a lot of harm," the sheriff explained.

"It will send me to the penitentiary, too, won't it?"

Sutter looked at the lovely young girl, with her touch of grave austerity. He knew well enough that no jury in the Southwest would send this white-and-gold bit of exquisite Eve to prison, and that if she testified in his behalf they would free Allan.

"It might," he said.

Evans smoked his pipe in silence. He was shrewdly aware that Allan had here an advocate far more potent than he.

"Then if he goes, I'll go."

"That's not the way to look at it, Miss Ellen. No use being foolish. What would your ma say? We got to think of everything."

"I'm thinking of just one thing, Mr. Sutter, that I'm not going to be a coward and keep quiet when I can help Allan."

The girl said it with such quiet conviction the sheriff knew she could not be moved.

"All right. You've told me your story. If I want you, I'll send for you."

"But you can't do that. You've got to arrest me. I'm like Allan, a what-d'you-call-it after the fact."

Evans laughed, with slow relish. "She's got you, Jim, where the wool's short. If she goes around telling this to other folks, you'll have to arrest her, looks like."

"Miss Ellen, you're trying to bulldoze me," the sheriff complained. "I don't have to arrest you. I won't. You know blamed well, Evans, if I arrested her, I might as well pack and get out. This town never would forget it."

"This town knows Allan didn't do anything but help a friend in trouble!" Ellen cried. "Do you think you can send him to prison for that?"

Not if this girl went on the stand for him. Both men were convinced of that. Even if she didn't, after the excitement had cooled down a little, they were of opinion that a jury would not punish loyalty, but would applaud it. Abstract law did not weigh very heavily on the frontier. The twelve men in the box would look at the boy and make up their individual minds as to whether he was a bad citizen.

Sutter threw up a hand in defeat. "All right. I'll turn him loose. If I want him later, I can find him. I've had half a mind, anyhow, to let him go. He's a nice kid."

"I think Miss Ellen had better not tell her story to anyone else," Evans suggested. "Think so, Jim?"

"I should say so!" the sheriff assented with energy. "She's done cracked the whip over me. It's time to quit."

"I'm awf'ly obliged to you, Mr. Sutter. When will you free Allan?"

Sutter looked at her and grinned. He took one little stab of revenge. "I'll turn him loose right off, so as he can keep any engagement he might happen to have this evening with a young lady."

The delicate tint in her cheeks deepened. "I don't suppose he has any," she said, to clear the record.

"If he hasn't he'll likely enough make one. I never did see a more limber boy. He sure moves fast when he gets started. I'll tell him, Miss Ellen, what a good lawyer has been working on me for him."

"Please don't," she begged. "I—I'm only doing my duty. I felt I ought to tell you."

"Hmp!" snorted Sutter. "I wisht I was young enough to have a young lady like you do her duty for me. I'll bet I'd rot in jail before one would lift a hand for me. I ain't a fool, young lady."

Ellen let that go without protest, unless a blush might be considered one.

Allan saw her coming toward him in the dusk his incomparable sweetheart, light as a feather-footed wood nymph. As she walked, the white skirt seemed at each step to cling to and model the slender legs and knees. Her very movements, so rhythmic and yet so individual, suggested music to him.

A strong, warm little hand pressed his. She lifted a small oval face, provocative in its tender mockery.

"Out again, Mr. Outlaw?"

"Thanks to you. Sutter told me."

She puckered a forehead, elfishly delicate in the half-light, to a mock frown.

"He does so like to talk."

In the girl was a burst of song. She tried to keep it decorously out of her voice. She had been too bold already. If he wanted her, he had to go the whole way. And he did want her. She knew that. His letter, that cry of despair, so restrained and brave, still lay where every beat of the heart was close to it.

He turned and walked beside her, adapting his step to hers. Her shoulder brushed against his arm. Vividly she was aware, in tingling pulses, of his masculine strength. She loved the rich bloom beneath the tan of his face, longed to touch the line of golden down on his cheek just above where the razor blade had moved.

"Male and female created He them." The words flashed through her mind, as Allan told her of his ride with the Tolts toward the border, of his assurance that they would get into Mexico safely. This long, lean man with the free stride was hers. He was to be her mate. All through her life she was to walk beside him. In sickness and in health, until death parted them. The joy of that knowledge was like warm wine in her blood.

It came to her that he was not going to speak. He was telling her of Dave, of his hope that the young outlaw would find a new way of life in another land. His manner was full of cheerful, impersonal friendliness. A flash of insight told her he was schooling insurgent emotions.

That was not what she wanted. After all, what did it matter about the first spoken word? He had cried it to her in the hour when he faced stark tragedy. Was that not enough? Why lose time, when all of life was so short a period to love and be loved?

She raised luminous eyes to his. Into the flow of his talk she broke, very gently. "I got your letter."

He stopped to look at her. "What letter?"

Then he knew. The jailer at Burke had forwarded what Allan had expected to be his last message to her. He was flung completely off his stride.

"I told him to send it if—"

"If they killed you," she finished for him when he stopped.

"Yes."

"Is it just as true . . . since they didn't?" she asked.

"It is just as true, but—"

"You said in it," she quoted, " 'Ever since I have been a little boy I have loved you; I shall be loving you when my last minute comes.' Is that true?"

"Yes," he answered simply.

"Oh, Allan, I've been such a fool!" she cried. "I

335

thought it was Dave. It never was. It must have been always you. How could I have been so wrong?"

Stormily the blood pounded through his heart. Could he have heard what he had seemed to hear?

"You said—" he stumbled.

"I said, if you want me—"

There was a lithe movement of her gracious body, and she was in his arms in shy, sweet surrender. He caught her close, in the savage joy of the conquering male, so that her slim, beautiful limbs were lifted free of the ground.

The song of larks . . . the ripple of running water sparkling with sunshine . . . the murmur of the wind in the pines . . . all things lovely and dear they would share together.

Center Point Large Print
600 Brooks Road / PO Box 1
Thorndike, ME 04986-0001 USA

(207) 568-3717

US & Canada:
1 800 929-9108
www.centerpointlargeprint.com